Blazing Ashes

By Alexa Whitewolf

Blazing Ashes

by Alexa Whitewolf

Copyright ©2019-2020 Alexa Whitewolf

First Edition

ISBN: 978-1-989384-11-4

This is a work of fiction.

Author's Note & Acknowledgements

This book, much like my *Avalon Chronicles* series, came to me in a dream. I only had parts and pieces of it when I decided to sit down and write it earlier last year. And let me tell you, it has been a journey. It forced me to dig deeper into myself than I ever have, and revisit a couple views of the world that were fully ingrained in me.

It also showed me the good, the bad, and the in between, word by word, page by page. You may find parts of it hard to read, but I hope overall you enjoy it.

To my family: this book wouldn't have gotten written without Steven's—my husband—never-ending support, and my two furbabies helping me with relaxing. When I originally wrote it, I was in ok health. Halfway through, after a nasty fall, I got a concussion and found myself bedridden for weeks on end, unable to do anything. Yet through it all, Katya's voice prevailed, and it brought me back from the brink of despair. Steven suffered through my grumpiness and writing blues, helping me even when he didn't realize it, and through it all, I managed to finish the story.

Huge thanks to Kristina, Candace, Siobhan and Donna for your beta reading. Your comments and encouragement kept me going when I doubted the story!

And to my readers, I hope, if nothing else, this book makes you pause in your busy life, and take stock of your surroundings ☺

Happy readings,

Alexa

Love isn't a chain.

It's a release.

Glossary

I didn't hold back on the Romanian in this one! Some of the translations are in the text, others are paraphrased, but here's a little helpful glossary in case you lose your way!

Da/nu – yes/no
Draga mea/iubirea mea/frumoasă/ Perfectă – my darling, my love, beautiful, perfect
Prietenă specială, da – special friend, huh
Vedere - sight
Scuze / bine – I'm sorry / good
Foarte bine – very well
Ce naiba / naibii – what the fuck / fuck
E viaţa mea, nu înţelegi – it's my life, don't you understand
Apa Sâmbetei – Saturday's water (I know this sounds weird, but it's explained in the book!)
Acuma - now
Zmeu / zâne / muroni – dragons and faes and vampires, the Romanian versions
Lumea Dintre – the Between world
Da, crezi – yeah, you think
Vino, draga mea – come, my darling
Nu aşa de repede, dulceaţă – not so fast, sweetheart
Ce vrei – what do you want
Bine ai venit – welcome
Ascultă. - listen
Cum te simţi – how are you
Vârful Moldoveanu – Moldoveanu Peak
Nefartatul – the Devil
Pot să fiu cine vrei – I can be whoever you want

O secundă – one second
E alegerea ei – it's her choice
Baba Oarbă – blind hag
Nu eşti de aici. – you're not from here
Prietene – friend
Bea tot. – drink everything
Dă-mi – give it to me
Cu grijă / noroc – be careful/ good luck

Chapter 1

The light shines briefly in my left eye and sure enough, the pain of a thousand knives bursts through my cranium.

"Effing hell, doc!" I yank my head away, waving uselessly to push him off, and he takes a step back. I don't even have to glance over—his disapproval at my tone is more than evident.

Well, too damn bad.

"I'm not sure what's going on, Katya, but I'll give you a prescription for a migraine relief pill."

"Great."

His lips purse at my less-than-enthused tone. "We've been over this before. Unless you let me do some proper tests, I have no way of seeing what's causing these headaches of yours."

"They're not headaches," I mutter, rubbing my temples. Some of the ache dulls, but not fully. All it would take is me looking at the neon lights, and it would be back, freaking driving me insane like it has been for the last two weeks.

"No, you say they're migraines, yet you don't have all the symptoms."

I try to glare at him, but a hiss of pain escapes me. The room wavers around the edges of my vision, and my stomach is doing the kind of somersaults I could do without. Forcing a deep breath in, I focus my sight on the dotted, ugly floor of the stupid walk-in clinic.

"Fine. Just give me the damn prescription. It's all you do, anyway."

His voice softens. "I could do more, if you'd let me." His pen scratches the paper as it scribbles something, and the tiny noise makes me wince again. "Honestly, Katya, don't you *want* to get better?"

"Of course I do," I say, and hop off the stool. Nearly ripping the prescription out of his hand, I walk out.

Rude? Bite me. Try being polite—let alone conscious—when every step brings you closer to the ground and oblivion. With each step, my vision grows spottier, and my feet act like they can't coordinate with my brain. Head wise, it feels like I'm constantly bouncing around between pain and darkness, or should I say between a hammer and an axe?

The way to the pharmacy is familiar—I'm in here almost every month, usually when the pain gets too much. And every time it's the same spiel, ending with *get some tests*. As if I want to be someone's guinea pig... No, thanks.

I trudge around to the pharmacy, slap the prescription on the counter and hope to hell they haven't cut off my insurance from my workplace.

Ex-workplace, I guess.

Ex-boyfriend, too, now that I think about it. But then, finding your guy banging the CEO's secretary, then taking a snapshot to show said CEO, tends to do that. And gets you fired in the process, apparently.

Don't judge. You would have done the same.

"Here you go."

The pretty blonde behind the counter looks like a fashion model, way more dressed up than she should be, with a perfect face of makeup. I scowl my thanks and pick up the package, thanking my stars. And nope, they're not lucky.

If they were, I'd have a job, a boyfriend and a damn good action flick waiting for me at home. If they were, I'd have Perky Pharma's platinum no-hair-out-of-place look and perfectly groomed appearance.

Instead, all I have is an empty apartment, a throbbing migraine, and my usual red curls and freckly face. Even my eyes are a washed-out sea green.

Parents, you ask? Foster care, I answer.

So what if I'm all alone in my Chinatown dingy place? Maybe I prefer it that way. Or maybe if

I keep saying it, I'll finally believe it.

Another step, and I nearly topple over. I lean against the wall, rip open the paper bag, followed by the pill bottle, and take two. Or, I'm about to.

"Don't!"

I jump, dropping the pills to the ground. Shit. I look around to yell at whoever startled me, but no one's around.

"Great. Now I'm hallucinating, too."

Much as it's tempting to pick up the pills from the ground, I can't lower myself to those standards. Who knows what's been on that floor? Instead, I reach inside the plastic bottle for two more.

"Don't!"

"What the effing shit!?" I look around frantically, this time clutching the pills in my hand so I don't drop them.

"You're not hallucinating."

It's like the voice is coming out of thin air. Nope, no *like* about it—it *is* coming from nowhere. I gulp, pretty sure my eyes are as round as saucers about now.

"Don't take the pills."

Ah, hell no!

Now I'm definitely taking them. My living situation is bad enough. I don't need to add mentally insane to the list of obstacles I have to overcome. Without hesitation, I pop the two white circles in my mouth and swallow them dry.

"What? Nothing to say?" I wait a second, then

mutter, "Yeah, didn't think so." I'm well aware of how crazy this sounds, talking to myself outside a walk-in clinic. I never used to consider myself delusional. Guess there's always a first time for everything.

≈ ♠ ≈

When I say I live in a dingy place in Chinatown, I'm not joking. Downtown Toronto is no billionaire's living quarters, especially when you make little above minimum wage. Or, *made.*

The apartment used to be flea and cockroach-infested, but I couldn't afford to be picky. Without a job, or much money in my bank account, not to mention a pissed-off ex-boyfriend, let's just say options were minimal. It's been three months since then, and the situation hasn't much improved.

My own stupidity is to blame for moving in with Bryan in the first place. But that's what happens when you're deprived of love in your formative years. You think you can survive without it, that you're tough as nails, then in swoops a Prince Charming that makes you lose your head.

Rather unfortunately for me, it ended in heartache. Hence the rush to search for a place, not finding anything within my means, and ending up in this bachelor studio atop a Chinese take-out place. The owner was kind enough to rent it to me on a probationary basis, at least for the first few months.

After my trip to the walk-in clinic, I stop by an ATM nearby to check my depressing account balance—nearing less than two hundred dollars, and still no job. *Guess that means it's more mac and cheese for me tonight.*

Sighing, I drag my feet to the back of the brick building, climb up the fire escape, and enter my tiny place. The inside is cozy enough—I bought everything second-hand. A green couch that's seen better days, a wall lamp, and an old-school TV. I've never been the crazy type about electronics, even my phone was an old flip-style one.

Something Bryan, my ex, always found endearing.

I wince, resisting the urge to smack the back of my head. Broken-hearted doesn't suit me, and I'm not about to become the type. Even if I should have seen the signs in his deciding to work later hours, become less interested in sex, and slowly distancing himself from me. But I guess I was too blinded by the life we had together, the illusion of a happy ending.

Resolutely, I take off my shoes and head to the corner where a stove sits next to a fridge vibrating hard enough to make the floor shake. I take out the pack of mac and cheese from the cupboard, check inside to make sure there aren't any uninvited guests, then pour the remainder of the contents into a pot to boil.

While my breakfast, lunch and dinner cooks, I start flipping through newspapers in search of various job ads. It's hard enough to find a job in the city without a degree. Now that I've been blacklisted by a powerful CEO, it's quasi-impossible. I guess said CEO didn't much like being made a fool of and retaliated on the person who brought the fact to light.

Luckily, I don't give up easily.

To my right, bubbling catches my attention, informing me my food is done. After pouring myself a bowl, I head to the couch and start munching. I'm hungry enough that it tastes like the best steak rather than plastic crap, and the whole thing is gulped down in seconds.

I have one more box in the cupboard, but it's supposed to last me until the end of the weekend. No way I can dig in now, no matter how bad my hunger is. Instead, I wash the bowl and place it back in the cupboard. If nothing else, I keep this place super tidy.

Then I drag myself back to the couch and drink about a gallon of tap water, in an effort to stop my stomach from growling. It doesn't work. My insides tighten, demanding food, demanding something I can't give them.

I'd been living the good life with Bryan, it's true. Since the moment we ran into each other at work, and he took too much interest in me, pursuing me relentlessly… I should've known he was a douchebag. But *should've* didn't stop me from making a stupid mistake.

My eyes shut but tears still peek past. The

hunger, the loneliness consumes me. I don't know who I pissed off in another life to be dealt this hand, but it sucks.

Burying my face in my elbow, I let it all out— the heartache, the helplessness, the pain. The pills seem to be finally working, because my head isn't throbbing as bad anymore. And eventually, my sobs lessen, and all that's left is anger.

Anger at this life, anger at myself for being so weak, for putting myself in this situation. *I'll get myself out of it and have the last laugh…* And then I fall asleep. If nothing else, I won't be lonely anymore for the next few hours.

≈ ♠ ≈

The dream starts out like most times. I'm walking in a forest, inhaling fresh air the likes I never have in the city. Butterflies fill my stomach, because I'm nearing somewhere—a meeting place. My steps falter, and I wait. It won't be long now.

A growl makes me jump, and I turn around slowly. Fur white as snow, eyes a mix of violet and grey, the wolf lifts his muzzle in the air, sniffing. Then he picks up speed, running like the wind towards me. He hurtles into me, and we roll over on the ground, me laughing and burying my face in his fur.

"I missed you, Bebo." It's not his real name, only a nickname I gave him, but that doesn't make this encounter any less realistic.

I've known him since I was a child, stuck in foster homes and trying to make myself small and invisible, so as to avoid the adults' rage. Bebo came to me in a dream for the first time when I was nursing a broken arm from my then foster-father. He licked the wound and stayed with me the entire night. When I woke up, I didn't feel alone anymore, but like I'd found the deepest buried treasure.

Only, of course, now I had two of them, all to myself. After I give Bebo a rubdown, and he's panting on the grass next to me, I drop my forehead to his. "Where's your master, Bebo? I could use some human company right now."

Bebo stares at me for a long, long moment, then licks the side of my face. His raspy tongue makes me laugh, and he gets up slowly. With one last look at me, he walks back into the forest. I know I won't see him again for a bit, as they never come together. Almost like they have a pact to share me.

With bated breath, I wait. Then the forest parts again, and he walks in. I'm pretty sure unlike Bebo, he's a fragment of my imagination, but what do I know? Dark hair, high cheekbones, Roman nose and a mouth made to kiss. Dark grey eyes smile when he sees me. He wears these shirts that are partly ripped, only adding to his appeal when those muscles get on display.

Forcing myself not to ogle too hard, I will my head to snap into focus. This is Vas, my friend. Since

I turned fourteen, he's been around, growing with me—except for that time he wouldn't come, years ago... Worst time of my life. But he's been back since, looking more ruggedly handsome than any friend has a right to.

And as I get to my feet, smiling my welcome, the thought hits me that maybe, just maybe, my breakup with Bryan wasn't all his fault. Maybe I had a part to play in it too, given every night for the past year I've been opening up to Vas, telling him things, trusting him...

I shake the thought off, and instead run to him, throwing myself in his arms. My head reaches the crook of his neck, and I bury my nose to inhale his earthy scent. Strong and firm, his arms come around me, holding me tight.

After a moment, we break apart. "How are you?" I ask.

He pushes a lock of my hair back, angling my face so he can see me better. "I should ask you that," he says darkly. "You don't look like you've eaten or slept much."

I shrug out of his embrace, glancing anywhere but in his gorgeous grey eyes. "I have, though. Promise."

Vas doesn't seem convinced. He stalks closer, tilting his head to the side. "That guy Bryan treating you right? Because if he isn't—"

Oops. I'd omitted telling Vas anything about Bryan since we broke up, becoming an expert at deflecting his questions. But now I'm a second too late in schooling my expression.

He pounces on it, his features darkening as he bites out, "What did he do?"

I shake my head. "Nothing! It's nothing. I promise. How about you tell me of your travels? You know I love a good story."

He won't be deterred, though, I can see it in the way he's slowly closing the distance between us. "Katya…"

The warning falls on deaf ears though, and I smile a big, pleading grin. "Please?"

Vas' eyes narrow on me, his expression so close to bursting past my walls, but I resist it. After another beat, he runs a hand through his hair in frustration, then holds his palm out for me.

I gladly rush back in his embrace, relishing the way he pulls me into his side as we start aimlessly strolling through the forest. It never rains, here, so the night is as quiet as ever, the moon peeking from behind dark clouds. In a soft, even tone, Vas tells me about his recent trip into some nearby mountains where he ran into a family of wolves.

His stories bring a different world to life for me, as they always do. I lose myself in the words, in the picture he creates. Of the father wolf hunting for his family, the mother wolf protecting the cubs, and his own innocent stumbling around their blissfully unaware family. He tells me how he redirected humans away from the lair, in an effort to keep the wolves' privacy, basically a Batman for the defenseless.

I'm not sure if it's real or not—how much of all of this is, anyway? —but it takes my mind away from hunger, loneliness, and despair at the world crumbling around me.

And as we walk, with each passing step, Vas lulls me deeper and deeper into the forest, and the sense of safety under his arm increases. I become aware of things I didn't, before. The scent of pine and freshness clinging to his skin, the musk of man and earth, the heat emanating into my side and warming me all the way from tip to toes…

Something else, too. Something primal. The lean muscle keeping me safe as much as captive, the deep murmur of his voice that does weird things to my stomach, *new* things.

No, not entirely true. I could lie to myself, but none of this is new. On the contrary. Since I was a teenager and he first showed up—a hot, young boy roughly my own age—I've felt this pull. Yet he's been in my dreams only, and reality demanded I find boyfriends that actually exist.

Still…

It takes me a moment to realize we've stopped walking, and even longer to catch on that Vas is no longer speaking. I can sense the intensity of his gaze on me, the expectancy in the air. My breath catches in my throat.

His eyes have gone dark, filled with something I can't understand. And the way he's staring at me, as if he wants to eat me whole…

"Vas?" I whisper.

When he doesn't answer, I bite my lip, tugging on the bottom to chew on it. A bad habit when I'm nervous, something I do unconsciously. This time, I'm aware of it, if only because of the attention Vas redirects to said lip.

The sensation in my stomach intensifies, and still we're standing, just staring at each other. Something crazy whirls inside me, almost reckless. I want to tell him, then, about Bryan. That we're no longer together, that I'm unattached and free as a bird. Free for him.

Unfortunately, I don't get a chance to. Before I can even open my mouth, something pulls at me. A pain unlike any I've sensed before, ripping my insides. My mouth opens in a scream that never escapes. Vas tries to grab hold of me, his anger gone in the wake of his panic, but none of that helps, and I lose him.

≈ ♠ ≈

I jolt awake, disoriented. The unfinished dream with Vas, the day's burdens, and then… A burning in my veins, like my blood is… boiling.

Moaning in pain, I fall off the couch, stumble about the apartment like a beast in dire need of being

13

put out. My head is killing me—again. I thought these stupid pills were supposed to help, but the throbbing has only gotten worse. My limbs are weak, my mouth is pasty, and the apartment feels like it's on a boat stuck in the middle of a storm.

I never should've fallen asleep, I think wildly, unable to narrow down a reason for this newfound agony. It makes everything more vivid, yet my thoughts are little butterflies I can't hang on to.

Another wave of pain rolls through me, and this time I cry out loud. No one will help me. The owner doesn't live here, I'm on my own... The idea runs through my mind that I might actually die here, all alone.

I gasp at the fresh agony, and blink—only I'm not in my apartment anymore. Rather, I'm in a park nearby, about a good ten-minute walk. How could I have gotten here, when just seconds ago I felt the cheap linoleum floor under my fingertips?

Glancing around, I seek someone out to help, but there's no one. *Shit.*

I curl onto myself this time, desperately gripping the earth as another wave, stronger than all the others, runs through me. My breath comes out in short pants, and my nails dig further into the wet ground. Only instead of abating like the rest, the wave grows heavier, and heavier... My vision narrows...

Then, the unthinkable happens and I burst into flames.

Chapter 2

A breeze hits my face. A soft swish of the air. The ground moves. I blink awake and stumble to my feet. The agony in my veins is gone, but did I imagine those flames? Has my brain fractured, some kind of psychotic break? Because I can still feel the heat scorching my skin, the tightness in my body…and yet it's gone, now.

My perception is different, as though my height has been altered and I'm smaller. Something else has also changed—I'm no longer alone. And the Adonis facing me is enough to get my blood boiling again.

Scratch that. *Usher*. 'Cause the caramel skin tone, strong jaw, chocolate eyes, holy fucking—

"Shit."

He takes the word right out of my mouth. I meant to say it, but I croak instead. Then I start flapping wildly. Croak? Flapping? I try to glance down my nose, and instead of human flesh I see the tip of a beak. When I open it as if to speak, it feels unnatural—I *must* be dreaming.

"You're not dreaming."

Even his voice is pure honey, pouring over me like whiskey on ice. Hot, *hot* whiskey, on about-to-be *very* melted ice.

The man laughs, then kneels in front of me. I get a closer view of the chocolate hue of his eyes, and the scruff decorating his jaw. He rubs it, as though in thought. "You are beautiful in your true form, Katya."

I'm too busy staring at his muscled arms to register the words. Then the naked chest. The faded blue jeans sitting oh-so-rightly on him. And the beautiful, angel-like wings folded on his back.

WAIT, WHAT?

I'm definitely not imagining them. Those things *move*. Massive, ivory-colored feathers stir in the breeze, then fold onto his back, still very much visible.

"You have them, as well." He chuckles, reaching out as if to pull on my hand.

Except when I look at it, it's not a hand he tugs on. It's a *wing*, dusted with feathers the color of fire. They shimmer under the light, and I squeak my shock.

"I see I'm just in time, Dante."

A second man enters the scene. He's all lean, solid muscle, with black hair falling in waves to his shoulders, and the iciest eyes I've ever seen. Unlike my bare-chested angel, he's dressed in an impeccable suit and could have easily walked off the cover of a magazine for the rich and ruthless. His British accent when he speaks pretty much adds to the image of some fancy aristocrat.

Wow this is some dream…

The man he called Dante sighs, drops his hand from my wing and turns to the newcomer. "Thirty seconds, D? Is that all the time I get alone with her?"

"Learn to share, *D*. We both have a hand to play in this."

They know each other, obviously. I only wish I could figure out if this is a dream, or reality. But if it's a dream, where's Vas? He's been a companion to my nights for as long as I can remember. Surely he wouldn't miss this delusion.

And it must be one. I mean, no way I'm some kind of shifter that can turn into a bird. Hell, if I was, I would've flown away from my crap life a while ago.

And yet… The flapping wings, my inability to speak, my new angle of viewing things, as though I'm super close to the earth… Not to mention my beak.

Maybe those meds were stronger than the doc told me. That must be it. As if on cue, the next part of their conversation shatters that illusion.

"I do not recall being the one to warn her off the pills." Dante smirks when his counterpart shuffles his feet, then shrugs.

"You know as well as I do, they would have

brought on the change sooner."

"And they did."

Blue Eyes scowls, pointing an index to his counterpart. "Angel or not, you're not all omniscient."

"Demon or not, *you* are still an asshat, mate." Dante mimics the faint British accent of his counterpart easily, then crosses his arms over his chest and the massive wings unfurl in obvious threat.

"They don't say asshat where I'm from, you wanker."

You might guess, by this point, I'm staring with my beak wide open at them, not believing what I'm hearing. Just as it seems both are about to come to blows, they turn to me.

"She's been in that form too long for her first time," Blue Eyes says.

"D, do not—"

The new D—not Dante—strolls over and puts one hand on my wing. I want to scream in pain, but it's only a faint shudder than runs through me, not the full-blown agony from before. Then smoke surrounds me, the scent of sulfur and cinnamon, and finally I'm no longer bird-sized but standing on two feet.

"Damn."

"You can say that again."

You know how in movies, shifters return to their human form naked? Not me.

Nope, I *glow*. With *stars*.

As if a dress has been made of tiny diamond-like stars just for me, then thrown over my body. It's embarrassing, but not like I can do anything about it. The strapless shape covers me, all the way to my feet. And no, I'm definitely not wearing undergarments. A corset of some sort … Whatever it is, it supports my boobs. But having those two staring at me with their jaws dropped, I might as well be naked.

I flush red to my roots, then it turns to anger as I realize I've got my voice back. "What the effing hell!? Are you guys crazy? 'Cause whatever drugs you're on, I want none of it. What the *hell* is this? I swear, if I don't get some freaking answers, there will be h—"

Blue Eyes moves fast and places a hand over my mouth, cutting off my tirade. Lips curled in amusement, he says, "I wouldn't say *hell* a third time, love. You'll be opening the gate to it, if you're not careful."

He removes his hand—luckily, as I'd been about to bite it.

"You did," I accuse.

Dante laughs. "He is a demon, Katya. He can do whatever pleases him."

I look pointedly at his angel wings, then the other guy's suit. For a dream, my imagination sure has come up with some awesome specimens of supernatural beings. *No harm in going along with it for a bit longer, right?*

Resting my gaze on Blue Eyes, I ask, "And why does it matter if I say it?"

"You're a Flama," he says, as if that alone should explain it. "Everything matters."

I blink, then whine, "But it's my favorite cuss word."

The two men share a look, and I half-wonder when we're going to move to the part of the dream that involves loads of pleasure for me.

"She is taking it fairly well," Dante points out, but he's frowning as though waiting for me to blow a gasket.

"What, the Flama thing?" I shrug. "I'm a redhead. I've been called worse."

This time, they flat out burst laughing. "What the h—" I stop again, and resort to stomping my foot.

"You can say it now. Just not three times in the span of a minute. And, love—"

"Call me love one more time, second D, and you'll meet her friend—hate."

He arches an eyebrow, while Dante still chuckles. "Second D?"

"The name's Daymun," Blue Eyes reveals, all perfect white teeth in a gleaming smile.

"Damon?" It suits him. He's dangerously irresistible.

"D-A-Y-M-U-N," Dante spells. "The Creator had a funny sense of humor."

I glance between them, missing the joke.

"How so?"

"Dante—poet who went through Hell. But I'm an angel. Daymun—his name is a mix of day and Amun, god of the sun and air in—"

"Ancient Egypt, I know," I interrupt. Being a bookworm has its perks. Not much else to do when you grow up isolated and weird, other than read.

I stare at them for a longer beat. And another one. Then my shoulders lift in a shrug. "Funny. Alright, you've had your joke. This obviously isn't a sexy dream, so I'm ready to wake up now."

Turning on my heels, I go to walk away, only to have them both rush to block my way. No amount of inspecting my surroundings provides me with a quick solution to escape these lunatics.

"You can't."

This is a bad moment to find Daymun's accent charming. He says *can't* like *cahn't,* and shit but that's sexy. And charming. How is it the angel's the one speaking all posh, and this one's so… so… tempting.

Demon, Dante had said. It would make sense then that he'd be temptation personified, I guess?

Lost in my internal debate, I almost miss Dante's next statement.

"We are linked to you, Katya."

My eyes narrow on them. "Are you reading my mind?"

More grins.

"In a way, yes. We feel your intentions."

I scowl at Daymun, then fold my arms across my chest. "This is a really, *really* horrible dream, but fine. I'll bite. How are we linked?"

"Our blood was used to awaken you in a human form," Dante says.

"And it can also be used to kill you."

There he goes again with the cahn.

Daymun's words are more ominous, especially when delivered with a straight face and unequivocal gaze. "Though, admittedly, silver can also hurt you due to its purified essence."

I gulp and take a step back. Not that it helps, as they mirror me. Every move I make, every breath, they respond in kind. And when the hair on the back of my neck rises, I'm starting to think this is no longer a dream.

Eyes darting around, I whisper, "This can't seriously be real. *You* can't be."

"We are," Dante says.

Daymun only stares, which makes me even more anxious. My heartbeat starts beating an angry rhythm, and my breathing increases. Behind my back, I pinch the inside of my elbow. Despite the pain, the two hotties are still in front of me, watching me.

"I realize you wish to bolt…"

Dante doesn't get to finish his sentence. The moment he opens his mouth, I'm turning on my heels and taking off. In high school, I used to run track and field. It was the one thing that kept me out of trouble and focused on what mattered.

Turns out, all those hours of training come in handy when you're trying to escape two crazies. My bare feet beat into the earth, and I angle my body forward so I can pick up even more speed. The starry dress—or whatever it is—floats around me, wrapping around my body as if to make running easier.

I'm panting by the time I chance a look over my shoulder, only to find no one chasing me. But the musk in the air is very real, and the soreness of my muscles tells me I'm really awake. So was I hallucinating again?

Maybe Doc was right, and I really should go in for tests...

The thought is removed from my head when I run smack into something hard. The impact jostles my entire body, including my teeth, and I fall on my butt in the earth. I look up into dark chocolate eyes. To make matters worse, Dante's wings are unfurled in the air, bristling with frustration.

On shaky legs, I stand, only to have another hand come up from behind. It wraps around my waist and pulls me to my feet against another hard chest—Daymun's.

"You should take more care, love," he whispers. "There are worse things to fear than us out here."

I jerk out of his grip and twist so I can keep

both of them in my field of vision. "What do you want from me?"

Dante opens his mouth to speak, but Daymun throws him a look. "Let me handle it this time, yeah?"

His faint British makes his words almost mesmerizing, and his looks all the more appealing. Not that I'm looking for a rebound, especially not a crazy asshole like him.

The blue eyes warm considerably, darkening a hue, when they land on me again. "Believe me, darling, it wouldn't be a rebound if we go there. I'd wipe any man from your mind."

His tone is soft, but the intensity in his words makes my toes curl into the ground. Dante clears his throat. "*Not* our purpose here, Daymun. Stick to the script."

"Script? You have a freaking *script* for this?" My cheeks feel hot again—what the heck is wrong with me, feeling attraction towards these crazies?

Daymun rolls his eyes at his counterpart and takes a step closer to me. I mirror his move and back away, leading to a flicker of annoyance crossing his features. "You can stop being afraid. If anything, we're the ones in danger here."

"Right." Sarcasm drips from me in that one word.

"I speak the truth," Daymun says. "And I swear I will never lic to you."

"Said every man, ever," I mutter to the wind,

avoiding his intensity. I still feel his gaze on me, almost caressing my skin.

Dante folds his wings, a move that somehow makes him more intimidating. Still bare-chested, he moves another step, his bulging biceps even more threatening despite his kind expression. "Why will you not even let us explain things to you?"

"Isn't that what I'm doing?"

"No," he says, in a way that implies he's disappointed. "And we already do not have much time. Daymun speaks the truth—always. It is simply the kind of demon he is, and the curse of his life."

I scowl at them. "Right, 'cause being a demon is definitely not a lie, eh?"

Dante unfurls his wings again, flapping them once, twice. The movement rushes a gust of wind in my face, with the scent of pine, honey and vanilla. I close my eyes, and a wave of warmth floods over me, cocooning me in a peaceful feeling. In the distance, a light shines...

"Katya."

My eyes open, staring into Daymun's icy glare. "Dante showed you his, now feel mine." He holds out his hand for me, asking permission.

Without really knowing what I'm doing, I place my palm in his. Heat suffuses me, with the smell of a crackling fire, cinnamon and a faint hint of sulfur. There's nothing peaceful about what surrounds me, but primal, wild and free.

Daymun pulls his hand from mine but doesn't

add distance between us. Neither do I.

Instead, my bemused gaze goes from one to the other. "I don't understand. What was all that?"

"We're immortals, love," Daymun says. "That's our essence you felt, which no human ever has. It's the most primal, precious part of us, but we shared it to show you we're not here to harm you." A beat of silence, as if to let me soak it in, then, "I'm a demon, born in the bowels of Hell, and meant to bestow corruption upon mortals. Dante here, he's an angel, crafted in Heaven, and meant to guide mortals to their ever-lasting peace."

"And together, we are your guardians," Dante adds. "Meant to help you on your journey, and aid with your choice."

I shake my head. Something's ringing between my ears, like an annoying sound that won't go away. "What journey? What choice?"

"You're a Flama," Daymun says. "And it's not a nickname. You're a species of shifter that was put on Earth eons ago, whose natural form is a phoenix—and not coincidentally, either."

"Two guardians are assigned to you and mark you with their blood. The way of the world demands a Flama awakens every five hundred years, on their twenty-fifth birthday," Dante adds. "Each Flama then has three weeks to complete its journey and pick a side—Light or Dark."

Something about that sentence feels

incomplete, like they've omitted the actual importance of the role. "Why? What's the point of all of it?"

"To purge the world of all its illness, its corruption, and bring balance."

I stare at Daymun. I mean, how would you react? There's nothing to say to that. Except...

"I'm not twenty-five."

Daymun shrugs. "And that's where the pills came in. They tweaked something in your system and brought the change on sooner. Which means you have five weeks instead to make your choice."

"I don't..." Still shaking my head, I lift a hand to my temple. I'm half-expecting the blinding migraine again, but it's not there. Only my thoughts, swirling around like so many butterflies, unable to sit still.

"It is a lot to absorb," Dante admits. "But that is why you have us."

"We're here to guide you."

I open my eyes again. "An angel, and a demon? Two guardians, for one puny human to make a stupid choice?" My brain kicks into full gear. "What else aren't you telling me? There must be more of a reason for all of this."

They share a look, but neither says anything.

I go over what they told me in my head. I'm some kind of shifter—a phoenix, a Flama —and I'm meant to choose a side. And I have two guardians, one a demon, one an angel.

The connection hits me full blast. "You're not just here to guide me," I say. "You're here to influence me, aren't you? One of Light, one of Darkness."

Daymun, true to his word, nods. No conniving about the gesture, no double-entendre.

Dante doesn't, not at first. Instead, he says, "Not influence, per se. Neither one of us can try to bribe you either way. But of course, we do have our own interests in the matter. The Creator wished to make sure your choice would not be tainted by other external factors."

"Except for you," I say.

Silence surrounds us for a beat, until I shake my head.

"I'm not having this. None of it."

Then I turn on my heels for the third time that night and walk away. When I hear their footsteps in the grass, I yell over my shoulder, "*Don't* follow me!"

Chapter 3

It was a dream.

I wake up snorting at my own lie, but whatever. Life's thrown enough shit my way, so what if now I'm having delusions and potentially turning narcissistic? Just another day in paradise.

Getting dressed is an ordeal when my head's pounding with each step. Thankfully, the outside is cloudy and gloomy—my kind of special.

In dark jeans, a clean shirt and jacket pulled over, I step out of my crummy bachelorette pad and put on sunglasses. Each step starts another throbbing in my temples. And it doesn't help that people won't. stop. staring.

As if they've never seen someone wearing sunglasses when it's cloudy outside. They've probably never suffered from a migraine in their life.

Ugh. *Cretini.* All of them. And yeah, my Romanian tends to sweat through my daily life, and *cretins* is my favorite insult, particularly more so when I'm having an incredibly shitty day. Not that I ever had anyone to teach me the language full-on, after being dumped at a church when I was four years old. But by then, I guess my brain remembered enough of what I'd heard growing up.

Over the years, I ran into a few Romanians, but being in foster care didn't make it easy to maintain friendships. I'm probably the only adult my age that can't boast a network of friends. Loner. Anti-social. Isolated. Been called that before, not that I care. Not that it gets to me.

And the longer I keep telling myself that, the more I'll believe it.

Walking slowly to the edge of the main traffic, I duck my head so I avoid the glare of glass windows and car headlights. A drizzle starts pouring down, soaking through my worn jeans jacket. That's what I get for picking comfort over practical. Double ugh.

As I duck into an alcove—the store behind is closed—I watch people pass me by. One minute turns into five, then ten. The drizzle is now full-blown rain, and I scowl at the sky. "Seriously?" Thunder answers me. Yup, whoever's up there has a bone to pick with me.

Oddly, the thought brings up my dream. The guys were scrumptious, I'll give them that.

Too bad my brain only conjured them on a whim. Because no way I believe any of the crap they were spewing. It was a dream within another dream—it must have been. So what if some of what they said rang true? So what if, while I was around them, my head didn't hurt?

It doesn't mean anything.

As I scan the people passing by, one in particular draws my eye. His ebony skin, faint grin, those chocolate eyes—a gasp escapes me. It's Dante! From my damn *dream*.

Only he's not in my head, but very much real and in a crowd full of humans.

I watch in shock as he makes his way through the throng of people, dressed in nothing but a pair of jeans, bare feet, and with those wings—*WINGS!* — protruding from his back.

Yet it's *me* people stare at? I glance around, but no one seems to notice him. Great. Just freaking great. Like I needed another reason to realize I'm losing my mind.

Then he's in front of me. "Hello, gorgeous."

I shake my head. "You're not real."

Sure enough, someone passes by in that moment and throws me a weird look. I want to shout at them to mind their own business but refuse to make matters worse for myself.

"Oh, but I am."

"No one else *sees* you!"

"Does that mean the unseen are not every bit as real as the seen?"

I shake my head, refusing to listen to him. At this rate, I may need to pull out my meagre savings and see if I can find a shrink. *Can you even get a shrink with a two hundred dollars budget?*

"Katya, wait." Dante moves in front of me to block my way when I try to make my escape. "You must listen to me, at least for a second."

I glare at him through the rain. "No, I really don't."

"This is real, all of it." He's fully ignoring me, rushing the words out as if trying to stuff them down my throat before I leave. It works—kind of. "Like it or not, you are an immortal shifter, placed on this Earth for a reason. Everything you have been through, your entire life, has made you into who you are, for a reason. To be what this world needs you to be."

That line from Batman and dark knights comes to my mind, but I shake it off. Grumbling under my breath, I duck into the rain, gasping again at its coolness. But I won't listen to him—not anymore.

I'm no one's savior, least of all the world's.

"You cannot run, Katya!"

Dante's shout echoes behind me, and all I do is quicken my step. Of course, like an idiot, I don't watch where I'm going—and bump straight into someone else. I glance up to say sorry, and back away. In my haste, I hit a pedestrian who topples into the street.

"Shit!"

I move towards the elder lady and help her

back on the sidewalk, just in time to avoid an incoming slew of traffic. She glares at me, but thankfully only stomps away while swinging her cane like an avenging angel.

And speaking of angels... Or rather, demons.

Daymun's the one I hit, and he's still standing in the throng of people, apparently unbothered as they all pass by him. Or, rather, through him. Our eyes meet across the distance.

"What do you want from me?"

I'm forming the words, but not actually saying anything. Not that it matters—people still give me odd looks. One blink, and Daymun's directly in front of me now. He smirks and those icy blue eyes glitter with the flames of the underworld.

"You, love. And we need you to start *seeing*, now."

Then his index taps the center of my forehead, and I sense some sort of energy—vibration—go right through me. That scent of sulfur and cinnamon tickles my nose again. My headache eases, then I blink and he's gone. I glance around, but Dante's nowhere to be seen, either.

"What the h..."

My mutter drifts off, and I shake my head. More hallucinations.

I get back to my original destination—the job fair I'd been meaning to show my face at. Only, considering I'm now as wet as a cat, I redirect my steps to the job search office a couple blocks away.

This time, I make sure to keep an eye out for people. Might as well avoid killing anyone.

Turns out, I should've kept my head ducked.

The first time, I thought it was an illusion.

The second time, another hallucination.

But by the fifth, I had to admit it's a helluva lot more than that. The faces staring at me—they aren't human anymore. They're skeletons, and some I pass and feel like not even a month of scrubbing in a shower would clean me. Others warm me with their spirit, and others still make me want to disappear.

What the hell is happening to me?

Forgetting all about not wanting to hurt someone, I duck my head and rush through the crowd, shivering and shaking. I can't be seeing this stuff. Not now. Not again.

Because if there's one thing running through me, one certainty I can't ignore, it's that this isn't the first time I've seen these faces.

I'm panting by the time I lean against the wall of the job search building. Soaked to the bone, shivering in my shoes, and feeling like my skin is heated. I glance at the back of my hand, and I swear the veins seem like red snakes are running through them.

Gulping a big breath, I try to calm my heartbeat. Surely I'm imagining this, too?

The lies are starting to get thinner, less believable, even to myself.

Closing my eyes, I think back to my childhood. To being a freak. Scared to sleep at night. Scared to go out. And then, at some point, all the skeletons I was seeing, all the weird vibes I was getting, they stopped.

That didn't stop middle school from being a nightmare. Both kids and their parents shunned me, bullied me. Teachers didn't see promise in my work. I've been raised to be no one, nothing—less than nothing. So if any of this is even real, why the hell would I be some kind of Chosen One?

Or maybe, the thought hits me, the faces never went away. Maybe I just got better at lying to myself. Either way, Daymun did something to bring them back. And if he did, that means he's real— regardless of whether anyone else can see him, or not.

Hands shaking, I ball them into fists and walk into the building, expecting to see more skeletons. I blink—it's gone. The faces are gone. Thankfully, everyone here looks human. A relieved breath escapes me, and I eagerly grab a chair by a computer and start googling jobs. I need a semblance of normalcy in my life right now, even if it may not last.

"Have you finally come around, then?"

I jump out of my chair, causing it to clatter on the floor. The girl at the info desk gives me a dirty look, but I ignore it and instead bend down to pick it up. Out of the corner of my eye, I glance at Daymun, looking resolutely devilish in the chair next to me.

A quick sweep around assures me we're far enough from everyone else that I can talk to him, without fearing I'll get kicked out for being crazy. At least, if I stick to whispers. Or so I hope.

I take a seat again and focus on the screen, aimlessly scrolling down the job listings. This page hides something else I'd been looking into—a google search for *flama* and *phoenix shifters*. Which, evidently, didn't turn up anything other than Daymun by my side.

"Are you still trying to ignore me, love?"

I kick my foot out to the side—surprised when it connects with his. My startled glare meets his, even as he releases a hiss of pain.

"That was uncalled for."

"You're being a stalker. It was very called for."

Daymun snorts, reaches down to rub his calf, then straightens up. He even makes the move appear sensual, but I'm not fooled.

"I thought mortal women were meant to fall for the whole bad boy act, or is that a myth?"

It's my turn to snort. "Yeah, a myth cooked up by bad romances and shit. Not real life. Been there, done that, bear the scars."

I exit the search tab on shifters, instead

focusing on the jobs. My clothes are still wet, but oddly my body seems to be exuding its own type of heat. Hopefully this means I won't catch a cold.

Daymun isn't so quick to drop things. "Katya, you can't go on ignoring us. Not only is it childish, it's also dangerous."

"*Childish?*" My voice rises, and I check it before continuing. "You're not real. You can't be."

"Tell yourself whatever you want, but we both know you're starting to believe it."

"Yeah? And what gives you that idea?"

He pauses, then says, "The skeletons? You saw them in your childhood, and you cannot deny it."

In my haste jerking to him, my neck protests. But I'm not interested in acknowledging the tinge of pain. What I need to understand is how he could've known that. It's not possible—I was alone. And even if he's playing some trick on me, I wouldn't have... I couldn't have...

"How the hell do you know that?"

Daymun presses his lips together, refusing to answer.

I lean forward, reaching for his shirt, ignoring the heat that comes through the silky material and his cinnamon scent. "Tell me how you know, you bastard, or else—"

"Or else?" His eyes are dancing with amusement, and I'm sick of it.

Without bothering to clear the history, I shut off the computer and take off. As soon as I'm out of the building, I take off on a jog—again.

I only make it around the corner before stopping, and this time, not because I've bumped into someone. Rather, more of a mental block. I've been running from so many things—heartbreak, poverty, loneliness, to name a few—but have never actually stopped to think. Self-reflect.

And heck, if now's not the time, when is?

Rather than rush back into the ongoing traffic of humans, I take the back roads and head to the park. It takes me a little under half an hour, but I make it just as the sun sets.

I should be afraid to be here alone, but I'm not. For one, I learned how to fight when I was young. There was no way around it, when you're a freak in a town full of idiots. And then when I was on my own, it came in handy to avoid perverts.

Really, though, the area is pretty devoid of threats right now. Unless you count the angel unfurling his wings under a tree, and patiently waiting for me to approach him.

I could turn the other way. But, really, why else did I come here, if not to hear what he has to say? On some subconscious level, I knew even as I woke up this morning that they weren't done with me, nor I with them.

So rather than take off, I force my numb feet to move forward, until I'm about two meters away from Dante. "How did you know I'd come here?"

He lifts one shoulder in a shrug. "The link. I sensed your need to stop running and figured you would return to a spot you were familiar with."

I tilt my head to the side. "You seem pretty sure of your assessment of me. What gives?"

His chocolate eyes close, as if it pains him to answer me. I realize why, once he tells me the truth. "Of course I know how you think, Katya… As does Daymun. We have been your guardians since you were a babe, it is only natural."

It takes a moment for what he said to sink in. Then I recall his words from last night… *Two guardians are assigned to you and mark you with their blood.* Rage fills me, boiling my insides. His eyes shift to the skin uncovered at my collarbone, and my palms.

"Katya…"

A quick glance shows me the red veins again—it must be happening when I'm in a highly emotional state. The realization doesn't dwarf the betrayal.

"All these years… You were there? But hidden?"

He nods, though I can tell he doesn't want to.

"What kind of a fucking angel are you?" My low hiss makes him wince, but I'm nowhere near done. "You come here, fucking with my life, expecting me to become some kind of savior for this place? Never mind the hell I lived through! Twenty-five years of misery, that you could've undone, that you could've freaking helped me with!"

Tears are running down my cheeks now, but I can't stop myself. Won't stop myself. "Who the hell do you think you are? Who the hell does Daymun thinks he is? And how in he—"

Dante's on me in a breath, his hand over my mouth, stopping me from uttering that third H word. I narrow my eyes on his and bite the flesh of his palm without remorse.

He lets go of me, but stays in my bubble, refusing to put distance between us. "Afraid I'm going to open the gate to the so-called Underworld?"

Dante's nostrils flare at my disdain, and a rush of satisfaction runs through me as he loses his cool. "Do you still think this is a game? After everything you saw today? Everything you lived last night?"

I step closer, my forehead to his chin. "Yeah, I think it's a fucking game. One you and Daymun are playing, to drive me insane. How else do you explain an angel standing by while I was traumatized, locked in closets, beaten to a bloody pulp, bullied through all my teens? How else do you explain having *two* immortal guardians, only to suffer like that?"

"We didn't have a choice."

The voice comes from behind me, but I don't move. "He's come to save you, huh?" I laugh in Dante's face, and only then step back to face Daymun. "Really? Two badass immortals? At least

41

stop lying."

His eyes flash almost dark. "I told you—I never lie."

"And I don't believe you!"

Whirling to Dante, I grab hold of one of his wings. "Are these even real? Or just something you threw on from a Halloween store?"

Despite my words, despite everything I want to believe, the feathers under my hands are soft like silk. And very much real. Dante's groan draws my eyes to his face. His jaw is clenched, his chocolate eyes dark, his hands curled into fists. Tension radiates from him.

Daymun's hand covers mine then and pulls it back. As he does so, his fingers brush up against a feather, and a zap like a lightning bolt shoots up between the two. I stare in shock, letting Daymun pull me away.

"What was that?"

"He's a celestial immortal, and I'm a fallen one. When we touch, nature objects."

I shake my head. "I don't…"

"Please stop lying to yourself, Katya," Dante says. "You have every right to be mad at us, for allowing everything that happened to you. But we couldn't reveal ourselves. Such is the law we were bound to."

"Why?"

"Will you even believe us, if we tell you?"

I glance between them. "Probably not. But try

me."

Dante sighs, and rubs his chin. All tension is gone from him now, leaving only that wise air, way too much for someone so young. "We mentioned before our connection, and how our blood is linked to you, and can also kill you."

He stops, clears his throat, but the rest of the words won't come out. Daymun rolls his eyes. "Pathetic." To me, he says, "At the beginning of time, there was nothing. Immortals were created first, much before humans. Then the mortals came, the jewel of the Creator's eye, and immortals got jealous. Especially those who realized humans were a danger to everyone—including this beautiful earthly realm. Some were banned, others remained but had to follow strict rules. But the Creator realized one set of banned immortals had the power to save his precious mortals."

He stops, staring at me, until I whisper, "You mean the Flamas."

"Indeed." Dante starts pacing, apparently unable to sit still. "Since Flamas were so powerful, the Creator bound the blood of an angel and of a demon to them, for eons to come, in order to control their journey, and ensure they would not destroy all that has taken eons to build."

I glance between them again. "I don't understand, though. If I'm to believe all this—and that's a big if—my shifter size is tiny. What gives me the power to do something like this? How can I save the world, cleanse it?"

The two share a look. "You can do so the way Flamas have always been able to—by opening the gate to Heaven, or Hell, and unleashing the curse within them."

"One to save."

"And one to doom."

I close my eyes at their words, but that doesn't stop them from echoing in my ears. *Save. Doom.* They aren't metaphors. They mean it literally.

When I open them again, neither guardian is in sight. Only me, the stars, and a crescent moon.

Chapter 4

That night, when I sleep, it's with impatience thrumming in my veins. It takes me way too long to get into a deep slumber, but when I finally do and the forest surrounds me, I run through it. By the time I reach the first expanse of land with no trees, I'm pacing back and forth, unable to rest.

"Katya."

I whirl around, and Vas is there. How did I not hear him? He's dressed like last time, but his eyes look tired, with dark circles underneath.

"You don't look so good," I tell him.

He shakes his head, releases a huge breath of relief, then pulls me into his arms, holding me tight. His heartbeat is loud against my ears, deafening the sound of my own pumping blood.

"What happened, before?" he asks as he lets me go, but still holds onto my shoulders. His grey eyes roam over my face, and his jaw tightens. "You're more tired than before, and thinner, too."

A blush creeps on my cheeks, I don't know

why, and I tuck a strand of hair behind my ear. "I don't know what happened. By the time I woke up, I was burning up, and then…"

Trailing off, I look anywhere but at him. I might've lost my mind in between our last dream and this one, but I clearly remember that moment, the intensity in his stare, the electricity in the air… In a way, it almost makes me wary to be alone with him again. Not because I'm afraid of anything he might do, but rather because I fear my own lack of control.

Vas has always, without a fault, been able to get into my soul. It's an addiction where he's concerned and makes me want to spend more time than is normal with him. That being said, how can I explain I had some kind of psychotic mental break? He'll run away, and despite only seeing him in my dreams, he's given me strength these last years.

I can't lose him, too.

Vas' hands tighten on my shoulders, pulling my attention back to him. "And then?"

"It's stupid. I've been hallucinating these things, this angel and demon telling me I'm some kind of shifter and savior of the world." A bitter scoff escapes me. "Can you believe it? Little old me, screwed over by the world at every turn?"

When he's silent, I look into his features, catching the oddest expression of panic over them. "What is it?"

Vas shakes his head and lets go of my shoulders. "That sounds…"

"Crazy, I know," I mutter and look away.

My head throbs, which it never has in dreams, but now it seems I can't escape reality any further. It's a weird kind of pain, pulsating and constant this time.

Vas sees me massaging my temples and comes to stand behind me. His hands go back to my shoulders, only this time he starts a slow massage, kneading my muscles and loosening me up. I can't help a soft hiss of pain as he finds a particularly stubborn knot under a shoulder blade, followed by a moan as he soothes it out.

I catch myself, blushing furiously again as his hands freeze. Embarrassed, I try to move out of his reach, but Vas shifts to my shoulders and neck, keeping me steady as he works on the tightness. Biting back more moans at the relief spreading through me is hard—he's *that* freaking good.

"You ever thought about doing this professionally?" I whisper, tilting my head to the side.

Vas chuckles behind me. "No, can't say that I have."

He continues alternating between soft and hard kneading, until I'm ready to melt in a puddle at how good it feels. The pulsating sensation in my head eases, becoming background noise.

And then… Vas turns it up a notch. I'm not sure what it is, exactly, that clues me in. Maybe his breathing changing, becoming harsher, or the way his hands suddenly feel more like they're caressing me, versus attempting to remove my pain.

His long fingers move right under my head, rubbing in circles from my neck to my ears, and back again. Another moan escapes me this time, and I'm powerless to stop it. Vas shifts closer, his chest to my back, and I feel him lowering his head. For a moment, I'm not sure what he's doing, but he ends up dropping the faintest of butterfly kisses on my ear lobe.

Faintest, and yet it sends a jolt of electricity through my body, straight to my very core. My body heats up, and just as I'm about to lean into him, arching my neck to demand more, Vas drops his hands.

A few more moments, then he steps around me and faces me, his expression unreadable. "Does that help your head?"

"Loads." I nod, hoping the darkness of the night hides my blush.

"Good." His expression hardens with determination. "Now, will you tell me the rest? What's going on with that Bryan guy of yours, is this all his fault or something?"

Tension radiates from him at the words, and I try to buy some time. "Where's Bebo? I miss his furry butt."

A flicker of amusement crosses his eyes. "I'll make sure to let him know. Probably out hunting, is my guess. Now stop stalling."

I sigh, run a hand through my tangled mess of red curls, then give up and whisper. "We broke up." When silence only answers me, I keep staring at the ground as if it's the most interesting thing ever. "Rather, *I* broke up with *him* three months ago, after he shagged the CEO's secretary. Lost my job in the process... And I'm in a bit of a pickle. That's why the tiredness, the migraines, and everything else."

More silence, then Vas' bare feet come into my field of vision. "I'm sorry," he says, and pulls me into his arms again. Only, this time, the embrace is different, like he's not holding back. It's hard to explain, but the way he slams our bodies together, not minding that I'm pressed up against all of him... It's like there are no barriers between us anymore.

I'm reminded of my earlier thoughts, about how part of the fault in the demise of my relationship with Bryan was also mine. Mainly, because I was confiding in Vas, spending time with him at night, though it was only ever as friends. Maybe to some extent that detachment was felt on Bryan's side.

When I pull back this time, Vas' brow is furrowed, and he seems about to say something. After an internal debate visible on his features, he kisses my forehead, lingering more than usual. "You need some proper rest." Then he grabs my hand and pulls me further in the forest.

We walk in silence for a bit, before reaching a spot where a hammock is set up between two trees.

A startled laugh escapes me as I glance between Vas and the makeshift bed. "This is yours?"

He grins back, then hops in and opens his arms in a silent invitation. I hesitate—we've only ever spent the night talking on the grass, and walking in the forest, but this feels more... intimate. Especially after that massage. How could he possibly know what turns me on, when all we've been is best friends for the longest time?

As if guessing my thoughts, Vas taunts, "You're not afraid of an itty-bitty hammock, are you?"

Rolling my eyes, I carefully get in, and after a brief shuffling that results in me elbowing him, settle against his chest. His arms close around me like it's the most natural thing in the world, and I'm asleep in minutes. But not before I register the hint of a six-pack under the abs of steel I rest my head on...

It's been two days since my freakish hallucinations whenever I'm outside, and my dream of Vas. I've searched online for some shrinks, but their quotes alone scare me. If money wasn't an issue, maybe I'd bother going. As it is, I'm more interested in paying the rent for my little shithole and putting food on the table rather than dealing with my head.

I also haven't taken the prescription for migraines since I saw the two Ds, and though the pain is unbearable, going on days now, it's almost become part of me. Hard to wish for no pain when you don't know what you're missing, right?

Against my better judgement, I've also gone back to the job place. This time, no demon or angel blocked my path or tried to talk to me. Maybe I really am crazy, or maybe they're giving me time to come to terms with it. But if that's the case, that would mean everything is real.

And I'm a Flama.

And I'm supposed to save the world.

How the hell can I do that, when I can't even save myself?

If it was up to me, I'd stay in my apartment all day long until the migraine disappears. But, that's not likely to happen. Sadly, I run out of options at about the same time I run out of food. Since I'm on a tight budget, that means no take-out either.

So I wait until the sun sets—like a vampire, yup—and get dressed to go to the grocery store. At least the lack of light will make it easier on my eyes, and head. This time, I opt for sweatpants, hoodie and worn sneakers. I keep my gaze glued to the ground, refusing to look at anyone and face my own insanity.

For the most part, it works. I'm able to get in, grab a cart, and head straight for the aisle of frozen meals. Cheapest meals, too. When you can't afford spices and basic veggies, might as well go for canned or frozen. Not the healthiest, but it kept me alive for the last three months.

Out of the corner of my eye, I catch sight of people around me. But I refuse to look at them directly, instead averting my gaze. I grab two boxes of pizza and some frozen lasagna, then head to stand in line.

An old lady is ahead of me, and I patiently wait for my turn, gaze glued to the dirty laminate floor.

Of course, I can't really keep doing that when I'm at the register. The girl there says some kind of total, and I glance up when I hand her the money. Only to then backtrack into the metal frame of the other cashier, hard enough to give myself a bruise in my lower back.

"What's wrong with you?" she asks.

What's wrong with *me*, says the creature staring at me with no eyes and teeth as yellowed as a rotten corpse. At the back of my mind, I realize I must be hallucinating again. But then I glance behind me, hoping someone else sees this. Only, they're all glaring at me like I've lost my mind, from gaunt faces with rotting eyes and skeletal bones.

"None of you see this?" I point at the cashier, whose eyes roll.

"Lady, look here—"

I don't wait to listen for the rest. Instead, I run out of there as fast as my feet take me, forgetting all about my food. Panting, I rush up the fire escape to my apartment, then slam the door and bolt it behind me.

It's not a hallucination.

The certainty vibrates through me, and I can't avoid it anymore. Pills or no pills, migraine or not, the fact of the matter is *something* is happening to me. And no one aside from the two Ds can give me a plausible explanation.

Unfortunately, that also means I have to hear it all, the full thing, and decide what I'm going to do—*if* I can do anything—afterwards.

But how does one go about calling two immortals?

The moment I think it, I feel them around me. The cinnamon and sulfur scent for Daymun, the pine, honey and vanilla one for Dante. They're not exactly visible, but surrounding me. My head feels ready to split into two, but I take a deep breath and push past the pain.

"Alright, show yourselves."

A moment later, both Dante and Daymun are facing me with mirrored expressions of patience. It throws me off, and tears prick my eyelids. They look so at odds in my small space, filling it up with their size and presence, and for the first time it strikes me that I'm not alone in this.

Sniffling, before I turn into a blubbering mess, I say, "What's happening to me?"

Neither guardian moves towards me, and I appreciate it. I don't think I could stand kindness right now, not when everything they've been trying to tell me the last days weighs on my mind.

Rather than physical comfort, they both provide something much more needed—mental comfort.

Daymun heads off to my stove and flicks his hand over it, causing flames to rise. My eyes widen at the display of magic, even as he picks up a beat-up kettle and pours water in to boil.

"Tea?"

My answer is a strangled groan, not that it seems to faze him. As he goes about the business of making me a cup, I turn to Dante. His dark eyes assess my mood, then he gives a short nod, almost as if it to himself.

"We promised we would be less, hmm, pushy this time around. Thus, rather than overwhelming you with information, how about you ask us questions?"

I gulp past my dry throat, and try to speak, but nothing comes out. Instead, I glance again to Daymun, standing over my stove—that he magically made work…

"It isn't magic." Dante's soft tone jerks my attention back to him. "Magic is a human concept. Immortals access what we call primal energy. Each group of immortals will have their own—or more than one."

I gulp again, and this time manage to speak. "Can you elaborate?" I'm surprised I sound so calm, given my pulse is in my throat.

"Of course."

Dante gestures to the couch, and I hesitantly move towards it, taking a seat. Daymun comes from the kitchen with a cup of tea, holding the steaming mug in front of me.

"As a demon from Hell, I manipulate fire," he says. "Some of my other brethren can also manipulate earth."

"And as an angel, I manipulate spirit, and air."

"Spirit?"

Daymun rolls his eyes. "He tends to have a calming effect on people. Taking away their pain, and all that."

The minute the words are out of his mouth, I'm reminded of my accusations to Dante, in the park. "So you guys are all-powerful, and immortal, not to mention you've got morals—even the demon. Why didn't you help me, then?" I look at the cup of tea, the warmth seeping into my skin. "You say we're linked, but you let me handle all that crap by myself."

"We could not," Dante says softly. "We were bound by laws much harsher than you could ever understand."

I choose to sidestep that, not wanting to think of how different my life would be, had I had them to rely upon in my childhood. "You said each group of immortals… What other things are affected? What other immortals are there? And what are these faces

I keep seeing, these skeletons? It only happened since you touched my forehead." The last is meant for Daymun, with an accusing tone.

Of course, he notices it and smirks. "I didn't do anything. You already had the *vedere*."

I jerk at the word in Romanian—*sight*—and his pronunciation. He's giving it a very supernatural tone.

"That's because it is," Daymun picks up on my train of thought. "Nothing is normal about what you are, and what you have been able to do since you were young."

"Gee, thanks."

"He means it as a compliment," Dante says with a glare to the demon. "It is an amazing gift."

"Right. That's why I had such a lovely childhood."

Daymun narrows his eyes. "If you hadn't hidden it from yourself, you would have been spared the migraines."

"Oh, so now it's my fault?"

"In a way." He shrugs.

"And why couldn't you two have told me that?"

"We're here to be your guardians, not your friends."

Ignoring the hurt spreading through me at his harsh tone, I change the subject. "How do you even know Romanian?"

"Picked it up over the years," he mutters, and

moves away. He stares out the foggy window of my fire escape, refusing to meet my gaze again.

I stare at his back for a moment, before moving on to another question. "What's the point of me seeing these faces, then?"

Dante answers, sounding contrite. "You have to understand, as a Flama, you see the soul within the person. You can choose to turn it on and off, like all gifts, but it is meant to give you a better idea of who is what—good, evil, human, immortal."

"Then how come it doesn't happen with you two?"

"Because we wear our souls on our sleeve. Who you see, that is who we truly are. Same will be true for any other immortal."

"That's not quite true though, is it?" Daymun snorts from his spot near the window. "Why don't you tell her the full thing?"

"We agreed not to overload her with information."

"Uh, hello?" I raise my hand. "I'm right here, idiots. How about you quit worrying about my feelings, since we're well past that? I want to know everything."

Dante glares at his friend's—enemy's?— back for a moment, before saying, "Vert well. It is a bit more complicated than that. While it is true that Daymun and I wear our souls on our sleeves, it is because we are linked with you. You will always see through our bullshit. With other immortals, you may not necessarily see their true face, at least not at first. As supernatural beings, we are also capable of hiding our real face for longer. But as a Flama, you will still be able to dig through, once you master it enough."

"And how do I do that?"

Dante shrugs. "Practice."

"So that's my affinity, for lack a better word?"

"Along with opening the gates, yes."

"Wonderful. So, pretty useless then."

"Not if you count what your purpose on Earth is." The whisper comes from Daymun's side, but I don't let him derail me again.

"What about the rest of immortals?" I ask instead.

"Well, vampires can draw souls out of people, and have a particularly easy time with air. Werewolves are good with animals. Fairies are great with earth and air. Elves, they are *particularly* good with earth and water. And zombies—" Shock must have shown in my expression, as Dante stops. "What is it?"

"You're talking about… fictional creatures."

"Nothing is fiction," Daymun speaks, his tone gentler than before. "All the stories you grew up with, the monsters, creatures and heroes, they're all real. Just not necessarily as you know them."

"That's… not possible."

"It is."

I stand from the couch then, sipping my tea and moving away from them. My head is whirling with thoughts, each crazier than the next.

"So everything is real?"

"Everything."

"All the creatures?"

"All of them."

"But... So why can't any of them do whatever it is I'm supposed to do?"

Daymun finally moves away from the window. "Because that's not their purpose on Earth, it's yours."

"Why can't another Flama do it, then?"

"Only one exists at a time," Dante says.

"Why?"

"Because your kind... They are meant to fix the balance of the world, but they also upset it." He hesitates, then adds, "That is why you have a timeline, whereby you have to do your duty. It cannot take longer, or the disruption will be even worse than before, and chaos will take over."

I sip the rest of the tea. "What happens to me then, after all is said and done?"

They share a look, and Dante answers yet again. "We cannot say completely. There are no written accounts of previous Flamas, only what was passed down verbally. All we know is what we were each told, before being named as your guardians— when you would awaken, what your purpose would be, and how to help you accomplish it."

My silence extends for a long time. I asked for the truth, and they gave it to me. I'm just not sure I can handle it.

"You said before that I have a duty, to this world, to what is happening. And that I only have a few weeks to make my choice."

"Yes," Dante says.

"The pills you took woke your gift up earlier," Daymun adds.

"How?"

"Because you've been pushing away all these thoughts for years upon years. The migraines were your mind's way of pushing back. Think of it as an elastic band. You tug enough times in every which way direction, eventually it snaps. The pills were always pushing your gift away... Until the band snapped. Your gift rose to the surface."

"All it means is, we have more time," Dante says in an effort to be reassuring.

I mull the words in my head a few times over. "And if I was to believe all this... What, exactly, am I embarking on?"

"A quest."

Images of flashing swords and knights pass through my head. Dante grins. "Not that kind of quest, gorgeous. More of a... spiritual one."

When my staring at them doesn't prompt the rest of the information, I scowl. "Elaborate, please?"

"It'll be meant to show you the sides of Dark

and Light," Daymun says. "The guardians are never privy to what is demanded directly, but we'll be there for emotional support, and as a well of knowledge."

"And when you are done, hopefully, you will have learned enough to decide what your true purpose will be."

"Whether I save or doom," I repeat their words from the other day.

Both stare at me, as if expecting me to make such a choice in the moment.

"How long do I have?"

Dante's expression is kind, but his tone is getting firmer with each word. "The sooner we go, the better, Katya."

"Why? And where are we going?"

"A place where legends still live, hidden from the rest of the world."

I shake my head, placing the cup with shaky fingers on the table. "I don't think I'm ready. I get why this is happening, what you've told me, but I can't wrap my head around it so easily. You guys don't get it—I'm not a hero. After everything I've lived through, I'm the last person you should entrust with the fate of humanity. I'm cynical, and have a hard time seeing the positives in this world."

When only silence answers me, I look up. They're both gone, leaving me alone with my thoughts.

Chapter 5

The following day is spent in a daze. I sleep a lot, and when I'm not doing that, I'm staring in the distance. No trace of either Bebo or Vas, but it's not like I have any dreams, period.

Late in the afternoon, police sirens pull me out of my trance. I've been doing nothing but thinking since the two Ds disappeared, trying to wrap my head around everything they told me.

It's impossible to. That's basically what the last hours have proven to me. Yet my rational, logical mind can't comprehend tthe creatures in the ratty books I used to read are actually real. Never mind the fact I somehow seem to trump them, yet I can't find a single piece of information on my kind, aside from what I've been told.

Take it at face value, a part of me says.

The other, much more cynical, points out my craziness.

Yet at the end of the day, there's really no way to accept all of this, and end up sane. Not when what really bugs me is not the weirdness of the situation, but the fact I'm supposed to make such a massive decision. That the fate of the world rests on my shoulders.

I mean, whoever the hell came up with that solution?

My eyes rise upwards, to the darkening sky. Dante had mentioned a Creator. I didn't ask for details, because I'm not interested. No higher divinity was around when I needed help, when I needed protection.

Neither were they, that same traitorous voice answers me.

And the thing is, I do feel resentment. It's a nasty weight in my chest, upset that all along I might've had another future, another life. Maybe I would've grown up smart enough to actually go through university. To not fall for Bryan. To not...

I shake my head. My reflection in the foggy living room window shows me tired eyes, gaunt cheeks, and lifeless green eyes. My hair is a mess—I haven't had proper, luxurious shampoo for a while, instead sticking with the cheapest crap I could find at dollar stores. When was the last time I even enjoyed a hot shower, without worrying about my water utility bill?

My muscles protest when I move from my spot, reminding me I've been immobile for too long. It's been ages since I've had something good... And just like that, an idea forms in my head. I'm also giddy with relief when I pull my sweater on and step outside of the apartment.

After all, what do I have to lose? If all this is real, and if I was to go on a journey, it's not like anyone would miss me, or care if I died along the way. Aside from this apartment, I have nothing tying me here. Least of all someone to love.

Thoughts of Vas rifle through my head. But it's not like I wouldn't see him in my dreams, right? He was still there when I moved in with Bryan, he's bound to still be around.

As for gaining something… Well, at the very least, I'd be traveling somewhere. In all my years on this earth, I've never gone outside of Toronto. So to be able to visit somewhere cool—wherever that is— will be worth it.

And if I'm to go on an epic quest, then I should at least see myself off properly. I probably won't need money when I'm out there saving the world—or maybe I would. Who knows?

Either way, I can figure out a way. I'm not alone anymore, not with Daymun and Dante around me. Unlike before, they're here to help—no rules holding them back this time. *I can do this. I can make something of myself. And if saving the world is part of the job, well, it's not like I picked me to do it. They'll figure out eventually I'm no one's hero.*

Grinning, I run down the stairs and back out to the grocery store. I pick one a bit further than my usual spot, since I don't want to make a fool of myself again. I don't even care about the faces, the people around me. Excitement burns my chest, and it's been so damn long I've felt this.

Even with Bryan, I'd always been afraid of a good thing coming to an end—and I was right. But this time around, it's like a new life is infused in me, and I'm relishing everything. From the wind in my hair, the chill on my cheeks, the bite of the musty air.

Everything is invigorating.

At the store, I don't bother with the frozen food section. Instead, I go to the warm food area and pick up a fresh chicken, a box of wedges and a potato and egg salad. Then I go to the toiletries section and pick up a ten-dollar shampoo. German. It smells amazing, and will do wonders for my ratty, shine-less hair. Last, I pick up a flowery-smelling body gel, a luxury I haven't had in ages.

With my supplies in hand, I go to the cashier. The guy stares back at me from under a skeleton just as ugly as the previous chick, but I don't care. Grinning and avoiding meeting his eyes, I hand him the cash, pick up my bag, and walk down the street.

I'm already relishing the idea of a shower— not a bath, I won't risk it in that bathtub. But a hot shower until the water runs cold sounds amazing. Without even realizing it, I skip down the street, practically whistling with happiness.

Maybe that's why I don't hear them at first. For the first time in forever, I let my guard down, and of course fate decides to have a laugh at my expense.

A few more meters down, and the hair on the back of my neck stands to attention. Someone's watching me. I turn my head to the side slightly and sight of two shapes following me.

A flash of lightning in the sky illuminates their faces—same weird, skeletal visions I've been seeing. Only, their aura is dark, more than anything I've encountered until now. Survival instinct tells me to run. Shivers run down my spine, and I quicken my step. I've always had bad luck, but this is my own stupidity. Rather than stick to the public area, I took a shortcut back home, and lost track of my surroundings.

That's the stupidest thing I could've done, and unless I run out of here, I'm going to pay dearly for it. No matter how I rush though, I can't shake them off. I see the end of the alley in the distance, the lights of traffic there, and give up on trying to be subtle. I was trying not to show fear, but I *am* afraid.

Their intent to harm is like a siren blaring in my ears, their aura pulsating in the wake of my shadows. I'll have one chance, and one alone.

So I run for it, full-legged. Not even my track and field saves me this time. Just as I reach the end of the alley, two other guys walk in, blocking the way out. I flinch, stopping in my tracks. Behind me, the other two close in.

I'm near the main street though… Dropping my bags, I give up all pretense and scream at the top of my voice. "Help!"

No one peers in, but I see people walking past the alley. Fuck this city and people's inhumanity. I drop my bag of groceries to the ground and clench my fists. Not going to go down without a fight, that's for damn sure.

"Whatcha doing alone so late at night, babe?"

"Yeah, you looking for company?" adds another.

Revulsion creeps up my spine and I grit my teeth. "Get the hell away from me."

The one behind me moves closer. "Don't think so, baby. You're just lush, aren't you?" He runs one hand down my front, groping me. I stomp my heel on his foot, then dig my elbow in his gut, as close to his groin as I can.

Cussing under his breath, the guy stumbles backwards, leaving me three more to deal with. The two in front of me move closer. Their skeleton faces are distracting, with empty eye sockets and worms coming out of their cheeks.

What you see reflects their souls, Dante had said. Well, these guys are obviously rotten to the core. Either way, their appearance is enough to throw me off, gaining them a few seconds.

When the first one grabs my wrist and pulls me close, I lift my knee—not fast enough. He avoids my kneeing him in the groin, and instead whirls me around in a chokehold. I let him pull me close—close enough to grind his erection against my ass.

"Keep fighting, babe, I'm gonna enjoy this."

Gritting my teeth, I let my head fall forward as if I'm giving up, and my body goes slack—then I shoot my head back with all the force I can muster. A sickening crunch rings in the air, followed by his cusses.

But I'm free. Contouring him, I make for the main street—only to have the other guy pull on my hoodie. I lose my balance, and he takes advantage to grab a fistful of my hair. His grip is tight, and he jerks me to the side, smacking my head against the brick. My vision goes dark for a moment, and when I'm conscious again, I'm on the ground.

The other two I'd hurt are standing, and all four surround me. Dread builds in my stomach. My hand on the ground is bloody, with fresh drops falling presumably from my head wound. My veins are red—the Flama, rolling to the surface.

If I could transform… If I could escape…

I close my eyes, hoping for the change, to no avail. It's too new, and up until earlier this morning I was still in denial. Even by being some Chosen One, I still end up screwed.

One guy kicks me in the gut, and I cough up more blood. Another kicks towards my face, and his foot connects with my jaw. I guess my beating their asses has removed any desire of raping me, but I can't find it in me to be grateful.

Not when all they want is to inflict pain on

me, on my body. Wrecked with blows, all I can do is curl up in a fetal position and hope they don't kill me. Hysterically, the thought crosses my mind—what would happen to the world if I died? Who would save it then?

And then something flashes in my mind. I'm not alone in this. But will they come, this time? And how can I call out to them?

The kicks stop for a moment, and past bloodied lips, I whisper one name. "Daymun…"

I don't know why it's him and not Dante that I call out to. Or, maybe I do. Maybe I know the wrath of Hell is what these guys need, and I want to see them suffer.

Something flashes, followed by the smell of sulfur and cinnamon, and then I hear blows—multiple hits. Something burns, making me cough. Charred flesh? I try to open my eyes, but they're both swollen, and I can't see much beside the black spots.

Then someone kneels next to me. I think I see a bloodied suit, and icy blue eyes, but surely I'm dreaming? I've never had a knight in shining armor.

"I'm not one," a familiar voice whispers. Darkness coats it, anger vibrating under the surface. And yet in complete contradiction, the hand touching my hair is soft, hesitant. "Katya…"

A sob escapes me, then another. I can't breathe, snot and blood filling my nose. Daymun picks me up, and against his warm chest I feel his harsh breathing, his held-back rage.

"Daymun, please. Please…"

My head falls against him, darkness pleading to pull me under, to make me forget about the pain. His strong arms hold me, tightening around me as if to protect. I squint into his face—contorted in pain, regret, and fury like no other.

"You are my priority, to get you somewhere safe, but I swear to you they will not escape." He sniffs the air. "No matter. I have their scents. They can run, but they cannot hide."

I must have blacked out, because the next time I squint my eyes, I'm surrounded by the familiar musty scent of my apartment. A gust of wind hits my beat-up face, followed by more cursing.

"No," Daymun says. "I've got this."

He brings me to the bathroom, and gets the shower running. With quick, efficient movements, he pulls off my clothes and supports me as I get under the hot water. I should be embarrassed, shy even, naked in front of a practical stranger. But I'm too detached, too drained by the night's events and the pounding in my head.

Everywhere the water hits me, I cringe, but I refuse to let out another sound of pain. Instead, I lean against the wall, trying to soak it in, and allow it to wash off the last hour.

This was supposed to be my night—a night to enjoy things I haven't in forever. To have a luxurious shower, a full stomach... Not get beaten up because of my own stupidity. Yet as always, whenever I let my guard down, the world has a way of freaking breaking me.

Gritting my teeth, biting the inside of my cheek, I stand in shame. Until Daymun touches my cheek, forcing me to turn towards him. "Katya, none of this is your fault."

"I should've been more careful."

His nostrils flare. "Not. Your. Fault."

I shake my head, and he helps me wash up, getting his suit wet in the process. His touch isn't sensual or seductive, rather efficient and caring, like he truly cares for me. It only makes me feel that much worse. Tears come to my eyes again, and I try to hold back a sob.

Daymun pulls me out of the shower then and wraps me in a massive towel. "Before I hand you to Dante, I have one more thing to say."

I look up at him, wondering what he sees now. I must be a mess of various rainbow colors, bloodied and bruised as I am.

Daymun tucks a strand of hair behind my ear. "Dante can help with the healing. Just tell me what you need."

I search his gaze, trying to figure out the meaning of his words. Something glints in his eyes, something he can't say out loud, something he can't incite me to. But my thirst for revenge answers his need for it, and I let the anger run through me, voicing it in a simple request. "I want their blood."

He doesn't fight me, just nods and squeezes my hand. "You'll have it, love."

Darkness welcomes me as he picks me up and carries me back in the living room.

≈ ♠ ≈

I jerk awake on a scream, shaking off the hand trying to offer me comfort. It takes me a minute of panicked panting to realize I'm safe, in my own house, with a guardian angel by my bed. He caresses my cheek, leaving a tingling behind.

"Where's Daymun?" I ask.

"Out."

At my confused look, he adds, "Cleaning the mess he made last night."

My eyes widen. "Because I asked him to?"

Dante shakes his head. "Believe me, Daymun wanted their blood even more than you did."

The thought of those men getting what they deserved doesn't leave an ounce of guilt in my stomach. Sure, if Daymun had been human, this would've been considered murder. Given he's not, can't it just be Hell expressing its wrath?

I think back to the attack. "Why… Why couldn't I change? How did Daymun even find me?"

Dante looks at the ceiling, then sighs. "He did not find you, darling. You called for him. In your hour of need, you called for him, and he was bound to come."

"Is that how the rule goes?" He inclines his head, something akin to sorrow in his expression. "So if I had called for you…"

"Then I would have come."

"But you couldn't show up without my call?"

"No. Angels and demons are bound to the spiritual world, where only you can see us, touch us. Otherwise, chaos would reign, and the two forces would take too much joy in using humans as pawns."

"So if I had known you were there when I was a kid, and if I had called to you…"

His expression is filled with regret. "We would have answered."

I bite my lip, only then realizing it doesn't hurt. I glance over at my hands and touch my head—nothing. "What happened to my bruises?"

"I healed them." When I only stare, he adds, "An angel perk."

I look back to the bedsheets, cursing against my bad luck. And wondering about the men Daymun went after…

"If it had not been him, I would have done it."

I stare at him in shock, and it takes me a minute to pull my thoughts together. "But…you're an angel."

"Nevertheless." His tone leaves no room for contesting. I'm left imagining him as an avenging angel then, and the image is all kinds of sinful.

Dante clears his throat, shifting me aside and

putting some space between us.

"Sorry," I mumble. *Probably not his type.*

"It's not that. You and me, Daymun and you… The link between us causes this. It enhances the connection, but you have to understand neither romantic option would work out."

"Why not?"

Dante shakes his head. "Only death awaits that path."

"Why?"

"Besides the rules keeping us in place, we are not compatible. Each one of us would try to change you, to cage you into what we believe is real. In time, you will see the truth of my words."

He sounds too damn wise, like he's lived millennia.

"While you slept, I have done some perusing, and I believe I have identified where we will travel. For your quest."

That draws my attention, given it had been the reason for my exhilaration last night. "What? Where?"

"Romania."

I'm stunned. I've never been there, though I carry the ancestry in my veins. Excitement at stepping on the land of my kin runs through me, obliterating the fear of the unknown. Images I've seen only in movies and books run through my head, of tall mountains and dipped valleys, rivers galore, and blanket of mysticism spread across…

"Why Romania?"

"The ground there is ancient. And bloody from many wars. In the mountains, there are caves… And enough mysteries to see which way you lean."

"And how did you figure it out?"

Dante grins. "We looked at a map."

Something about his words tells me there's more to this choice, but I don't push. I'm slowly learning they'll each tell me stuff in turn, when they deem me ready for it. And with the attack, it's not like my head's in a space to overthink.

Instead, my thoughts turn to something else. "Dark or Light," I whisper.

"Mmm."

"What you said before, about my choice and what I have to do… You said it would lead to opening the gate for Heaven or Hell and releasing the curse within either one."

Dante only watches me, a wise gleam in his chocolate eyes as he waits for me to finish.

"And Romania… These mysteries awaiting me, are they meant to show me something? Some kind of trial by fire, to see which way I lean?"

Dante nods without adding more explanations, and then he lets me sleep. Flashes run through my mind—the fear from earlier, the brutal attack — and I pull the blanket closer to my chin.

He may have healed my wounds, but my mind, that's another thing. And despite myself, I wonder if there really is a point to my going through these trials, when I'm obviously already leaning more towards revenge than saving.

Tossing and turning, I finally pass out of sheer exhaustion. And when I dream, it's of messy brown hair and grey eyes, a tattooed back with a living phoenix... and then the man turns into a wolf.

≈ ♠ ≈

It's light outside when I wake up next. No dream of Vas, and it's just as good. I don't think I could lie to him about what happened, never mind explain everything else. Someday, I'll have to, but I need more time.

The two Ds are in an angry whispered conversation, of which I'm the subject. When they don't stop, I clear my throat. "What's going on?"

They both turn to me but hesitate in answering. Until, as usual, Daymun jumps head in. "We need to leave this place. And, preferably, erase all traces of your existence here."

"What?"

"We have a plan. Once you've packed the necessary, we will burn everything down."

"You'll do *what*?"

Daymun sighs. "If you're to be who you are meant to, there can be no trace left of your overall human existence."

"But..."

I'm not sure at first what has me so

apprehensive. Except, maybe, for the fact it's so...final. Will I really never return to this life?

"No," Dante says in response to my thought. "After the weeks are up, the Flama is never seen again by mortals. They ascend to the Ether, a sort of resting place for your kind."

"You mean I'm going to *die*?"

Daymun rolls his eyes. "No, love. You'll live, but in a place where your immortals thrive. Once your duty is done, there will be no reason for your existence on Earth."

"What about you two?"

They shrug. "We go back home. Heaven for Dante, and Hell for me."

I glance around at my crummy apartment, the last three months running through my head. "And if I do none of this?" It's a whisper, but I realize it's been ongoing at the back of my mind.

Dante seems panicked at the thought. "You cannot shrug off your duty to humanity, Katya!"

Daymun lifts his hand to pacify him before he can continue and walks over to me, kneeling beside the bed. His blue eyes are devoid of emotion, yet his voice is soft. "Our lives are linked with yours. If you refuse to do your duty, we will cease to exist, as will you. *That,* I assure you, is a fate worse than death." He pauses, narrowing his eyes slightly and lowering his voice. "Besides, do you really think you can avoid your fate, love? Do you even want to, after last night, when it's obvious humanity needs to be taught a lesson?"

He holds my gaze for another moment, then straightens up. Dante throws him a wary look, but they both keep silent as I look around the place again. I can't deny Daymun's words spin on a loop in my head, reminding me of the pain, the attack… But also of the sheer relief I felt at being able to call upon an immortal to wipe those inhuman people off the Earth. And to think I have that full power now, for the rest of humanity?

And yet a part of me dreads leaving all this behind. It's not much of a life, but it is mine. "And I'll never return here?"

"Never."

Their words sound like a death sentence, but I nod. After the attack, and everything else, do I even want to come back to it?

No, not really. Whatever's out there, that's my new life. And nothing else.

Chapter 6

It's one thing to say I'd never come back to this life. It's another thing altogether to see said life burn up in flames. Which is what I'm doing within hours of the last conversation with the two Ds.

Around a corner, hidden in an alleyway with both of them by my side, we watch the apartment I've lived in for the last three months burn into flames. Dante says he's made sure the store underneath won't be affected, and I hope he's right.

I took the remainder of the cash in my tin box and followed them out, with nothing but a backpack filled with clothes and toiletries. *Good thing I never did get that food, I guess.* The thought is random as it runs through my head.

"What now?" My whisper carries, but the two don't say anything until I turn to face them. "How am I supposed to get to Romania with less than a hundred bucks in my pocket?"

Dante grins and flaps his wings, the gust of wind hitting me straight in the face. "What do you think these are for?"

I gape at him. "You expect me to fly in your arms for eight hours? Hell, no!"

Daymun snorts. "Not in your human form… You would never survive. We'll get you to shift back to Flama, then take off." With a roguish grin, he adds, "At least that way, if Dante drops you, you can fly away."

I'm nowhere amused by the assumption, and my panicked gaze meets Dante's. He rolls his eyes, and his tone is as reassuring as can be. "Nothing will happen to you, Katya, I vow it."

With one last glance over my shoulder, I follow them further into the alley, and the park that lays beyond it. Memories of my beating rush through me as the darkness closes in on me, but their presence here is reassuring.

That, and I've sworn to myself I'll never land in a similar situation, ever again.

Once we get to the park, I check around to make sure no one is there. My two guardians face me, their expressions patient even as I fiddle with my hair, then fingers, until I finally stop fidgeting and look at them.

"Okay, what do I do?"

Dante takes a step forward. "Do you remember what brought the change on the first time?"

"Not really. I woke up with everything burning in me."

"Can you recall that?"

I wince at the memory. "Kinda hard to forget."

"Let that memory fill you. Even the pain."

"Especially the pain," Daymun adds.

My glare has no effect on him. And, really, I owe him my life—but does he have to be so annoying? With a heavy sigh, I close my eyes and think back to that night, only a few days ago.

Insane how fast your life can spin out of control, right?

The agony, the stretching of my muscles, it fills my mind and I cringe. Dante whispers something that sounds like "It's working," but I'm already too far gone to hear him properly. Then my vision narrows, flames burst around me, my body feels like it's melting... and I'm back to being bird-sized. They both kneel next to me, grinning.

"Not bad for a second time," Daymun says. "I'll see you in the woods."

Woods?

I croak towards Dante, but he only sighs at his demonic counterpart. With one hand, he picks up my backpack. With the other, he gathers me to his chest, letting me move around until I'm comfortable and not squished. My size, with the long flaming tail trailing down, is about the length of his torso. Surprisingly, it doesn't burn him, which I take it to be another angel perk.

"Good?" he asks.

I nod my tiny beak, and his wings unfurl. "Hang on, darling." It has a nice ring to it.

The wind surrounding us intensifies, and then we're going up, up, the city below becoming smaller and smaller. Humans turn to ants, and then we're bursting through the clouds, higher still, until we're completely hidden.

Bye bye, my old life. Hello…whatever the hell awaits me now.

≈ ♠ ≈

I must have fallen asleep. By the time I blink, Dante is still flying, the strong and steady beat of his wings being what lulled me to dreamland in the first place.

When he feels me stirring, he loosens his grip a little, enough so he can tilt his head downwards and meet one of my eyes. "Do you want to try it?"

I glance below and want to vehemently deny such desire. But, in truth, I'm itching to spread my wings and feel that freedom. So I nod, and he grins in approval. Instead of continuing on our route, we stop in midair, the beat of his wings holding us up.

"I'm going to slowly let you go. First on my hand, then you can take off. Just capture the wind under your wings, and your body will do the rest."

Doubtful it'll be that easy. Obviously, I can't voice that.

Dante does as promised. Little by little, his

arm moves away from his chest. My talons grip the skin, drawing blood, but he doesn't let that faze him. Then I unfurl my wings, beat them once, and again… And then I'm flying.

The rush is exhilarating, like the best high a drug could provide. I've never tried any—my body is a temple, and all that—but I did get massively drunk once. It had been amazing not worrying about anything, forgetting all the past troubles and shit I've had to go through. But this… it feels a million times better.

My surprised gaze meets Dante's, and he points onwards. "Follow me."

For the next hour, I fly with him, sometimes above him, sometimes below. At one point, his voice carries over the wind. "You can do so much more beyond this, Katya. Phoenixes have healing abilities through their tears, not to mention they can carry massive loads. Your Flama form is also not always this small. Your mind controls it, and you are limiting yourself because of the birds you know. Think bigger, wider, and it will make flying easier. Let your emotions rule you."

I glance below, finding him flying on his back, as though he's swimming in the air. *Show off.*

For a beat, I'm afraid to try something so unpredictable while in mid-air. But then I realize the way Dante positioned himself is so he can catch me if I fall, so I let go and trust him. It's a hard concept for me, but if ever I was to trust anyone, it should be my guardian angel, right?

I try to wipe from my mind images of hens and hawks and think bigger instead. Eagles, vultures, mythical creatures. My mind segues into being alive, and strong, and untouchable... Flames burst around my wings, and the rest of my shifter body, but not once do I falter from mid-air.

By the time they're gone, and the smoke has cleared, I'm three times my regular size. My startled gaze meets Dante's, and he's grinning ear to ear.

The high that I did something right—that I might actually be good at this—increases, and my flaps get more confident as I thread through the air. And then... something catches my attention. I'm not sure what it is at first, like a ringing in my ears, but I follow it and deviate off the path.

Dante calls out to me, but I ignore him, instead flying faster, willing the wind to take me wherever it is. Something is wrong—infinitely so. And when I finally emerge from the clouds to look below, I realize what it is.

A large ship is sinking, filled with containers and what looks like oil barrels. The force of the water underneath has pushed the metal cages open, and plastic and garbage contaminate what used to be a beautiful patch of the ocean. Surrounding the area, I see two dolphins trying to battle their way through the thickness of the water, and the sludge of the debris, and fail.

Eventually, after useless fights, they stop and float away, getting dragged under the mess. I try to move forward—it had been their beautiful song that drew me here—but Dante flies in my face, his expression shuttered.

"We cannot do anything for them, Katya."

I cry out in refusal, in pain, and try to move past him but he unfurls his wings to stop me. Despite my increased size, he's still way larger than me, and slightly intimidating.

"I know you want to help them, but their lives are already lost. And they are not the first."

Tears fall from my eyes, even as he forces me backwards, and away from this mess. One more thing humanity touched, one more thing it ruined. I shouldn't be surprised anymore. People barely care about their loved ones, so why would they give two shits about nature and what we're doing to it?

Another hour of furious flying goes by, and I start looping in random circles. Dante appears in front of me and opens his arms in invitation. After a slight hesitation, I go in and snuggle. Though I'm larger now, he still has no problem hanging on to me and my backpack. His stamina must be something else, and I have no way to match it right now.

"One day, you'll be able to," he says above me.

I croak softly into his chest and let my tiredness lull me to sleep.

≈ ♠ ≈

When I find myself in the forest, I panic for the first time in years. Vas has always been a friend, a great listener, and someone I could always count on. But seeing him now, when I'm halfway across an ocean in the real world and going on some quest, I don't know how I can explain myself. Or worse, lie to him.

Regardless of how I eventually absorbed the impact of the news, it's something harder to communicate to another person. And yes, Vas is a figment of my imagination, but he's been a long-standing figment and he's more real than any person I've met.

Not to mention after last time, and falling asleep in his arms, something feels changed…

Put on your big girl panties, Katya, I admonish myself. *Vas will understand.*

With a stomp to the ground, I straighten my shoulders and move further into the forest. The clear air surrounds me, and I hear an owl in the distance, followed by rustling of leaves. Tonight, this place feels alive, vibrant, as though trying to pull me in.

It's with relief I reach the familiar meadow, but no one is there. I wait for long, long moments, then finally head through to the other side, trying to remember where Vas' hammock had been. After a few misses, I find it—but it's empty.

I hesitate, then climb into it and let the soft material swing me back and forth. It's cozy, and it smells like pine and Vas—familiar. Without realizing it, I nod off.

Something wet licks my hand, and I jerk to a start. *Sleeping in a dream and waking in the same dream, that's a new one.* Getting to my knees, I peek around the hammock to what had touched me, and find...

"Bebo!" My eager cry earns me another lick, this one more insistent.

To anyone, he'd look ferocious with those canines glinting in the moonlight, and the predatory gleam in his violet-grey eyes. To me, he's just another friend, a comfort in a lonely world.

I grin at him and tap the side of the hammock. "Come on up, boy!"

Yes, I realize he's not a dog, nor do I recommend trying this with a wolf you run into. Bebo and I, we're special. Always have been, even when I was young.

He jumps in and settles on my legs with a tired oompf, and I stroke the fur around his ears. Like a cat, he leans into my touch and rubs himself on my knee, closing his eyes.

"Where's Vas?" I ask him.

Those engaging eyes are half-open and stare at me, as though he knows but he's not about to tell me. I bite my lip, and whisper, "Is he mad at me? Is that why he's not here?"

He continues staring, and when I stop petting

him, he nudges my hand, begging for more. "Is he mad at me?" I repeat, realizing how stupid it sounds carrying on a conversation with a wolf, but Bebo listens.

He tilts his head to the side, as if asking, *Why would he be mad?*

And before I know it, that's all it takes. The words pour out of me like a dam breaking, and I tell Bebo everything—Bryan, the migraines, the shittiness of the last three months, and my guardians' appearance.

When I'm done, big, fat tears roll down my cheeks, and I've got a feeling my face is all blotchy. Bebo gets up slowly and steps over me, then licks my face clean, and lets me bury my head in his neck. Wordless comfort exudes from him, like so many times before, and I let it soothe over my loneliness. My eyes drift close once more, and I let sleep take me away.

Somewhere in the midst of it, I think Bebo moves off me. Then a groan echoes, followed by soft footsteps on the grass. A hand touches my forehead, tucking my hair in a familiar way.

"Oh Katya, why couldn't you tell me sooner?" It's Vas' voice, filled with so much yearning and regret, that I want to open my eyes, to tell him...

But then I fall deeper into sleep and let everything else fade away.

≈ ♠ ≈

The next time I wake, it's because we're losing altitude. Beneath us, the clouds disperse, giving way to a massive landscape of green. I stare in awe at the majestic mountains, the valleys that dip low, an undulating river emerging the closer we get.

We dive lower still, and I wonder if humans can see us. As if guessing my thoughts, Dante says, "No. They only see what they want to, and barely ever look up."

It seems we're headed towards a particular pinnacle, where I notice ruins. Further down we go, and the ruins turn out to be some type of fortress. The lay of the land, the river nearby, triggers a nugget of information in my mind, but I can't place it.

We land in the woods underneath it and Dante sets me back down, along with my backpack he'd been carrying. He kneels next to me, and says, "Alright, you can turn back to your regular form. Just picture any part of your body clearly, and it should trigger the change. If you picture yourself with your original clothes, it may also work."

He stands and moves back, and I do as he says. Luckily, he was right, and I do get the clothes I had on before. Reaching into my backpack, I pull out a jug of water and drink until my throat feels less parched.

Dante declines it, and Daymun chooses that moment to join us, appearing from nowhere and making me spill water everywhere.

Glancing between us, he dusts some speck of dirt from his still-impeccable dark suit and says, "Well?"

"Easy," the angel shrugs.

I get the feeling there's more to their exchange. "Did you expect trouble?"

Daymun arches an eyebrow my way, noticing the clothes. "Figured out the change? Good job, celestial. For once, you did your duty right. And no, love. No trouble, at least not yet."

"What does that mean?" I ask.

An annoyed sigh, an impatient tap of his foot. "Once word gets around that you're here, we may have unwanted visitors. That's why we chose this place."

Which reminds me… I glance around, at the dense forests, and bite my lip. Something's really familiar, but I know for sure I've never been here. *Have I?*

"I read about it!" Bringing my startled gaze to the ruins I can see upwards, I say, "Vlad the Impaler loved this place." Most people nowadays know him as the true man behind Dracula. I had a bit of an obsessive phase growing up, and knew there was much more to him, ergo, obsessive reading.

Vlad had been a prince, a ruler of a part of Romania then-called Wallachia. He'd been held captive by the Ottoman empire in his youth, but eventually used them to regain territories all over Romania, until he was betrayed. His rule of fear had him impale his prisoners of war around his castle, leading to the whole Count Dracula legend. And while I'm not a fan of psychos, there's always been something…. genius-like in the way he got his way, back then.

My eyes widen as they take in everything, especially those ruins. "1400 steps to get to it… We're near Poenari Fortress, aren't we?"

Daymun nods, a slight smirk on his lips. "The bookworm rises to the surface… Yes, we are."

"And you chose it on purpose, you say?"

"Yes," Dante answers. "And you are correct. Vlad Țepeș, otherwise referred to as the Impaler, fell in love with this place because of its location. Or so legend says."

"The reality," Daymun intervenes with a smirk, "is that not only did he like the location, but he knew the land was blessed. An angel died here, eons and eons ago. As did other immortals. For the weak of mind, the land can drive them insane. It did so to Vlad's first wife, after all. But for the strong…"

He lets the sentence trail off on purpose, baiting me, and of course I bite. "What does it do for the strong?"

"It enhances their healing, protects them from evil and, some say, focuses their affinity."

In the aftermath of his declaration, I can't help a shiver run through me. Dante throws him an annoyed look, but I refuse to be daunted by such mythical words.

"Wonderful," I say with as much sarcasm as I can muster.

Daymun shrugs and walks a few steps away. It's then I notice a small pile of wood accumulated near a massive tree. With a flourish of his hand, a fire burns through the wood, the flames filling with warmth and temptation.

"Get some sleep," Dante says softly. "The journey must have been rough, with a lot to take in for your first few days. You're safe here, and we'll watch over you. Tomorrow, we can get the lay of the land. Tourist season is over, and the closest town isn't for miles, so we should be left alone."

I unroll my sleeping bag and do as they ask, leaving them to guard me. You would think a meagre cover in an unknown forest would be enough to keep me awake, but I pass out almost immediately, lulled by an odd sense of safety. Seems I'm getting better and better at this trusting thing, at least where they're concerned.

≈ ♠ ≈

Hours later, the same can't be said. An owl hooting woke me up, and now I can't go back to sleep. The two Ds aren't sleeping either, instead keeping watch in silence and giving me space, as if they realize I need time to digest everything they've told me. So when I wander off, neither tries to stop me.

They must be really sure about those

protections they mentioned.

My footsteps sound loud, crunching over fallen leaves in the moonlight glow. My fate's unknown now, as far as anyone's concerned. Or do I even have one? Am I still Katya, or simply this Flama creature? Am I meant to completely reinvent myself?

My feet kick at pebbles and dirt, and I go on, and on. It's close to the end of October now, and the air is chilly here. Yet the woods welcome me like old friends, their pine scent filling my nostrils. The moon gives enough of a shine that I can see my steps and not break my neck. Owls hoot nearby, and other creatures move in the darkness.

I should be afraid. I should be wary. I should feel something other than what I am, which is... complete belonging.

It's like this place is where I've been meant to be my entire life.

Emerging from a clearing, I stare at the shadow of the fortress. It looks menacing—or, it should. Yet I have an intrinsic need to go closer, to breathe its musty air, touch those stones that have seen so much.

And why not? It's right there within reach. Nothing stops me.

It feels free not having a phone hooked to me, or the usual business of the city. Before long, I'm too engrossed in the landscape to realize I've already trekked through the forest and am near the ruins. A bridge made of wooden stairs leads the path, and then I climb upwards. But I don't go to the main event, rather follow the path as if led by some unknown force. First around a corner, then inside a short tunnel.

It's manmade, or maybe not. Moss covers the walls, and if I didn't know better, I'd think it's some kind of sewer. But the only scent I catch is that of freshness, the woods, and…cinnamon?

Pulled by some unknown need, I go closer and closer. Then I touch my hands to the stone, and it vibrates under my fingers. Words float on it, written in Romanian, though I automatically translate them.

I am Flame;
Flame is Light;
I am Fire;
Fire is Sight.

I whisper them aloud, and a shiver runs through me. Ominous words, but not more so than the quest bringing me here. When I lower my hand, they disappear, as if only revealed in a special light.

Stepping back from the tunnel, I head back to the other side. This time, I go all the way to the river, relishing its soft current. The water is cold when I touch it, but that's not surprising, given we're in October, after all.

A rustle by the bushes draws my attention, breaking the spell. The emerging wolf is as white as the moon. He stares at me for a long moment, then turns its muzzle up in the air as if it's sniffing.

I'm frozen, my mouth agape, trying to understand what I'm seeing. Because rather than yellow eyes, like you see in movies, he has the most incredible grey eyes specked with violet.

"Bebo?"

His muzzle turns towards me again, and I remain rooted to the spot. *This can't be...*

"You're not real," I whisper. "You were in my dreams, hundreds and thousands of miles away from here."

My voice is trembling, choking me, and I have to clasp my hands together to stop their shaking. Bebo—or whoever the wolf is—lowers his head and laps at the river, but those grey-violet eyes never leave mine.

I wonder how much trouble I'd get into if I try to pet him?

He does growl then, as though catching my intent. *Bebo never growled. It's not him.* Relief spreads through me, but rather than leave or move closer, I sit back on my haunches, palms open, and wait. Little by little, he inches closer to me, sniffing the ground near me, then my knee.

One bite is all it would take to finish me—I'm distinctly aware of that. Yet I'm more curious than I am afraid. I remain immobile, willing my body to be as still as a statue.

The wolf sniffs my hands next, then his

tongue comes out to lick me. It's raspy, and rough, and completely unexpected. A sound like a squeak escapes me, and he turns those incredible eyes toward me.

We stare at each other.

"How did you get here?" I whisper, figuring since he hasn't eaten me yet, it's safe to speak.

He tilts his head to the side, and I berate myself for talking to a wolf. I mean, how crazy am I? But then he glances over his shoulder, almost as if pointing to the woods, and back at me.

"The woods?"

He nods.

I'm pretty sure that's not regular wolf behavior, and again he reminds me so much of Bebo, of his demeanor around me. Then I remember what Dante told me—about immortals. My heartbeat increases, and I gulp past the sudden lump in my throat.

"Are you… an immortal?"

The jaw opens—and I swear he's grinning. Then he's gone, taking off into the woods, and towards the howls I hear. I stay frozen for a moment longer, then glance at my hand, where he'd licked.

After washing up and drinking some of the clear water, I head back to camp. I'm not even sure how I find my way through, only that my feet seem to know where to go. I've lived all my life in the city, but these woods feel more like any home I've ever had.

By the time I get back to my guardians, the sun is starting to rise.

"Where did you go?" Dante asks.

I point at the ruins. "Over there."

Without waiting for more questions, I go into my sleeping bag to doze off for a few more hours. The murmur of their voices lulls me back to consciousness before I'm fully asleep.

"Did you catch that earlier, too?" That's Dante's low timbre, all right.

"Yes."

"We should warn Katya."

"And if it's not him? There are others, you know. The hills have eyes in this part of the world."

Silence lingers, and my eyes grow heavy. But they're not done talking, and my curiosity gets the better of me, chasing away the fog of sleep.

"A world soon coming to an end." Dante sighs, and I catch a deep sadness in his words. "It is unfair, putting this pressure on only one person. Is it any wonder some lose it?"

"I don't think it's the pressure, as much as the potential of havoc. Besides, you know humans. Dodgy as hell, selfish bastards to top it off. Ready to stab each other until the sun rises."

"Do not let that rub off on Katya."

"Rub off?" Daymun snorts, and his voice takes on a dangerous tone. "Do you really not think she's seen for herself what this world has to offer?

Not just recently, with that attack, but even before."

"She has, yes, but there is still time to show her the good."

"What *good*, Dante? You may be an angel, but even you've lost faith in this lot. They're ruining the earth, attacking each other, committing sins against morality and nature itself. No amount of celestial benevolence can save them."

Dante is silent, at least for a moment. I can almost imagine his sage expression. "Salvation always finds a way."

"That's rubbish, and you know it. Selfishness and greed have corrupted most of what we know. I don't even have to tap into any demonic powers to convince people. All they need is a tiny nudge, the barest of touches, and they do as they want. Then blame Hell and all its beasts for their weakness."

Hate resonates purely in what he says, and I can't help but agree with most of it. I can imagine Dante's angelic side yearns for humanity to be saved. But I don't know how I'll ever make the choice, when I have so little faith in it myself.

"All of them, even *him*, are the same. Do you think if it all rested on his shoulders, that he'd live up to the expectation? At least Katya can." I'm surprised at Daymun's faith in me.

"I think the real question would be, if he had the chance to save millions by sacrificing his own, would he?" Dante counters.

"Maybe. Maybe not. He *was* military. But

damaged, and nowhere ready to meet Katya."

As sleep overtakes me again, I try to ignore the thousand questions in my head. Damaged? How? Aren't I, in the end?

And most importantly, who is *he*?

Chapter 7

Hours later, I wake up dazed. It takes me a moment to realize the brightness of the sun is hidden behind massive trees, and somehow, I've remained in the shade. Another sweep around the area shows I'm alone, no sign of either of my guardians.

I crawl out of my sleeping bag, aware I badly need to pee—and wouldn't mind a shower. I grab a change of clothes, my soap bar and a towel, and head to the river.

Back in my teens, I ran away from a foster home at one point. I'd caught the husband leering at me one too many times and sensed the incoming danger. Despite being on the streets, I still had to show up to school, so I learned to clean up and take care of myself with the barest necessities. It worked for a bit, until the social worker saw through my lies and assigned me to another home.

I think of that time as I near the river, musing that living in these woods, waiting for my instructions, is kind of like that. After checking to make sure no one's around, I make quick work of my clothes and hop in. Teeth chattering at the water's coolness, I scrub myself quickly, then dry up in record time and get dressed.

From my old apartment, I only saved a few pairs of clothes, so I'll have to figure something out soon. In the meantime, I untangle my hair, comb it quick, and pin it atop my head in a loose knot. Then I dump my dirty clothes in the water and wash them by hand with the soap, before hanging them on a nearby branch to dry.

I don't like polluting the water, but I take solace in the fact the soap is fully biodegradable, naturally made, and I've only used a tiny bit to wash out the dirt.

It's not summer, but this later fall isn't as cold as I'm used to, either. With a bit of luck, the clothes will be dry by nighttime—if we stay in the area, that is.

The thought reminds me I need to check in with the two Ds and figure out what they meant last night about *he*. I woke up thinking about that, and I'm not about to let it go so easily. And then there's the matter of my quest. How am I even supposed to start with that?

Sighing, I kneel next to the river one more time to brush my teeth, then get back up and head to camp. Daymun is back, but no sign of Dante. My demonic guardian, on the other hand, has some kind of meat on a stick, and he's turning it right and left atop the fire, attempting to cook it.

"Is that for me?"

Daymun frowns at the piece of meat like it's the most complicated thing. "Yes, if I can get it to cook properly."

Stifling a laugh, I walk over and take it out of his hand, then place it further from the fire, where it's not being charred. Daymun watches me for a few moments.

"Don't you eat?" I finally ask.

A shrug is all I get. "We have other sustenance."

"Like what?"

Daymun gives me a piercing look. "You really wish to know, love? Fine. I feed off emotions. And Dante feeds off faith."

I scoff, but his serious expression tells me he's being real. "Wow. Okay. Well, um, thanks. For the food, I guess."

"You're welcome."

He goes to step away, now completely disinterested in what I'm doing. But I'm not done talking. "I heard you last night."

He freezes, and glances over his shoulder at me. "Oh?" Despite his unaffected tone, I can tell I've hit a nerve.

"Yeah, when you both thought I was asleep. You were talking about humanity, how it doesn't deserve to be saved. You also mentioned someone."

Daymun faces me then, his blue eyes

unreadable.

"You said you'd never lie to me," I remind him. "So, I want to know who you were talking about."

His jaw clenches, and for a moment I think he'll go against his so-called morals. But Daymun surprises me yet again. "We think another immortal is around. He's ex-military, goes by the name Mateescu."

That name… It sparks something, a nagging at the back of my head. Too much has happened for me to focus on it, especially given every new moment around the two Ds raises more and more questions.

"You sound very familiar with this…" I trail off, unsure how to pronounce it.

"Mateescu," Daymun says. Only, he says it like Mah-tehs-kuh.

"Mateescu," I repeat, rolling the name on my tongue. Easy enough the second time around.

"What did you tell her?"

I whirl to see Dante land behind me. And by his narrowed look, he doesn't seem happy that Daymun revealed anything about our uninvited guest.

"Only what I asked," I say, but my defense falls flat. I try to change the subject instead. "Where were you?"

"Making sure we remain alone here, away from tourists." His gaze meets Daymun's. "Why the chattiness, demon?"

"Don't start," Daymun warns. "She has a right to know."

The smell of charred meat hits my nostrils and I pull the kebab off the fire. I wave it in the air to cool it off, then start nibbling on the sides. The meat melts in my mouth, and I close my eyes to better focus on the taste.

I haven't had anything this good in ages—never mind actual meat. Thinking back to the wolf last night, I wonder if he was scouring the area for food. The thought makes me curious, and I leave my two guardians bickering, while I slip off into the woods once more.

≈ ♠ ≈

Within the half hour, I'm back by the river where my clothes are drying. The remainder of the kebab is in my hand, and I'm scouring the area, looking for pawprints. I catch some large ones deeply imprinted on the other side of the riverbank and hop on some stones until I reach it.

By some miracle, I manage to avoid splashing myself with water, and also keep hold of the kebab. But once I'm on the other side, I wonder about the smartness of my impulsive move.

And then something moves in the shadows, and white fur peeks through, and I forget all my hesitations. Kneeling down, I lower my gaze to the ground and hold out the kebab with the other hand.

"Want some? It's freshly caught."

Silence alone answers me. I nearly jump out of my skin when I sense the meat being tugged from my hand. He neared me without making a sound—the perfect predator. Yet his gaze holds no malice when I meet it, only gentleness.

I'm not surprised, really. As the wolf lowers to the ground and nibbles on the meat, I watch him. Joy fills my chest. I've always had a bond with animals, more so than humans. If anything, they've been around when I needed help, unlike my own kind.

But they're not really your kind anymore, are they?

Before I can ponder the thought further, we're no longer alone.

"Move away from him, Katya."

Both guardians arrive out of nowhere, startling the peaceful moment. The wolf leaves the meat and jumps up but doesn't run off. My gut churns at the prospect, and when I turn, it's not to take their side. Rather, I'm facing off against the two Ds with the wolf at my back.

I never said I was smart, did I?

They're both surprised and mad, I can tell by their expressions. But I'm going to stand my ground and protect this creature against them if I have to. He's innocent in all this.

The wolf pants behind me and without even

looking, I can tell he's angry. Sure enough, his growl echoes in the air, then he steps by my side. *Bebo.* The thought wildly runs through my mind again at his defensive stance, the paws dug into the ground. No matter how I try to shake them off, the similarities keep hitting me.

"You have one chance," Daymun says.

I snort. "Or what?"

Only, it's not me he was talking to. I realize it one second too late, then Dante lifts his hand and a blinding light escapes his palm.

It hits the wolf next to me and he whines low, bending under the weight.

"Stop it!" I yell and throw myself in the light's path—see previous comment about not being smart—and the full brunt of it burns my back. An anguished cry escapes my throat, and I fall to my knees, vaguely registering the two Ds fighting over hurting me. Vaguely.

Because I'm focused on something else. Namely, the human feet now facing me versus the wolf paws. My brain feels sluggish, the burn in my back aching with each breath. It takes me longer than it should to realize those feet used to belong to the wolf, meaning it hadn't been a wolf at all, but a shifter I'd been conversing with.

And unlike all those paranormal books, he's not naked. Sadly. My eyes travel slowly upwards, noticing he's wearing a pair of jeans, and a tank top that's seen better days. The sun hits him straight in the face so I can't see him properly, but what I do notice looks freaking scrumptious—and I thought I'd seen hot with Dante and Daymun.

As I kneel there, staring at him, he joins me on the ground and gently pulls me to my feet. His hand goes over my back, checking for injuries, and I hiss in pain. He pulls me in his arms, and his body trembles with rage.

I feel it in his tone when he speaks. "Vați pierdut capul, sau ce naiba! Îi faceți rău ei numai ca să-i dovediți că sunt lup!" *Have you lost your head, or what the hell! You'll hurt her just to prove that I'm a wolf!*

And it goes on. It's Romanian, with a hint of something so exotic it makes my mouth water. He's yelling at the two Ds for being completely irresponsible, not to mention selfish immortals.

The anger, his scrumptiousness, none of that explains my utter stillness. Like I'm a rag doll in his embrace, unable to think or move. Nope. But that voice... The feel of his arms... The familiarity...

Before he'd pulled me in his arms, I caught a flash of rugged handsomeness and eyes of grey and violet, but it was all too fast. Now I shift in his arms, finally coming to. The voices around me are raised, and my head pounds threateningly. Not enough to drown out that *familiar* voice, though.

"Vas?"

He bows his head towards me, recognition

flaring in his expression, and the arms around me tighten some more. "I can explain, I swear it."

Gaping at him, I try to gather my thoughts into a semblance of—something. *How is this possible? He was never real! It has been dreams only, for years upon years...* And yet here he is, in flesh and bone.

The cacophony of shouts from my guardians makes my throbbing head worse. I don't want to step away from him, so I just turn in his arms enough to look at the two Ds. "You two, scram. I need to talk to the wolf."

They're not happy, but they listen. Almost too easily... Or maybe it's because they feel bad about hurting me. Whatever the reasoning is, I'll get to that later.

And then Vas lets me go, taking his heat with him. "This is not how I wanted to introduce myself," he says, "but they gave me no choice. The light was not meant to hurt me, Katya, it was meant to force me to reveal my true form."

When I say nothing, he shifts his stance, as though restraining himself from reaching out for me. "I'm getting carried away, I apologize." A hint of Romanian still tinges his English, unlike in my dreams where he spoke without an accent. Or maybe I just never remembered one. "My name is Vasile Mateescu."

Vas. Vasile. My best friend. The immortal Daymun mentioned, by his last name only. And

Bebo... They're one and the same.

"Vasile..." *Vah-see-leh*. It feels too damn right on my lips. "But, the dreams, they... I don't understand."

"It was all real," he whispers, as though afraid to scare me. "We've been connected from the very beginning, you and me. Always meant to cross paths, to meet." He stops himself, as though he wants to say so much more, but he's afraid of my reaction.

And he should be. Something's boiling under the surface of my skin, and I glance at my hands to see the red of my veins once more. Oddly, the burn on my back hurts less. Am I healing? Is that even possible?

"What they did, what you did...." I trail off, unable to form a proper sentence.

This is my friend, my confidant, the only person I've ever been vulnerable with, because I always thought he was a figment of my imagination. Only, he's not. He's real, standing in front of me, his features filled with so much emotion I can't make any sense of it.

Vasile runs a hand through his messy hair—a darker brown in person, almost black. "I am a wolf, your guardians were right. I didn't mean to scare you..."

He trails off, because I've started giggling. Then I start laughing. He's staring at me like I've lost my head—and I kinda have, I guess. I should be fuming, but after turning into a Flama and flying across the ocean, this is just the cherry on top of the cake.

Bebo is Vas. Vas is Vasile Mateescu. Mateescu is Bebo.

When I don't calm down, he tries to come closer, lifting a hand, and I flinch out of his reach. He doesn't scare me. But it's a reflex I didn't even know would happen.

His eyes darken, and the air grows thick with tension despite the sunlight bearing down on both of us. "Who hurt you, draga mea?"

I'm not his *dear*. I'm not his anything. But somehow, his tone—it unleashes what I've been holding back. But it's not at him I'm angry—rather, at the two people who should've been honest with me from the start.

I know my rage is almost irrational, but the knowledge does nothing to calm it. Stomping on the earth with a vengeance, I make my way back across the river and to my little campfire. Dante and Daymun are on opposite ends of the ashes, and both stare at me as I approach.

"Katya, I apologize—" Dante starts, but I lift up my palm towards him to shut him up.

"I don't care about that. Worse has been done to me, you've seen it happen when I was a kid, so don't act all kind now." It's a low blow, and hurt flashes across his expression, but I'm too far gone to care. "I want to know the rest of it. Whatever you held back in the park. Tell me *everything*."

They share a look at my order, then Daymun shrugs. "Fine. I will if you won't."

He leans back against the tree, an utterly bored expression on his face. His eyes flicker to Vasile, silent behind me, but he doesn't ask him to leave. Instead, he says, "What do you know of this world?"

Impatience tinges my tone when I answer. "What all humans do. Where are you going with this?"

Daymun purses his lips, seeming to reconsider. "Very well. You remember what I told you, about the immortals? Well, what if your worst nightmares really existed?"

"Come again?"

"Werewolves. Shifters. Vampires. Goblins. Dragons. Fairies." He pauses. "All of them, and not like in the movies. But in full gory, darkness-fuelled reality. And what if everything humans are polluting, is affecting them and making them angrier? More chaotic? More evil?"

"That's not possible," I counter, glancing again at Dante. His pained expression at Daymun's botching of the explanation would seem almost comical.

Almost.

If, say, I wasn't thinking I was crazier than I already am.

"What if I told you," Daymun straightens up like a feline and stalks towards me, "that your world has simply forgotten their existence? But they live still. In the shadows. In the people they can sometimes possess."

"I would not believe you."

My bravado slips at his victorious look and I step away.

"And you would be wrong. Come with me."

He grabs my hand and drags me to the woods, but Vasile interrupts. "That's enough.'"

"She needs to know."

"She does."

"She needs to *see*," he insists on a growl.

To my surprise, tame Vasile growls right back. "And she will. In time. But don't you think you're pushing it?"

They stare at each other for a bit, then Daymun releases his hold on me. I rub my wrist thoughtfully, then turn to Vasile.

I search his gaze, trying to figure out his role in all this, but end up only saying, "Thank you."

He inclines his head. "Do not hold it against him. He may be hardheaded, but he wants you safe."

"We both do," Dante says. His gaze is speculative on Vasile.

"How do you guys know each other?" I ask them bluntly. When they act all shocked I figured it out, I snort. "Please. The way you talk to each other, feed off each other… This isn't the first time you've met."

Daymun comes back to my side with a new sweater, and gestures for Dante to join him. "Would you heal her back, already?"

Vasile steps a bit away, leaving Dante room to maneuver. Last time he healed me, I'd been asleep. This time, I feel that essence of his surrounding me, then a faint blueish glow catches my eye from behind. My back stings at first, then Dante's hand is on the flesh, kneading it, caressing it. I bite my lip, and coolness suffuses my skin as he keeps at it.

When I jerk my gaze upwards, I catch Vasile's. The intensity is there, same as last time I saw him. I remember that last dream, where only Bebo showed up, but I thought I'd heard his voice, too.

Gulping, I ask, "Were you there? In the last dream? Bebo was you, right?"

Vasile nods, confirming everything I've already figured out.

Silence lengthens for a moment, then two. Dante steps away from me, his soft sigh informing me the healing is done. Sure enough, when I move my shoulders, I don't feel the tightness of a wound anymore. I grab the sweater from Daymun and head into the woods, just far enough to get changed without either of them seeing me half naked.

Once I'm done, I head back in their midst. "What about the rest of my questions?"

Dante shrugs. "We don't really know him. We know *of* him, particularly his last name."

"So you never knew that during all my childhood, and teenage years, *and* adulthood, I've been seeing him in my dreams?" Shakes of the head answer me. "Fine. How do you know of him, then? From whom?"

"Our handlers," Daymun says. "Dante and I, we each answer to a higher being of our order. They're the ones who give us information bit by bit. Mateescu's name, because of his ties to this place, runs around in our circles."

I shake my head. "I still don't see the bigger picture, not like you do. What exactly am I supposed to do? You mentioned a journey, but not the specifics. Now we're here, in Romania, a country I was born in but know nothing about… And out of all places, you've brought me to the fortress of a well-known and rather bloody historical figure. Why?"

"Because the three of us have a job to do."

Right. Mission impossible is more like it. "Purge the world of evil, you mean."

Dante grins at my less than delighted tone. "Precisely."

Something else occurs to me. "You said before my phoenix form is no coincidence. That my kind alone are able to perform this task for a reason."

"Yes," Dante says. "Besides your innate strength, ability to lift large loads and healing tears, phoenixes can be reborn from the ashes. This makes you, for lack of a better word, indestructible."

"Unless someone gets ahold of your blood, shoves it down my throat, and kills me with it," I point out.

Dante's expression loses its amusement. "Yes, that is true. But your resilience makes your kind the perfect candidate. And, there is the matter of the corruption of the soul."

"The what, now?"

"Put it this way. Most immortals are born already leaning towards a side—Light or Dark. Flamas are the only beings born with a choice."

I frown at the new nugget of information. Never have I really felt like I had a choice in what happened to me, but maybe that part only applies to the supernatural portion of my life. "Choice? But…why Flamas?"

"No one really knows," Dante says. "Some say all immortals have this choice but grow up in an environment where they automatically think they do not, thus end up picking the side of the majority without realizing it. Other say the Creator, when he made the Flamas, was less strict on account of their beauty. That their fire blinded him."

Daymun snorts then. "Right. I've heard a different side, mate. More along the lines of the Creator royally screwing up, and accidentally imbuing the first Flamas with celestial essence. Which is why they're able to transcend death via their phoenix form, like you and me. Also why they were attracted to the gates of Heaven and Hell in the first place, and discovered they could open them."

I rub my temples then, throwing a glance over my shoulder to Vasile. He's been quiet, observing the scene and taking it all in. In that moment, I want nothing more than to hear his thoughts on all this craziness. Then I remember he's not even supposed to be real, and a pang of hurt flows through me.

With an effort, I push it aside and turn back to my guardians. "Regardless of the real story, what do these tales have to do with it? What you said before, I mean. About monsters and stuff."

Dante throws a look at Daymun, who shrugs. "I tried it my way. You finish it."

"You're impossible," Dante scolds him like an older brother. Their dynamic still confuses me, but not as much as their intense expressions. "How good of a cook are you?"

I gape. What is it with these guys?

"Average."

"Bear with me. Would you try out a new recipe without first knowing all the ingredients and reading the instructions?"

"Of course not."

"Same concept applies."

At my bemused gaze, Vasile clears his throat and steps in. "If I may… I believe what your guardians are trying to tell you is the monsters in this world equal the ingredients. Challenges equal instructions. The cooking equals the quest, meaning the purging."

For a moment, I'm stunned once more at how much he knows. Then I'm reminded he is—was—Bebo at the time I told the wolf everything about my Flama heritage, and my guardians, as well as this quest. *Also, he's obviously not new to this immortal thing.*

"I—"

"You know what she is?" Daymun interrupts.

"Of course," Vasile says. His tone gives away nothing, neutral as all hell. It's annoying. "Not like you two tried to hide her trace at all."

"We had other things on our minds," the demon snaps.

"Regardless, Katya. The point is you cannot do what you need to without understanding the totality of the world you live in. Good *and* Evil. And you cannot start the purging without an idea of the different ways it was done, and of what affects it and your alignment with Dark or Light."

That, of course, was Dante. Could have been Einstein for all I care. I'm still left picking my jaw off the ground, staring back and forth between them. They're waiting for me to say something, but all I want is to run away and pretend this is a nightmare.

Daymun's lips twitch as if he heard me. *Busted.* And oh, right. They still need an answer.

"Challenges?" My squeak is cringe worthy.

ALEXA WHITEWOLF

"No one said anything about *challenges*."

Chapter 8

Silence follows my accusation, then Dante takes up explaining things to me again. "The decision resting on your shoulders is massive, Katya. And because both aspects of Light and Dark are involved, it'll take you experiencing them in order to realize which to pick."

"Three of them, to be exact," adds Daymun.

"What kind of challenges are we talking about?" When they'd mentioned quest, I stupidly thought it meant a retreat of some sort. Meditation. That kind of stuff.

"I'm not sure," Dante says. "This area is filled with legends, and you would have to meet one of each immortals—Light and Dark—in order to make up your mind."

A breath later, Vasile speaks. "I may know that which you speak of."

"No one asked you, wolf."

I don't quite understand the hostility in Daymun's tone, nor do I care. I turn to Vasile. "Okay, then tell me."

"The wall you touched earlier, with the writing—"

"How do you know about that?"

"Because he's been watching you."

Vasile glares over my shoulder at Daymun, then says, "Perhaps we should have this conversation alone."

"No way." Something about Daymun's unwillingness to leave me alone with Vasile seems puzzling.

I turn to him, biting my lip. "I want to. For a bit. We'll stick close, I promise, but I need this. I don't know him like you guys do, with whatever reputation you have in mind. Vas—Vasile—he's been there for me when no one else was." *When neither of you were,* I think, but don't say it out loud.

Turns out, I don't have to, because they get the message and step out of our way. My need to talk to my best friend is outweighed by my yearning for answers. And right now, he has them.

I follow Vasile, and after we've put a couple meters between us, and the guardians, I ask again. "Go on."

Vasile throws me a side-glance. "They are right, you know. I was following you."

"I know, but it's not like it's the first time. The dreams we shared…" At his bewildered look, I shrug. "I guess I knew deep down that no wolf can have grey and violet eyes."

He grins, and that alone transforms his face into something gorgeous enough to cut off my breath. "You have no idea how many times I wished to tell you." We pause in our steps and he tucks a strand of hair behind my ear. "Especially as you got older, and my wolf form desperately wanted to interact with you. We grew up together in dreams, practically. And then with the years passing by, there were guys, and then Bryan, and I didn't want to ruin your happiness." He sighs, and his hand drops from me. "I was selfish."

"Maybe a little bit," I say, then step closer. "But you did hurt me, you know. When you disappeared that one year and didn't give any explanation."

Vasile looks away then, and I notice the shift in his body. His muscles are tense, his jaw is rigid, as if he's fighting some memory. I recall what Daymun said last night, about him being broken. And then the other part, about being *ex*-military.

My jaw drops. "Is that where you went? To the military?"

His head jerks towards me, and his eyes roam my face. Slowly, he nods. "Da. I had my pack by then, but we had skirmishes with the Russians. You had met some guy, and I was frustrated that I hadn't told you the truth and hid so many things from you. I couldn't sit back and watch you be happy then, so I ran away. I was so tired most nights that I couldn't be bothered to reach out to you in dreams. And then, before I knew it, a year had passed."

The intensity of his words as he tells me leaves my mouth dry, and my heart pounding in an odd way. Thoughts of him in the line of fire, of me not knowing he'd been in danger, of the possibility he could have died—it all makes it hard to breathe.

It also changes the tone of the conversation. If I'd had anger brewing under the surface at him not telling me the truth, it's gone now. What purpose would it have served, when I wouldn't have even believed him?

"How did you get out?" I ask.

He shrugs. "Explosion. Shrapnel hit me. They deemed me unfit for duty after."

I can't help moving closer, lifting my hand to touch his cheek, sensing the stubble there. "I'm glad you survived it. That you came back in my dreams."

Vasile says nothing for a bit, then clears his throat. "The wall from earlier, that writing was not accidental. It was put there by an old creature, a zmeu that lives nearby here."

"A zmeu?"

"Sort of a dragon, if you will."

"Okay… So why would a zmeu put a message there?" Vasile throws me another side-glance but remains quiet. I stop walking. "Are you saying it was put there specifically for me?"

"Not you, specifically, but whichever Flama came to these parts. Katya, how much did your guardians tell you, besides what they touched upon now?"

"That I'm a Flama, here to save or doom the world, and that I need to come to Romania to figure it out. You heard the rest of it back then."

"Did they mention the immortals, and the danger you face?"

"I mean, they told me how each immortal has an affinity for something, and I'm guessing this won't make the trials any easier."

Vasile shifts his stance, and I see then what they meant about military. Even as we're standing, his eyes are darting around, assessing the surroundings. He's ready in a second to shift to a protective stance. *They were wrong,* I realize. *I'm safe with him, even if he's not the strongest.*

"That's not what I mean. Every immortal grows up with the story of the Flama. Like a boogeyman, if you will. Something parents use to scare the kids."

I snort. "If you saw my shifter form, you'd understand there's nothing scary about it."

Vasile shakes his head. "Gazing upon a Flama is a privilege not many get."

"What? Why?"

"Because people are greedy, and immortals sometimes more so. They crave your power, your blood, and would give anything to influence you. And Flamas, like most immortals, have a weakness that can get them killed."

"With the blood of their guardians, right?"

Vasile nods. "Yes. And the last time that happened, the world was nowhere better for it."

"What do you mean?"

He sighs. "You heard of the age of the dinosaurs?" When I nod, he adds, "It was no meteor that brought about the ending for them. It was the death of a Flama, from way back when they hadn't been confined to the Ether. Since then, each one is more wary than the next."

"But... I don't understand. The two Ds also said only one Flama is born every five hundred years. How would the new Flamas know about the past, and what they're supposed to do? I mean, it's not like they can communicate, or like there's some kind of instruction manual to this."

Vasile avoids my look then.

"Is there?"

"Not a manual... but a journal. My family has been keeping it. That is why I'm familiar with your guardians. That is why I knew who, and what, you are."

"And that's why you're known in their circles..." I gulp. "Can I see it, then?"

Vasile nods. "I will bring it to you. But you have to understand, aside from this, Flamas have a way to communicate. I'm not sure how, exactly, but it is possible. And that is how the message has gotten passed through generations."

"That still doesn't answer one question. Why would other beings try to kill the Flama?"

"Because they think if they do, what the Flama does will be stopped, and this world will still exist, enabling their corruption. Only, it doesn't work out like that. All I know is even if the Flama is killed, the end still comes—sometimes worse. But it won't stop them from trying."

He turns to walk again, and I'm quiet then. Following in his footsteps, I keep turning everything he said over and over in my head. Then Vasile stops, sniffing the air. The moment after, he rushes to me, jerking me against his body, and dragging me between him and a tree.

"What—"

I tense against him, but then realize he's hunched over as if trying to protect me from something. Or hide me.

"Fenix… Te miros."

I gulp. *Phoenix… I can smell you.*

"What is that?"

Vasile looks down at me, and despite the tension, his gaze drops to my lips. The moment lengthens, and then he moves off me, and he's gone. In the distance, I hear growls, and hits as if someone is being thrown against a tree.

I rush towards the noise and find Vasile fighting with another man. No, not man. He's pale, his blonde hair shaggy and falling around his gaunt face. Aristocratic features, but dirty. And then Vasile throws him again.

This time, when he gets up from the crouch, I see the fangs. *A vampire!*

Vasile punches him, and I gape at his fighting skills. The vampire is faster—way faster—than him, but he can't get past Vasile. Every step, every punch is purposeful, forceful, the muscles bulging under his shirt.

My stomach coils, and then Vasile grabs the vampire by the neck, and twists it. In the next movement, he rips it from the rest of the body and tosses it to the side, proceeding to dismember the remaining cadaver. When he turns to me, I see he's gotten blood on his shirt, and a few scratches.

"Are you okay?"

He nods. "Can you start a fire?"

Though I find the request odd, I do as he asks, gathering wood quickly. It's only moments later that I realize the point of the flames. Vasile comes and pulls out a pack of matches, then tosses the head in, followed by the body. A sweet, charred smell fills the air.

Without the burning, that creature wouldn't have been really dead.

I gulp, the seriousness of what just happened hitting me. That's bones and flesh burning up in there. An actual… corpse. "Was that a vampire?"

"Nu, un strigoi," he whispers. *A strigoi.* "I suppose you know them as vampires, but remove from your mind the idea they have a soul and sparkle."

I shake my head. "Wasn't even going to go there, not after what I just saw."

"Good."

Vasile watches the fire burn the creature, and I watch him. He seems unfazed, as if it's a daily occurrence for him. It probably is, given where he lives. Me? Having grown up in a busy town, with the rule of law everywhere around me... Well, let's just say it'll take a moment for my breathing to return to normal.

We hear footsteps, and soon enough Daymun and Dante emerge onto the river bank, their gazes glued to the fire.

"Rogue strigoi came after Katya," Vasile says. "I took care of it, but there will be more."

My guardians share a worried glance, then Dante says, "We expected as much, but this land should have offered more protection. No matter, we will be more vigilant and stand guard. However, you will have to begin your challenges as soon as possible, then."

I remember their words that night, not too long ago, about how these woods have eyes. It's enough to shake me off-balance, but I refuse to show fear. "Well, what am I waiting for?"

"A full moon."

Of course.

≈ ♠ ≈

It takes a good two hours for all remnants of the vampire to turn to ash. Vasile stays with us through it all, while I nod on and off against a tree. When I finally fall asleep, I dream of his lips on mine and my toes curl in desire—then wake up quite fast from it.

Vasile's still by the fire, which has turned to ambers now. His eyes are trained on me, unreadable in the night. "Will you be alright? I need to head off for a bit."

I take stock of my body and nod, then notice his own gashes and scratches are gone.

Vasile adds, "Dante healed me while you slept."

"Good thing, too." Then I remember his question, and say, "I'll be okay."

He straightens up and turns to leave, but on impulse comes back and kneels next to me. His hand cups my cheek, and I automatically turn to nuzzle his palm.

"I will come back," he says, then leaves softly into the night.

Confused and more than a little tired, I munch on a granola bar from my backpack and snuggle back to sleep. The woods around me are alive with noises, but somehow it all turns into a soft melody that lulls me to sleep.

Not even a few hours later, Daymun shakes me awake. "We need to show you something."

Through the woods, I follow them until we reach the fortress. I look up at the imposing shadow, then behind me at the two Ds. "I thought this was private land."

Daymun snickers, while Dante grins faintly.

"What's so funny?"

"Money buys access," is all Daymun answers as he strides on.

"But we're actually bringing you somewhere else."

Intrigued, I follow Dante, with Daymun closing the way. I trip, and Daymun grabs me before I make a fool of myself. Turning to thank him, I notice he's looking around, eyes darting and nostrils flaring.

"What is it?" *Are we being followed?* Shit. I'm about to panic, then his expression eases into a thoughtful one.

"Nothing, love. It's only the woods. Keep going."

We walk, and walk, and walk some more…

"Are we there yet?" I pant, whining like a petulant child. My muscles are used to city terrain, not what feels like the world's tallest mountain— though I know it's not. My sneakers slip occasionally on the ground or wet leaves, and I try to be more careful so I don't end up hurt before my quest has even begun.

For all answer to my question, Dante steps

towards some large branches and pulls them apart, revealing what's beyond.

Ruins. Smaller than the main fortress, but they fill the land in a circle, and I walk towards them in a daze. The air is thick here, and my eyes land on what's in front of me, but without really seeing it.

Instead, I'm seeing a mansion, light, laughter. Fingertips graze a stone wall, a mouth on mine, lips on my neck, sounds of passion…

A cough behind me startles me, and I blush. "Stay out of my head." I know they can both hear me.

Soft laughs answer, and I ignore them to continue my perusal. *What the hell is this place?*

"I've been here before."

Certainty fills my statement, completely at odds with my initial confusion. And it scares the shit out of me, making my pulse race. My breathing comes in short gasps, even as I try to make sense of it. First my dreams were real, and now…

"What was that, love?" Daymun moves closer.

"I've seen this… lived this. Through the eyes of another."

"We don't follow."

I turn to see them share a concerned look. Great, I'm making even my angel and demon guardians think I'm crazy.

Just peachy.

Nonetheless, it's like I can't stop the words coming out. "All of this. The ruins, everything. I've been here before."

But how? When?

"That's impossible, we've watched you since you were a child," Dante breaks my thoughts.

At the same time, Daymun's expression clears and he snaps his fingers. "It *is* possible!"

Dante throws him an annoyed look. "Again with the suppositions."

"Listen, you celestial wanker, I know you deal in fact, but it's possible."

"We should not be clogging her mind with maybes."

Daymun scowls and is about to keep insisting when I butt in. "Tell me. I want to know."

Dante sighs and gestures for the demon to continue. "I believe you're picking up on the soul imprints of those who lived here. It's something only a few can do, and I've never heard of a Flama capable of it, but it would account for this oddity."

"Why can only a few do it?"

Daymun purses his lips as though he's about to say something sour. "Only elves can, on account of their connection to the earth."

I glance around, almost expecting them to pop out of nowhere. "Are there any here?"

Daymun shakes his head. "They're pure beings, and the corruption of this world scares them. They've taken to living on a parallel realm, much like other immortals."

"Okay… So then if feeling the dead isn't my affinity, why did you bring me here? And how am I able to see all this?"

"Because of your kind," Dante reveals. "What you do, your purpose, you need to see past, present and future. Your gifts would help you with that."

"And that's why we're here," Daymun adds.

I sigh, already dreading what I will hear next. A noise rustles and I turn, almost thinking I see glowing grey-violet eyes, but darkness alone shimmers. Instead, I say, "Vasile said his family has been guarding the journal of a previous Flama."

They share a look, and Dante nods. "It was lost over the ages, and uncovered by the Mateescu family, yes. They have been its guardians ever since."

"Is that why you brought me here? Knowing we'd meet?" It would only make sense, given they've been with me since my childhood.

Both shrug, in an identically comical fashion.

"In a way, yes," Dante eventually says. "We thought he might be able to shed some light on a few things, given we have so little to go on."

"And is that normal?" When they stare at me in confusion, I gesture between them. "You're my guardians, supposed to guide me and influence me on this journey. Shouldn't you have all the answers?"

Daymun barks out some laughter, but Dante is calm when he speaks. "No. The Creator… He believes if we knew everything about to happen, it would only give us an unfair advantage over you and ruin your chances of eventually coming to your own decision through free will."

"More like he prefers to punish us, alongside you."

"Punish me?" I frown. "For what?"

But they both fall silent, and Daymun avoids my look as if he said something he shouldn't have. I could press him for more, insist he tells me everything since he can't lie, but my head is already throbbing from all this information. I remember another thing Vasile told me.

"I don't understand something. He also said Flamas can be killed with the guardians' blood. But, how would that happen? I see you two, and you wouldn't let anything happen to me, regardless of where my decision goes, right?"

They both nod, and it's Daymun who answers. "Very true. However, we can also be killed. If someone knows what they're doing, we would have no choice. And in killing us, they make us vulnerable."

I bite my lip. "And this, here, do I really have to let it all sink in?"

"Perhaps only enough to give you a better understanding of the world you've stepped in. To some extent, love, I think you haven't quite grasped it."

I think back to the last twenty-four hours.

"Seeing Vasile with that strigoi, I'm sure I have."

"That was too close, and will not happen again," Dante assures me.

More promises. They're so quick to hand them out, not knowing I've long ago stopped believing in them. But, if it makes them feel better, I'll continue to. At least where they're concerned.

Without answering, I kneel on the ground and try to prepare myself for soaking the memories in.

Chapter 9

My hand digs into the still-wet ground, and I sense an odd rumble. But nothing happens after, and I glance over my shoulder at my guardians. "Am I supposed to say or do something?"

Daymun snorts "You're not a witch, so no amount of Latin will get this going. Just give it a moment."

I want to snap something at him, but then I think back to what they haven't yet explained. "This full moon thing... Why do we have to wait, exactly?"

Dante shifts on the balls of his feet. "Do you not know what the date is, a week from today?"

I frown at him, even as I try to think back. I'd lost all track of days before we left, and with the migraines that plagued me... Then it dawns on me. "October 31st."

"Cue the realization."

Ignoring Daymun, I focus on my reluctant angel. "Why this date? Why now?"

"The veil between the worlds is thinner,

Katya. It's in every legend you've ever heard, surely."

"Yeah, and I also know it only lasts a day and a night. By November 1st, everything is back to normal."

Their shared look cues me in that, nope, everything doesn't go back to normal. Feeling idiotic with my hand dug into the ground, I go to move, but I can't. My hand is stuck in the earth, as if it's being gripped by something and won't be let out.

"Umm…"

"Breathe into it, Katya," Dante says.

When I'm close to hyperventilating instead, Daymun kneels next to me, getting his suit full of mud in the process. He puts two fingers underneath my wrist, right on the pulse, and breathes in deeply, then out.

"Go with it, not against it," he whispers.

I throw a look at him, but his focus is on my buried hand. A slight frown on his face, he's the picture of statuesque beauty. If nothing else, the distraction is enough to stop a panic attack, and by the time I glance back down, my breathing is in sync with his.

"Good girl," Daymun says. "It's nothing to be afraid of. Earth reacts to you, and it has been a full five hundred years since the last Flama has graced these lands. If nothing else, the land is a bit… clingy."

With a half laugh, he stands and backs away.

I try to remember what I'd been talking about before. Without turning their way, I say, "So, the date significance?"

"It is not just the world of the dead and living with the veil thinned out," Dante says. "Rather, the same is said for immortals who hide in their own realms and dimensions away from the regular folk."

"But that's still for only one day. Twenty-four hours."

"Only in the case of a regular Samhain," Daymun says.

Dante throws him a look. "Must you use the pagan name?"

"Must you get annoyed every time I do so?" As if to drive his point home, he repeats, emphasizing the pronunciation. "Sow-win."

I roll my eyes and snap my fingers with my free hand. "Oi, both of you! Since I've got my hand stuck in the earth, can we at least focus?"

Had anyone told me a month ago I'd be bossing around an angel and a demon, I would've laughed in their faces. And called them crazy. Now, what does that make me?

Contrite, Dante rubs the back of his head and shifts again. His gorgeous wings flutter, then go back to a resting position. "What Daymun meant is, this is no regular Halloween. On the year the Flama walks the Earth, Hallows Eve becomes a twenty-one-day event. A full moon starts six days before Hallows

Eve, and by the time the cycle is done, the moon is back to full. Mortals are only aware of the one day, but the immortals, well…"

"They know it's time to party." Daymun's bitter tone doesn't escape me.

"Does that include demons?" I ask.

He laughs dryly. "Perceptive, aren't you, love?" At my glare, he clears his throat. "No, it does not. Demons have to guard the gates of Hell to keep all the other creatures down there. Likewise, angels guard Heaven to keep their kin away from temptation."

"I'm lost. So then…"

"Vampires, ghouls, dragons, zmei, balauri, shifters of all kinds, faeries, elves, mermaids, sirens—"

"Okay, I get it!" I lift my free hand at his list, and thankfully he stops. My head is spinning. "So, they can all enter as they please, mingle with humans?"

"And take whatever they wish."

I shrug. "Maybe it's not such a bad thing."

Dante frowns at me. "How so?"

Daymun, I can tell, has already guessed my meaning, but he remains quiet. Leaving me to stammer through my response. "I just… Erm…" A sigh, and I try from the top again. "Is it so bad if humans are shown for a couple days that there are stronger beings than them around?"

"What does that accomplish?"

"Put fear in them," I whisper to the earth. "We've been destroying so much of this planet, always acting like we're the apex predator now that dinosaurs are extinct. We take joy in imprisoning the defenseless, letting out the guilty, even abhorring nature. Maybe it's not so bad that someone teaches us a lesson."

The silence behind me warns me I've put my foot in my mouth—again. But before anyone can say anything, something nips on my buried hand.

"Ow!" I can feel blood trickling down, then the earth around me changes.

Fire swims under the grass, but without really burning—rather, it's illuminating the land. My hand is freed, and I yank it out, turning to yell at them for the stupid joke—only I'm alone. Yet I'm still in the forest. But the air is different, foggy and sparkly all at once, like a blanket of fairy dust.

I inhale deeply and can smell an ocean breeze, cinnamon and cloves, and so much more.

"Dante? Daymun?" My voice echoes, but no one calls back to me.

For a moment, I debate whether I should be moving, or trying to, from the spot. Then I see no reason not to. After all, I'm here to learn something, right?

Step by step, I head further into the mist. It parts around me, like it won't touch me. I glance down at my hand, noticing the red in my veins—the

Flama must be close to the surface again.

Then the mist is gone, and I'm standing... I don't even freaking know where. The fortress is gone, but I'm on the riverbank of a river. I don't know if it's the Argeş one surrounding Poenari Fortress, but... What am I even looking at?

The land on the other side is split into two. One part is charred, burnt to a crisp, nothing living. The other is inundated by water. I'm seeing both, but they're not real... are they?

And then in the mist, an echo starts, and I hear those same words I'd read before:

I am Flame;
Flame is Life;
I am Fire;
Fire is Sight.

I stumble back from the river, realizing what this is. The two choices, the two paths I'll have to eventually take. One more step, and my foot gets buried in the earth. I can't move, staring at the two options, my mind sidetracked, and I'm losing it, losing it...

"Katya, wake up!"

I snap to, nearly decking Dante in the jaw. They're both peering down at me as I lie flat on the earth.

"You alright, love?" Daymun asks.

"What happened to me? The river... It was

charred and inundated…" There was something weird about it, foreboding almost. I struggle to get to my feet, accepting Dante's help and staggering to keep my balance.

They share a look at my question, before Dante says, "You have seen into the Ether, then."

"The what?"

"It is the place Flamas go to afterwards, and sometimes when they do astral projection—throw their spirit out into the universe, while their body remains here. When you connected with the earth, you saw what was, or what could be." Dante pauses, then adds, "You should not stay in there long, ever. It is dangerous."

I stare at them some more, blinking back tears this time. Unable to understand this well of emotions, all that runs through me is pure exhaustion, as if I've run out of batteries. "I'd like to go back to camp now."

Thankfully, they know me enough to help guide me, and let me rest.

"Katya…"

A whisper, a soft touch on my cheek, and I blink awake. The sun is up again, but barely, and Vasile is standing over me, his expression open and grinning. "Come with me, *frumoasă*. You've had a long day yesterday, and a walk will do you good."

Seeing him soothes something in me, with last night's emotions gone. Maybe it's the bright sunlight filtering through the trees, or the birds singing and the air feeling so damn fresh. Or maybe it's that Vasile kept his promise and returned… Whatever the case, I go with the flow and shake the last cobwebs of sleep.

I don't feel particularly beautiful—as he called me—when I struggle to my feet. Before we go anywhere, I grab my toiletries and head to the river to brush my teeth and splash some water on my face. My reflection shows a mess of tangled curls atop my head, with a few escaping crazily.

Not much I can do about it. After I take care of business in the woods, I head back and grab another granola bar. Dante is gone, and Daymun is busy doing whatever he does. He spares me a glance, a glare to Vasile, then goes back flipping through a black book. No bigger than his palm and bound in thick, worn leather, I don't quite understand why it attracts my eye. And then I remember Vasile speaking earlier of a journal detailing a Flama's journey.

"Is that…?"

Vasile grabs hold of my hand and squeezes. "Later. Let's walk."

Reluctantly, I follow him into the woods, and down some path he alone seems to know.

It feels odd, walking hand in hand like we're about to go on a date. And yet, not so odd? Much like in our dreams, Vasile spends the morning showing me every corner of these woods, and then it's almost midday. But I haven't seen anything of him, in particular. Does he really live in a hammock in the middle of nowhere?

As we dive under a particularly low branch, his hand switches to my lower back, helping me navigate the treacherous ground. "Why the frown, *frumoasă*?"

A faint smile pulls at my lips. What is it about this guy? He's not model gorgeous, rather scruffy looking. He's not as buff as Dante or full of danger like Daymun. Rather, he's lanky. Like he could be a teacher somewhere. But strength emanates from him, a quiet reassurance that answers my soul's need of belonging.

Maybe it's that, more than anything, which pushes the truth past my dry lips. "You've shown me everything, but not much that's personal."

His unique eyes glitter. "Nothing is more personal to me than these mountains." He takes a step closer, and another, and then my back is to the tree. His forehead drops to mine, his nose nuzzling mine. "But if it's personal you want, *draga mea*..." He trails off, leaving it up to me.

Memories of that night in the hammock, of falling asleep in his arms, drift through my head. His body had felt so good, so solid against mine. I'm distinctly aware of that strength I just mentioned, his arms bunched on either side of me, the intensity in his gaze.... A ragged breath makes its way to my lungs.

I must have taken too long to respond, because Vasile laughs and steps away. "*Vino,* follow me."

A hesitation, then I listen to his command and trail after him.

About an hour later, we pass through the last of the woods and emerge into a village, of sorts. Four—no, six—decrepit houses are spaced sparsely, each with their own land. Some chickens and kids run about. Clothes are strewn over ropes, drying in the wind. The houses look more like cabins, built in the old school way with mud and wood.

To anyone else, it would appear poor. To me, the thirty or so weathered faces and the smiles that greet Vasile are richer than the best gold in the world.

He speaks something to them, though I don't catch most of it. My Romanian isn't perfect, and when he speaks so fast, it's impossible to get it all. Then someone asks about me, and Vasile turns to me, holding out his hand.

"This is my very special friend, Katya. She's visiting."

"*Prietenă specială, da?*"

We'd been surrounded mainly by old women, kids and two younger women. But at the mention of my name, one of the men working in the distance inches closer to us. He's the one who spoke, repeating Vasile's endearment of special friend. His eyes, an odd mix of yellow and green, settle on me with both wariness and hope.

"Mihai, don't start," Vasile warns in a half-growl.

But his friend doesn't listen, instead moving nearer. He grasps my hand in his, as if assessing me. Then he lets go and this time his smile is less forced. "She'll do."

He turns away then and speaks to one of the younger women. I catch him asking for food, and she nods, then leaves.

Vasile is left shaking his head and pulls me into his side. "Sorry about that."

"About what, exactly?"

"Mihai, he... has a particular thing with people. He reads them."

I glance at the taller guy, a million questions on my lips. One, unfortunately, passes through with no filters. "Is he a gypsy? Is that why you brought me here, 'cause it's a Romani village?"

"Excuse me?" Mihai whirls to us, eyes narrowed and appearing a hell of a lot more threatening now. "How can you show such disrespect?"

"I-I—" Shit. My mouth is cotton candy, and I stammer out an excuse.

Luckily, it's only us three standing in the middle of the place now, but damn, could I have made more of a mess? Insulting Vasile's friend, no less!

And I should've known better. I learned long ago that when people hear Romania, their ignorant minds either think of Dracula or gypsies, and if you've got a darker coloring it's always the latter they throw on you. For me, despite my fair skin, the ragged clothes and unkempt hair made me an easy target for the kids at school and their parents to slander.

Pulling myself out of my own headspace, I seek out Vasile for help. Only then do I realize he's pressing his lips together as though he's trying hard not to laugh. My glance then shifts to Mihai, noticing the same expression on him.

"You're... You were joking? You're not mad?"

He shakes his head, letting out a booming laughter, which Vasile echoes. I almost want to punch them, but I'm too busy flushing beet red with embarrassment as everyone turns our way. Mihai, of course, adds to it.

"She thought this was a gypsy village!" His uproar is picked up by everyone else, and soon I'm surrounded by laughter, without getting the joke.

Vasile intertwines our fingers again and waves his hand over to quiet everyone. Most go back to their various tasks—sewing, making food, chopping wood—but Mihai sticks around.

"*Scuze*, that was too damn funny. But to

answer your question, *nu*, we're not a Romani village. We are nomads, but of the Dacian kind."

I tilt my head, trying to rack my brain through massive amounts of information I've stored there over the years. My love for books comes in handy once more, as I pull out one fact. "Wasn't Dacia the name of this region, under the Romans? But… it was a kingdom, too, way before that. Celtic ancestry?"

Mihai nods, surprised I knew even that little. "*Foarte bine,* Katya. I'm impressed. Da, my people were the free Dacians who refused to stay under the Romans, and continued their rituals, and lifestyle outside of what the Empire wished. Their descendants are spread throughout Romania, but our particular tribe decided to settle here. We like being close to the land." With a wink to me and a look to Vasile that I can't decipher, he walks away.

I have so many more questions now, the facts of that historical time bouncing around in my head. But I decide to leave it be, for now.

Vasile grins wider and tugs me a tiny bit closer. "Feel like staying for a while? Mihaela just went to grab us some food."

Remembering the woman Mihai spoke with, I chuckle. "Sure."

He introduces me to a few more people as we go, but not all of them speak English very well. They seem to appreciate my efforts to stutter in Romanian, which somehow only serves to enhance the feeling of belonging that's been with me since we landed.

And for the first time, no headaches threaten me, or anything else. No quest exists, no Flama duty to uphold, no fear of the future. Just... me.

We're walking back up the slope to the fortress when it happens. My head starts throbbing, bad enough I stumble and would've kissed the ground without Vasile's help.

I groan in his arms. The migraine moves further into the center of my vision, blurring everything. Even the food in my stomach is rolling around, eager to come out. My mood, happy until then, dips dangerously close to depressed at the knowledge this pain isn't done with me just yet.

"Headache?"

I nod, and something akin to agony crosses his features.

"What is it?"

Vasile shakes his head. "Nothing. This isn't about me." Instead, he drops his forehead to mine again. "It's about you."

And then he does the most unexpected thing, and kisses me. It's not passionate and it doesn't make my toes curls. It's not one of those things that you read about in romance novels. Instead, it's... deeper, on an emotional level I didn't expect.

His lips touch mine, move with mine, and it's like he's touching my very soul. Like he's feeling my pain, cradling it, and pulling it away. I've never been held like this, kissed like this, and emotion clogs my throat even as I press our bodies closer, demanding more. *I need this.*

I don't know for how long Vasile kisses me, as he makes me lose track of time. But when he pulls away, I blink and can actually see around me. The pain isn't fully gone, but it ebbed away, as did the darkness of my mood.

"What did you do?"

Before he can answer, another voice does.

"What he was trained to."

I glance over my shoulder to find a frowning Daymun. His words make no sense. "Huh?"

His icy glare goes past me, straight to Vasile. "Enough games, wolf. I'd say it's rather time to tell her the truth."

"What truth?"

For modesty's sake, and because my demon guardian seems ready for a fight, I put some distance between and Vasile. But I can't make myself let go of him completely, not after that kiss, so I keep our fingers intertwined.

"He's not here by chance," Daymun says, still holding onto the black book. "He's here because he's your mate."

Chapter 10

"I… what?" My hand drops from Vasile's.

Daymun's words, delivered in that cold tone, can't be real. And yet the truth of them is etched on Vasile's features. Long gone is the easiness from earlier today, instead replaced by wariness—and a heavy dose of anger, if I'm to guess by the glare directed at Daymun.

"You could have delivered it more softly," he says. There's a growl somewhere in there, but it's muted.

Meanwhile, I'm still trying to wrap my head around Daymun's declaration. If I'd ever believed in fairy tales and white knights coming to the rescue, it had been squashed out of me in my youth. Any entanglements I've had with the opposite sex have only ended in disaster, with Bryan being the latest.

So to me, the concept of a mate is as foreign as can be. Not to mention scary. Sure, Vasile's been in my life as a wolf since we were kids, and in human form since we were teens. He knows my darkest secrets, has been a great confidant, and I can't deny the attraction between us. But…a *mate*? It feels so final, and yet another thing I need to assimilate without freaking out for their benefit. It feels like that's all I've been doing since I found out what I am, and it's not getting any easier.

"What do you mean, a mate?" I finally whisper.

"As in, he's the one destiny has chosen for you," Daymun says, almost as if relishing the confession. "No other will suffice."

"Like… an arranged marriage?"

I stare at Vasile, but he doesn't deny any of it. Betrayal seeps through me, making my limbs and heart heavy. For years now, I've spoken so freely to him, and he never mentioned any of this. Purposefully hiding it from me. Not once did he let his guard down, it seems, whereas I have plenty of times.

He tries to step towards me, but I shake my head, shoving him away. "No. *No!* It's bad enough I can't control anything anymore, least of all the course of my life, and you're telling me even the guy I screw has been pre-ordained?"

Dante strides in then, eyes narrowed at my shouting. He opens his mouth to say something wise enough to calm me down, but I'm not having it. "No! You can take your fucking quests, and everything else, and go back to where you came from. I'm done with this. *Done!*"

"Katya, it doesn't work that way," Dante says.

"I. Said. I'm. *Done!*" The fire in my stomach curls into my blood, then into my skin and something similar to an explosion takes place. Fire swallows me whole, burning me up, and then I'm smaller, back in a phoenix form. It takes me a moment to realize what happened, then I take off, storming the skies before any of them can stop me.

The coolness of the wind, and the beauty of the landscape, are a salve to my bleeding heart. Why did Daymun have to complicate the one simple thing I had going on?

He's looking out for you, a voice at the back of my head says.

Only, it doesn't feel like that. It feels like he's trying to drive us apart, though why, I haven't the faintest idea. And, regardless, Vasile should have said something earlier. He could have even told me when I first met him face-to-face in the woods here.

One more person lying. One more relationship fractured. Because I'm not planning to be anyone's mate. And despite my earlier words, a part of me feels bad abandoning the quest. Only, I've learned to watch out for myself first and foremost, because no one else will.

Dejected, I keep flying around, taking in the mountains, valleys, and the crisp night air. Sometimes I go low enough for my fiery tail to almost hit the top of the trees, but I avoid creating forest fires. At other times, I'm almost above the clouds. The freedom—I'll never lose this. Not for a guy, not for anyone.

I'm not sure how long I stay gone, flapping my wings aimlessly and letting the current carry me around. Not even sure where I'm going, lost in the feel of the wind, the earth beneath me. The only thing that calls me back is the howl of a wolf, a sound as familiar to my heart as my own bird cry.

By the time I reluctantly touch land, and turn back to human, it's only to faint in Dante's arms from the exhaustion of the change.

≈ ♠ ≈

You would think that being so exhausted, I'd sleep until the morning. But, nope. My Flama spirit has other ideas in mind.

So imagine my shock when I suddenly find myself hovering above my body. My new form is translucent, and I'm wearing a washed-out version of my jeans and sweater from the real world. The only thing bringing color to my ghostly shape are the red veins I notice on my hands.

Below me, the two Ds are fighting with Vasile. Well, Daymun seems to be. Dante is holding back, assessing the situation.

"*Ce naiba!* Did you have to tell her now, of all times?" Vasile shouts at my demon guardian, his fists clenched, and body turned as if protecting my unconscious body.

"I promised I would never lie," Daymun says smoothly. "Your little black book was rather informative on what grounds and what doesn't ground a Flama, so you must have known how important it is she realizes the truth."

I was right, then. Daymun *was* protecting me. Some of Vasile's anger ebbs away, and he runs a shaky hand through his hair.

"It's not like that! *E viaţa mea, nu înţelegi?*" *She is my life, don't you understand?*

His startling outburst makes my heartbeat pick up. In fear, in exhilaration, I don't even know. *I don't want this,* I try to remind myself. *You don't even know how old he is!* And yet, my idiotic pulse still races, wanting to hear more. All the barriers have fallen, Vasile is laying out his emotions for the world to see. Maybe something in them will convince me this isn't all bad, that it's not yet another way for fate to fuck me over.

Unfortunately, I don't hear much else. Their voices become muted, as if someone's muffled the sound. Meanwhile, my body's level to the ground, floating on its own. It's a weird sensation, not going to lie. Like everything's been shed from me, and I'm free—flying. No longer tethered to anything.

The thought rings alarm bells at the back of my mind, but I push it away. For years now, I've been weighed down by the world—trapped. Now I'm free and can go anywhere. I glance again at my guardians, and Vasile…

My gaze moves to the mist in the distance, the sparkles in the sky, and the stars above. I recognize it for what it is—the Ether. And though I'm afraid of what I saw last time, my curiosity gets the better of me. My translucent form floats upwards, higher and higher….

I'm not sure how long I've been in this Ether. My mind's been busy replaying what they told me, the latest freaking development in this quest. On some level, I realize I'm acting like a child. Probably worrying them sick.

With the mist and sense of eeriness surrounding me, it's easy to recall Dante's warning about this place, how I shouldn't stay in it too long. But it's hard. Because here, I'm protected. No strigoi, no quests, no mate waiting.

And why does that bother me so much, when Vasile is practically made for me? Because it scares me shitless. I don't need months of therapy for a psychologist to tell me I've got abandonment issues, and that having something so permanent as a mate shoved in my face is the perfect way to make me lose it.

Something shifts in the mist. The woman stepping out is my age, but her eyes hold the wisdom of age, as if she's been around for a while. Blonde hair falls in wavy curls to her shoulders, and she's wearing a long skirt and the type of shirt I've only seen in old depictions of Italian Renaissance fashion.

"Who are you? And how are you… here?"

"I am Flama, just like you."

My eyes narrow on her, searching her expression for the lie. "I thought only one lives every five hundred years."

She only stares at me, a smile playing on her lips, as if she's humoring me. And then it dawns on me. "You're not alive, are you?"

"No," she says. "I am an imprint left of the girl I used to be, before the quest took over my life much like it did yours." She beckons me further, her smile soft and engaging. "You must see this, if you are to move forward with your choice."

"I don't…"

My hesitation doesn't bother her. She floats closer, then grabs my hand and pulls me in the mist. It parts to reveal the sea. Its waves are frothy, sloshing back and forth as the tide rises.

The sand under my feet is soft, and I let her drag me to the edge. A full moon shines down on us. "Where are we?"

"Still in the Ether," she says. "But you are seeing through my eyes now."

The waves rise up, almost ominous and large enough to wipe out everything. Yet they don't drop back down and crash over me, instead remain standing tall, intimidating and ominous.

"What—"

Before I can finish my question, something moves in their depths, and I realize it's a memory. Almost like the sea holds the secret to what happened when this Flama made her choice. Mesmerized, I walk closer, stepping into it until I'm covered to my hips. The water is cold, icy even, but it also grounds me.

The images are a jumble at first, like one of those optical illusions. Yet when I focus on them, they smooth out and play like a movie. I see the Flama coming to this same beach, her face bathed in tears. In the distance, two men are watching her—one with wings, the other in a suit. With a start, I realize they must have been her guardians.

She heads into the water like I have, until it covers her waist, then withdraws a dagger from the folds of her skirt. Its blade glints in the light, and I watch as she cuts her palm, and the blood drips into the sea. Her lips move into a murmur, but I don't have to hear the words to realize what she is muttering.

I am Flame;
Flame is Life;
I am Fire;
Fire is Sight.

A shiver racks up my spine, but I still remain unmoving, watching the rest of it play. Her blood mixes with the water, turning it a shade of burgundy that should be impossible. Only a few drops have fallen, but it's like the entire sea mourns her.

And then she throws her head back and looks at the sky. More words pass her lips, then the water rises around her, progressively taller and taller, bypassing the size of the largest tsunamis. It hovers in mid-air, as though awaiting a signal. Then lightning strikes the sky above, a blaze illuminates a crack in the clouds, and wings emerge—loads of them.

The water rises to impossible levels, darkening the images. The last thing I see is the Flama's peaceful expression, bathed in fresh tears.

I stagger backwards, the waves drop to their previous regular size, and it's like nothing happened. Yet I'm shaking, trembling, teeth chattering and arms wrapped around myself. I drop to the ground, unable to stand any more.

The Flama watches me, waiting.

Eventually, I ask, "What made you choose salvation?"

Those had been angels coming from Heaven. She chose Light, in the end, and there must have been a reason. Yet her answer is not what I expect.

"I saw something worth saving," she whispers.

When I next look up, she's gone. And so is the sea, the cliff, and everything else. I'm back to the regular Ether, surrounded by mist and sparkles, and nowhere closer to where I need to be.

≈ ♠ ≈

For hours it seems, I walk the Ether once more. Then a shiver runs up my spine, and the mist parts, revealing another woman. She's unlike the first one, a dark glint in her eyes that makes me uneasy. Her hair is cropped short above her shoulders, unevenly as if done with a knife, and she's wearing some kind of Amazonian costume. Scares decorate her arms, and a bow is strapped to her back.

"The Savior must have spoken to you, then?"

I gulp, her husky voice a tad intimidating, as is that direct stare. "Is that what she was?"

This one shrugs. "That's what I call her."

"And who are you, then?"

Her smile is cold as ice. "Haven't you guessed? I'm the Destroyer."

My shocked expression must have given me away. "Another Flama, then. You chose the other path?"

"Very well." She jabs her thumb over her shoulder, pointing the way. "Follow me."

My feet stay rooted to the ground. "I don't think I want to see this."

Her snicker echoes around me. "As if you have a choice, Baby Flama."

I follow in her footsteps, until once more the mist parts, and this time we're walking over charred ground. Fire is an unforgiving mistress, and the land shows it. Barren, filled with grey ash, it speaks of desolation.

When I hesitate, she grabs my arm forcefully and shoves me forward. I turn to tell her off, but my feet have kicked dust from the ground, and it swirls around me in a very unnatural way, almost as if trying to blind me.

The Flama backs away from the whirlwind, her expression cold as she watches me. Then I lose sight of her as the dust thickens and obscures my vision completely.

Just like with the water, images assail me. The Flama is flying above this land, which still shows grass and life. She lands, almost rolling unto herself, and it's only when she morphs to her human form that I notice the bloody gashes on her back.

In the shadows, two shapes watch her, and I make out an outline of wings and a suit. Then the Flama pulls out a similar dagger from a pouch and cuts her palm. Her face is a cold mask filled with hate. She mutters the words I've heard before.

I am Flame;
Flame is Life;
I am Fire;
Fire is Sight.

And then she looks at the ground and says something else. No hesitation, no second-guessing. I only recognize three words that pass her lips: *Hell, Hell, Hell.*

Dark lightning runs across the sky, thunder shakes the ground, and then it breaks. Out crawl creatures—demons. Each one uglier than the last, their skeletal faces staring at me through the memory. Shivers run up my spine, and it feels like the ashes are in my lungs now, preventing me from breathing.

Right when I think I'm about to pass out, the ashes drop around me, and the images fade away. The Flama stares at me from afar.

"When was this?" I ask her.

She smirks at me. "Does it matter?"

It doesn't, not really. What was done, was done. And all I can do is gain knowledge from it. So I ask her, "What made you decide?"

Much like the other Flama, she gives me a vague answer. "They did not deserve salvation."

Unlike her, she doesn't stop there. Instead, the woman moves closer to me, meeting my gaze with her dark eyes. "You've been hurt, haven't you?"

Memories of the attack in Chinatown linger on the edge of my consciousness. "Yes. What does that have to do with anything?"

"Everything is connected, Baby Flama. Everything. Your choices will stem from your twenty-five years on this Earth. But I wouldn't choose so fast, if I were you."

I gulp. "What do you mean? I was told I have five weeks, because I awoke earlier."

She throws back her head and laughs. "You are lucky, then. But still, five weeks is not much, given the scheme of things."

"What do you *mean*?"

Instead of answering, she counters with another question. "Do you really think there will be a life for you, after? Regardless of which way you choose? They took you away and destroyed your previous life for a reason…" She walks away, her last words echoing the mist. "So you would have nothing to miss."

She disappears, and the mist surrounds me once more, taking away the scent of charred flesh and earth. I turn in a circle, her words ringing in my head. I'm not meant to survive this, then. I should have realized, should have clued in, but…

This quest will kill me.

The truth, plain and simple, is here. And the last tethering I feel to Earth shifts, as my feet carry me further and further into the mist.

≈ ♠ ≈

You cannot stay too long in the Ether, Dante had said.

I should've listened. Because now I'm lost, and I don't know how to find my way back. The mist hasn't parted for hours—days? I've lost all track of time, which unfortunately gives me way too to think about.

Like my incoming death.

"Get over yourself, Katya." My whisper is too loud in the silence. "What's one life, when millions might be saved?"

Not that long ago, I told my guardians I quit.

I hadn't meant it, not really, but what if I had?

If I don't give in, if I don't do any of what's expected of me... What if I just stay here, refuse to take responsibility, and let the world keep heading towards where it is? After all, it wouldn't be my fault if everything comes to a collapse. It's already been heading towards that, even before I got involved.

Why should I save it? Or cleanse it? Why should I care, when this world has done nothing for me? Ever. All I've met in my twenty-five years is pain, agony and more craziness. Nothing is worth saving... Except for maybe the animals. Along with Bebo—Vasile—they've always been there for me, from stray dogs to cats and everything in between. When I ran away, when I needed comfort, they were there to shelter me and help out, more than humans ever did.

So, why should I care?

The answer is in my core. Because much as this world has screwed me over, it also made me stronger. And, there is good to be saved within it... At least, I imagine there is. I've yet to see it.

Vasile springs to mind. Is he counted among all those who have wronged me? Should he be, for hiding this mate thing from me? Part of me wants to never speak to him again. But the other, stronger part, reminds me we've been friends for ages, long before fate threw us together in real life. And... despite my fear, maybe I owe it to him to not be a complete bitch.

The mist swirls around me then, distracting me. And from within comes another voice that makes shivers run up my spine. "If you do not achieve your task, the Enlightened Ones will."

Then the mist draws into me, choking me, and it feels like a threat—a warning, to do what I'm meant to. In the distance, a wolf's howl draws me back, and someone reaches for me…

≈ ♠ ≈

Gasping like I've just come from underwater, I get to an upright position. Vasile is kneeling by my side, frowning at me.

"Are you okay?"

I nod as he pulls me into his chest, automatically relishing the feel of safety. Yet my thoughts are buzzing annoyingly, and I'm already shifting so I can glance over his shoulder. "What was that?"

Daymun shrugs. "It had been more than thirty hours, and you were getting lost. I had to bring you back."

So it was him who reached for me… The memory of the pull makes me tremble. "It seemed like the Ether was trying to suffocate me."

His narrowed eyes meet mine. "It wasn't the Ether, but those who control it."

Vasile brings a bottle of water to my lips and I drink fully, soothing my parched throat. "Who controls it?"

"The previous Flamas."

"I don't understand. You said the Ether is where previous Flamas go to live, after completing their tasks. But the two I met were dead." Accusation drips into my words, and I sense Vasile shift.

"That's what you told her?" He sounds incredulous. Then he reaches in his back pocket and pulls out a small black book, the same one Daymun was reading through previously. "This was passed down from generations through my pack. An account from a Flama who lived to tell the tale."

Vaguely, I wonder how he retrieved it from Daymun. In the scheme of things, it doesn't really matter. I pick it up gingerly out of his hand and open it, careful with the yellowed pages. The writing is small, curled, elegant—a woman's. Gulping, I rifle the pages. It's all in Romanian, and I can't believe in coincidences anymore.

"What's the connection to Romania?"

Dante moves forward, leaving the sidelines. Head bowed in thought, he says, "We did not lie to you, Katya. You were already so overwhelmed—we had no choice but to filter what we told you. We did come to Romania knowing it would help with your quest. It is not always so—some Flamas go to the North, the South, all corners of the world. But Romania has a particular connection—*Apa Sâmbetei*."

I frown. *Saturday's water?*

Dante nods, lifting his gaze to mine. "It is the World Ocean. A legend we will tell you another time, but let it suffice to say the origin of Light and Dark stems from those waters."

"And where is this, exactly?"

Daymun shrugs. "Hidden, on another realm—or plane of existence, however you wish to think of it. Accessible from here. And we had to follow that connection, love. The world is getting quite corrupt with each passing day, and even other places that could have served as the perfect spot for your dodgy trials would no longer do. Here, we have the advantage of protected ground, and of extra time."

My thumb caresses the cover of the journal. "So you brought me here knowing all this. Knowing about Vasile, too. But what about the Ether?"

Dante rubs his jaw and takes a few moments to compose his reply. His angel wings shift restlessly, an indication of his internal agitation. "You recall us mentioning the Creator and his immortals, then the mortals shaped after?"

"Yeah, and you said some immortals were banned." He nods, waiting. A light bulb goes off in my mind. "You meant Flamas!"

Vasile grabs my hand in his, squeezing it. I don't have it in me to yank it away as he says, "That's what the Ether is—both their prison, and their ever after. One is only born in the human world at the five hundred years mark, and only because the Creator makes it possible."

"The minute she is born, two guardians are assigned, and with their blood bound to her. And after her purpose is achieved, she is returned whence she came," Daymun says.

This reminds me of the two dead Flamas, forever stuck in the Ether. "That's why you told me not to linger in there."

The trembling of my body increases, and my pulses races. If I had remained there longer, if Daymun hadn't brought me back…

I duck my head, burying it in Vasile's chest. His arms come around me and he rocks me back and forth, his palm rubbing soothing circles on my back. My fast-beating heart cools down, and I pull back, a sudden resolution clear in my head—even if it is ruled by fear.

"I can't be mated to you."

His jaw clenches at my whispers. "Tough luck, *frumoasă*, because it's not something we can choose."

I shake my head and get up to my feet. "No. It's already been made clear to me that I cannot step away from this path set in front of me. But that doesn't mean I have to play to everyone's tune."

My glare settles on my guardians. "Why didn't you tell me this quest would cost me my life?"

"Because it might not," Dante murmurs. His chocolate eyes are filled with regret. "It is different for every Flama."

"Not according to the two I just met."

Shaking my head at their paltry excuse for an explanation, I shove the black journal into Vasile's hands and stalk off into the woods.

≈ ♠ ≈

The ground is hard under my butt, cold even, but I don't mind it. I've been watching the sun set from atop Poenari Fortress, basking in the shadows cast on the land. Though I'm sitting on the stones of the old fortress, my eyes are on the empty staircase leading to it. No soul breathes around here, and I relish the silence even more.

The recent events have given me a lot to think about. And, much like in the past, my solace comes in the form of an animal. This time, a hawk flies above me, before perching itself on a wall near me. One golden eye turns to me, its feathers bathed in moonlight.

"I can't do this," I whisper to it, admitting the deepest fear of my heart. "This quest, what I'm being asked to do, I don't even know how to start."

The hawk croaks, then his gaze shifts over my shoulder. Moments later, a soft voice says, "Then let me help, Katya."

I don't move as Vasile takes a seat next to me. His hand is close to mine on the cool rock, our pinkies almost touching.

"What are you, following me now?" A bitter

scoff escapes me, and out of the corner of my eye I see him wince in pain.

"Da. I have no qualms in admitting that. If nothing else, I have to protect you."

I turn, meeting his grey-violet gaze. "Why? Because of some dreams we shared?"

He smiles then, ruefully. "I know you've been through a lot, and you're brave to even attempt this crazy quest. I also realize you have a sense of responsibility to this world, even though all it's done is hurt you."

I look away, refusing to register the emotion in his gaze. "How old are you, even?"

"Three years older than you," he says in a level tone. "Does it matter, given we're both meant to live longer than a human existence?"

"You are," I whisper. "Not me. Not according to what I just found out."

Vasile reaches for my hand then, clasping it in his much larger one. His heat permeates my skin, warming me from head to toe.

"I know you're used to standing alone against the storm, whichever way it comes from. But you don't have to anymore. I'm here for you, Katya, in whatever shape or form you wish me to."

Words refuse to pass my lips, but I don't move my hand from his grip. Vasile shifts closer and wraps his arm around my shoulders, pulling me into his chest. Without saying a word, he holds me.

The hawk croaks one more time, then flies into the distance. And in that moment, I wish I could fly away, too. Away from these problems, away from everything else... away from him.

Only, I know that last part is a lie. Because being in his arms feels too damn good, like it's a place I've been looking for, but never found. I can deny it all I want, I can fear it to the end of time—my time, anyway—but the truth is staring me in the face.

It feels... like I've come home.

Chapter 11

We must've fallen asleep, because when I blink awake, I'm surrounded by Vasile's heat. It can't have been more than a few hours, as night still envelops us. But at some point during this time, he cushioned my head on his bicep, and we're as intertwined as only two lovers could be. He made sure I'm half-sleeping on him for comfort, but the hard ground has to be incredibly unrestful for him.

I tense and pull out of his reach, but the movement makes his eyes snap open. We stare at each other for a bit, then I break the contact and reach for a bottle of water he brought in a corner, to cleanse my mouth. When I'm done, Vasile does the same and spits it out.

Then, he gets to his feet. "You shouldn't be alone, especially given how close we're getting to Hallows Eve." He pauses, as if he wants to say so much more, but finishes with, "If you need me, you know how to reach me."

The moment after, he's gone down the stairs,

171

and I watch his form disappear into the darkness. Pain spreads in my chest at his slumped shoulders, and the quick way he made his exit. I must've hurt him by my pulling away, but I just can't wrap my head around it.

It would be easy to give in to my body's demands. But a relationship is built on more than lust—there's trust, honesty and respect. Vasile definitely had the first and last, but he kind of screwed up on the middle one. And while half of me is aware I'm using this one mistake against him as an excuse to avoid closeness, I also refuse to blindside myself.

The idea of having a mate, something so forged in forever, is scary as fuck. I'm nowhere ready to get married, never mind now that I know I'm going to die in a few weeks. What would be the point? Yes, I have a small chance of survival, according to my guardians. But really, given how much this world has screwed me over, who's to say it'll actually play in my favor this time?

A flutter in the air stops my dark thoughts and my gaze rises up. Angel wings cloud my vision, but they're not the silver feathers I'm used to seeing with Dante. Rather, they're ivory, glinting with the moon's light.

The guy lands next to me, dressed in jeans, bare feet and bare chested. *Angel attire, I guess.*

He glances around as if expecting to find someone else, then his green eyes settle on me.

"Where is your guardian?"

Not liking the tone, I cross my arms over my chest. "Guardian*s*, I believe you mean, since I've got two of them. They're around."

His features have none of Dante's openness, rather remain rigid and unimpressed by my sarcasm. But if he's not daunted by me, neither am I by him.

"Who are you?"

His expression darkens further at my insolent remark.

I take it as a bad sign and am about to take off when another angel lands next to me. This one, I know, and am relieved when one wing wraps around me, as though shielding me.

"What are you doing here, Gabriel?" I should note Dante's tone isn't very warm, either. In fact, it's the coolest I've ever heard it.

Rather than answer, Gabriel scowls. "Care to explain what she's doing alone, rather than with you?"

"Not everyone likes to suffocate their charge," Dante throws back.

Gabriel takes a step closer, his wings unfurling in a threatening manner. Dante doesn't budge, instead lifting his chin in defiance.

"Your task is to influence her towards Light, not stand around cavorting with some demon."

Dante's tone turns icier. "I will thank you not to tell me how to do my duty. Unless you have an actual reason for your presence here, leave her be."

He moves us back, and we head for the stairs. I glance back, and Gabriel's still there, glaring at our backs. After nearly breaking my neck on the next step, I stop trying to keep an eye on him, and instead follow Dante.

In complete silence, we trek back to the campsite and arrive just in time to see Daymun arguing with another man. He has olive skin and dark eyes, he's dressed in a leather suit, and his expression is foreboding. When he notices us nearing, his eyes flash red, but Daymun interferes before he can move.

"Enough. Return to the bowels of Hell, I have this in hand."

"You had better."

The other demon disappears as if erased by the rising sun. First his feet go, then his legs, then his torso, and finally his head. It's the weirdest thing to witness.

"Is that how you move around?" I ask Daymun.

"Yeah," he says, rubbing a hand over his face. His suit jacket is off, and he's rolled his shirt to his elbows. This only makes him look hotter—I never said I was made of stone. "Angels fly, we dematerialize. All demons can do it, but not all can exit Hell to enter here."

"So who was he?" I press.

"An inconsequential arsehole." With a grimace, he adds, "Who unfortunately is my superior." Daymun then turns to us. One look at Dante, and he rolls his eyes. "Let me guess. Some angel visited you, too?"

Dante nods.

"I don't understand," I say, glancing between them. "You said this place had protection in place and would deter others from coming. That it's also why my seeing those faces has abated. Why all these visits then?"

"To remind us of our task," Dante says. He sounds like he's got the weight of the world on his shoulders, and for the first time I snap out of my little bubble and realize these guys have a lot to lose, too, and not just their immortal existences if I stop in my task.

Reminded of my words from yesterday, a deep wave of shame rolls over me and I bow my head. "I'm sorry," I whisper. "For earlier. For saying I wouldn't do this, that I was done. I was just overwhelmed and… It's not fair to either of you."

Silence reigns supreme for a few moments, then Daymun snorts. "Much as I appreciate the sentiment, that's the least of our problems right now."

My shame evaporates in an instant and I roll my eyes. *Leave it to Daymun to be annoying in a moment like this.* Clearing my throat, I ask, "Why are you being reminded of what your task is, then?"

Daymun shakes his head, then jerks his

thumb to the angel. "This one's idea."

"Not entirely! You brought it up."

"And you executed it," Daymun points out as he dusts his pants.

I stomp my foot on the ground to get their attention. "Executed what?"

Holding his palms up as though not to spook me more, Dante says, "Do not get upset again."

"I can't promise that."

He drops his hands, his wings extending behind him. "A Flama's life is precious, but it is also very short, as you found out. We do not know what change the quest will cause in you, but we know what you have already survived."

"What does any of that have to do with anything?"

"After the attack—"

"—and even before—"

"—we decided rather than follow the old pattern of influencing you, tugging you apart even more than we already have, that we would instead help you find something to ground you."

I stare at Dante, waiting for him to finish his thought, but he only stares back. And then it dawns on me. "Vasile… You mean my mate?" I shake my head. "No, that makes no sense. Daymun, you didn't like him from the beginning, and Dante, you forced him to show me he's a wolf!"

My voice has risen now, enough so they share an alarmed glance.

"We knew from the beginning," Daymun says as he catches my eye. "It was a play, one Vasile had no idea of, and one we needed to put into practice for you."

I want to be angry at being manipulated like this, at falling right into their trap. And yet... Glancing between them, I realize the full implication of what they said. "You chose to go against your orders, and instead give me happiness for however long it would last?"

When they both nod, I want to crawl under the nearest rock. *I've been such an ass.*

Dante notices it. "Why the long face?"

"You guys gave all this up, and I've just been moaning and groaning all along. And... I might've hurt Vasile. At least, bad enough he left."

"Then go to him." Daymun shrugs at my surprised look. He's the last person I expected to give advice on romantic issues. "Tell him the truth—that you fucked up because you're afraid. He'll understand, believe me."

I gulp past my dry throat, and glance at the sky above. The sun is pointing over the horizon. "How long do I have until Samhain?" With all the sleeping and supernatural shit going on, I've officially lost count of the days.

Daymun smirks at my use of the pagan name and throws a victorious look to Dante. "Less than two days. October 31st is tomorrow, which means you have until the full moon rises that evening. You might as well enjoy it while you can."

I'm already picking up my bag. On impulse, I rush to each of them for a hug. "I'll be back by then." Before they can change their minds, I take off into the woods.

≈ ♠ ≈

Running through the forest feels too damn familiar to my dreams. Yet unlike how easy it was to find Vasile in there, I find reality is quite different. The area is massive, and despite me calling out his name repeatedly, he doesn't show up.

And then minutes roll into an hour, then two, and I stop long enough to realize I'm not quite sure how to get back. My plan pretty much consisted of finding Vasile, but I never stopped to consider what would happen if I didn't.

Luckily, the sun is fully up now, and worst-case scenario I figure I could easily switch to my phoenix form and fly back... I mean, the skies are easier to navigate than the ground, right?

With a sigh, I stop in my tracks and drop to the grass, leaning my back against a massive tree. "Freaking hell." I catch myself, not wanting to accidentally open the gate, but it's hard when it used to be my favorite word.

Something snaps nearby—a twig. I jerk to my feet and peer around the tree, only to see a large black wolf emerging from nowhere. He sniffs the air, and his dark brown eyes settle on me. I back away slowly, unsure if I'm dealing with another shifter or a real wolf.

Growls behind me make me turn, and I catch sight of three more wolves. For a moment, I'm fooled into thinking they're regular animals. Then I notice the eyes—blue, hazel, brown again…

More shifters. Shit. They warned me to be careful, that this place has eyes, and now I've managed to seriously put myself in danger.

One wolf gets brave and inches closer to me, taking a deep inhale of the air around me. I stay still, trying not to provoke them. *Maybe now would be a good time to shift and get out of here.*

Before I can put my plan into effect, something moves in my periphery and Vasile lunges—in human form—through the air, then tackles the wolf closest to me and shoves him away. Dusting himself off, he stands with his back to me.

"Not yours," he growls. "Get out of here. *Acuma!*"

The wolves share a look, not appearing convinced. Vasile crouches low, and his tone is harsh when he speaks again. "Beware the Dacian curse if you hunt in their territory. *Nu vreți un război, da?*" *You don't want a war, yeah?*

That, more than anything, sends them running for the woods. Only the black wolf lingers around, eyes glued to me, before finally taking off.

Vasile waits another beat before turning to me. "Katya, why didn't you call for me? These woods aren't like in our dreams, real dangers exist here."

He sounds exasperated, but I don't care. He's *here*, and that's all that matters. Without overthinking things—again—I take one step, and another, then throw myself in his arms. Vasile automatically hugs me back, though I sense his confusion in the slackened hold, as though ready to release me at the first sign I don't want it. This reluctance makes me want to kick myself, and I miss his tight hugs all the more for it.

"I'm sorry," I whisper in his chest. "I didn't know how to call to you. Not like we have cell phones here, you know?"

He snorts above my head, and one of the hands rubs my back soothingly. "Nu, we don't. But we do have fire. And, Katya—"

I pull back so I can look into his incredible eyes. The violet hue is dark, almost overpowering the grey. I know from the years spent together that he gets like this when he's really emotional about something.

Reaching my hand to his cheek, I ask, "What is it?"

"You've made your feelings clear about the mate part, but the thing is, it's a benefit, something you can tap in. As a Flama, the land here calls out to you, responds to you. As do its creatures. And as a wolf shifter, my affinity is for all creatures of Light."

As if to illustrate his point, he removes one hand from my back and lifts it in the air. Within seconds, a hawk comes and perches himself carefully on Vasile. I stare in wonder, and the bird tilts its heads and lets me reach out and touch his feathers. With an affectionate nip at Vasile's neck, it then takes off again and we both watch it soar away.

"So all I have to do is reach any animal here, and you'll get the message?"

He nods, and I file the information away for later.

After a few more moments of hugging in silence, Vasile looks down at me. "I know what you've lived through, how hard it has been for you. If I wasn't clear last night, let me say it again. My purpose here is not to cage you, or try to change you, or even to distract you from your path. It is to support you in everything that you want, and more, *iubirea mea*."

"I realize that." My eyes shoot back to the sky. The words are on the tip of my tongue, but it takes all my courage to push them out. "In all the years we've known each other, I've never felt trapped with you. It always felt like... like I was coming home."

Vasile reaches for my chin and forces me to meet his gaze. "As it did for me. And it still does, Katya. I'm sorry for not telling you about this mate

181

business, but please don't let this one mistake be the only thing you know me by."

I clear my throat and shake my head. "I won't. I'm not. The reason I came in here, is because I was looking for you."

He stills then, so impossibly frozen I can't even tell he's breathing. Then his nostrils flare, as though he's taking in my scent. "Why?"

"Because for as long as I've got left here, I want to *live*, too. You've always made me feel safe, and happy, and loved. It was easy to say you betrayed me, because it was harder for me to accept the truth. That being your mate is the calling I've felt in my bones since I first saw you."

He lets go of my waist then, but only to cup both my cheeks and rest his forehead against mine. "As did I. For years, it killed me having to pretend the dreams weren't real and keep my distance in the hopes our paths would cross. Not even the military could wipe you from my mind, and believe me, I tried. I will lay down my life for you, my beautiful phoenix. Know this, and trust me as you once did. Fully."

Before I can answer, he drops his mouth to mine in a sweet, heart-wrenching kiss. His lips move over mine, cajoling, teasing. When I grip his shirt in my hands, Vasile deepens the embrace and that's when I feel it all the way into my toes. A tingling, a sense of rightness—the axis finally shifting.

≈ ♠ ≈

For the rest of the day, Vasile shows me the forest his way. No danger, no unwelcome visitors. Instead, we hike everywhere, and he takes me to a small lake for a leisurely swim. The water is surprisingly lukewarm. By the time we're done, I'm starving, and he hunts us a rabbit, cooking it over a low fire. I devour most of it.

And through it all, we talk, and laugh, and banter back and forth. An easiness surrounds us like I've never felt with Bryan, or anyone else. And now I know why.

By the time evening comes around, Vasile leads me to another part of the forest, and to his real-life hammock. I laugh at the irony and fall asleep in his arms much like I did that one night. Serene, peaceful rest was what I should've gotten.

Instead, I wake up a few hours later, noticing the darkness deepening. An odd aura fills the air, like something is happening—and then I realize what it is. October 31st has arrived. Shivering, I snuggle back against Vasile. The veil between worlds has officially lifted, and the realms are accessible to all. Which means my trials are not that far off.

≈ ♠ ≈

The next morning, after freshening up and feeding me again—berries and homemade bread and butter from Mihai's village—it turns out I don't have to explain anything to Vasile.

"I felt the change when I woke up this morning," he says. "It's never been this intense, though. Practically raises the hair at the back of my neck."

I nod, munching on the bread. There is nothing more to say, and we try to enjoy the rest of the day with more hiking. Kissing distracts me for the most part, but by the time the afternoon draws to a close, not even that works anymore.

Vasile returns to the campsite with me, joining Daymun and Dante right as night arrives. They pause in their conversation to look at us.

Daymun breaks the silence first, pointing at the sky. "It's time for your first challenge, love."

When I make a move towards him with my bag, he shakes his head. "You won't need any human belongings. Just yourself."

Sighing, I drop my backpack to the ground. Before I can move further, Vasile tugs on my hand and whirls me back in his arms. He grasps my chin and drops his mouth to mine, savoring the embrace as though we have all the time in the world. When we break apart, I sense his reluctance to let me go like a tangible caress.

"I'll be okay," I whisper.

He squeezes my shoulder in response, then takes a step back. The move might look easy from the outside, but I can see in his eyes the pain it causes him. He's afraid for me, and with good reason. *I haven't got the faintest idea what the hell I'm doing.*

Rather than say that out loud, I turn to my guardians and follow them into the woods, leaving Vasile behind. We don't walk for too long, and I realize after a few moments they're leading me back to the ruins near Poenari Fortress. I hesitate to enter the stones, recalling the imprints of the souls who lived here before.

"Are you saying the first challenge is here? Or in the Ether?" *So Vasile was right, when he talked about the zmeu.*

"We do not know, darling," Dante says. "You will have to chance it. Just remember, nothing is as it seems."

Daymun adds, "And if you need help, call out to us." He walks to me and drops a necklace around my head, with a pendant in the shape of a teardrop of fire. I recognize the stone as tiger's eye, though its purpose eludes me.

"Thank you."

I turn to the path ahead and straighten my back. By the time I glance behind, they're already gone, and I'm surrounded by the mist. But I don't stay in the Ether for long. With a few long strides, I emerge in different mountains—the slope goes downwards.

Telling myself to get a grip, I follow the path outlined in front of me until I reach a little valley. A river flows through it, and I walk on its shores, eventually reaching a cavern hidden deep within. I duck in the small enclosure, and after a bit of squatting and walking, I emerge into a larger cavern.

A gasp leaves my lips, echoing all around me. The walls are painted with glorious pictures of battle scenes, but that's not what attracts my eye. Rather, the pictures all depict the same kind of creature. I easily identify it as a zmeu, a dragon-type monster from Romanian folklore.

Is that what I'm meant to fight in here?

The thought makes me shiver. In these pictures, the zmeu has dark scales, and he's massive, easily five times the size of the soldiers. His tail is spiky, his talons sharp, and the muzzle is more angular than a dragon, with a jaw that—at least in folklore—can snap you into two like an alligator.

Bottom line is, I'm nowhere equipped for the battles outlined on these walls. If anything, I'm more likely to become dragon food. And from what I remember, the zmei love themselves some maidens.

Slightly more depressed at my imminent demise, I follow the path until I pass through two other caverns. The third one is the dead end—in more ways than one.

In the middle of it lies the zmeu. Just like in the pictures, his enormous body is curled up in a sleeping form, like a fox. The scales on his back are only a few feet away from the cavern's ceiling. In the darkness, I see odd things glinting, probably his treasure horde. A pond shines in the farther distance. And as I stare at the zmeu, my breath starts coming out in short, panicked pants, disturbing the silence enough to wake him.

He lifts his head, opens two bright blue eyes and stares at me. His jaw drops, showcasing teeth as tall as me. His wings flap, easily taking over the entire cavern. One extends over me, blocking the way out. The membrane vibrates with held-back strength. And the tail, spiky and so damn dangerous, rattles closer to me as he stretches.

"I… was told to come here," I whisper.

If you'd told me a month ago I'd find myself in Transylvania, hunting down a recluse zmeu, I'd have told you to piss off.

And yet here I stand, facing the damn monster, my heart in my throat, close to praying to a Creator I don't believe in, if only he'd help me get through this.

"I thought your kind were extinct," he says in a low rumble.

I blink dazedly at his growling tone echoing around me. "You… speak?"

"Of course. *My* kind was here long before yours, human."

"I am Flama." I surprise myself in clarifying.

Something akin to a chuckle escapes him, along with a few puffs of smoke. I step back, dreading the fire he could accidentally sneeze on me.

"You have not yet grown into your powers, eager one."

Gulping past the lump in my throat, I will my voice to be strong. "That's why I'm here. So, what's the challenge?"

The zmeu looks at me, tilting his head like a snake would. "What do they call you?" he asks, taking me by surprise.

"Katya."

"You are in a rush, Katya. Is there a reason?"

"I'm really not in the mood. My time is counted to figure this out, otherwise my guardians and I are dead!"

I didn't mean to shout, but it's too late to take it back.

The zmeu watches me silently, then says, "How can you even start your challenge, when you do not realize what world you have stepped into? When you lack the knowledge for it?" His head tilts to the other side ever-so-slowly. "I could take one bite out of you, and you would be unable to defend yourself."

I refuse to back down. "True. But I can't go back where I came from. Nothing's left of my old life."

"Is that why you're here, then?" His head lowers, and he moves it so one eye blinks at me. "Because you have nothing better to do?"

His tone is taunting, and I grit my teeth. "Why do you refuse to give me my challenge?"

"Because you have yet to prove you are worthy."

"What is it you want from me, then?"

"Acknowledgement of the power you possess, for one." At my confused gaze, he backs up. "Before this world, another existed. Creatures lived together—the law of the jungle prevailed, and there was honor. The Enlightened Ones came. Proud, advanced, wise, they gave us the tools to live, to survive. Since then, only bad use was made of them. That is how your kind was created. To purge by extinction or purification."

I've heard that name before, the Enlightened Ones, but it was in the Ether.

"Who are these Enlightened Ones you speak of? And why couldn't they do what the Flamas are now tasked with?"

He ignores my first question, instead saying, "Because they loved all of Earth's children and could not harm them. When they were hunted, they left this world with a promise. If the Flama does not do their job, they will return and annihilate everyone."

Could this get any worse? I thought I had the fate of three in my hands… Now it's the entire world? *And who the hell are the Enlightened Ones?*

"I don't know how to do what is being asked of me."

"Let me show you what lies beneath…"

I watch warily as the zmeu moves to the middle of the cave, where the sparkling pond lies. Inch by inch, I follow, hesitant to look within its depths. When I do, I see our reflection, mine tiny besides his. Then the bastard pushes me in, holding me underwater with his paw.

The upper half of my body is submerged, and water fills my every cavity. Water splashes everywhere as I fight, to no avail. He's bigger. Stronger.

Impulse makes me want to reach for Daymun's necklace, but I'm panicking at not being able to breathe, and wanting to draw in liquid rather than air.

Then I hear his voice. "Stop fighting and look. Listen. *Feel.*"

With no other choice, I do as he demands, praying I don't end up drowned under his massive paw, so far away from what I love.

Chapter 12

For a moment, all I'm aware of is the water in my throat, clogging up my nose, my eyes, my everything. My body rebels against the paw on my back, jerking and trying to free itself. Claws dig in through clothes, into flesh, and my mouth opens in a silent scream.

Which, if you're underwater, is practically the worst thing you can do.

"Feel. Listen. *See.*"

Echoes of the zmeu's voice reverberate through the water, and my body goes slack against his hold. I close my eyes, forcing my lungs to continue living, and then... I let go.

No other explanation exists. I stop struggling, stop trying to drag air in my lungs, and instead go slack. Only, I don't die and float away towards the light. And it's not in the Ether I end up, either, but somewhere else. Somewhere I've never been before, yet that feels too darned familiar.

I'm staring up into a kind, weathered face—a

priest, if I'm to guess by his collar. And judging by the angle, he's holding me in his arms. Blue eyes wink at me as he strokes his beard. "Where did you come from, little angel?" He picks me up and shows me to a woman.

She's also got a wrinkled face, but she's younger, and looks up at him with hope. "God has answered our prayers."

"This is much more than that, Elena," he says. "It is a second chance."

They can't be more than fifty, and I'm obviously the baby. But this can't be real, because it's not the life I've lived... Unless my entire existence has been a lie.

I know I was dropped off at a church, but I was older, a four-year-old toddler. And no kind couple took me in, rather I was thrown straight into the system, bounced from house to house, each one worse than the last.

Images file in front of my eyes like a movie, and then stop. I'm older now, on skinny legs. Running down the stairs, ignoring a woman's voice warning me to be careful. I emerge into a kitchen, where a massive cake is laid out with two candles spelling out *10*—ten years old.

The woman from before, Elena, smiles at me. "What do you think, sweetie? Do you like it?"

"It's AWESOME, Mommy!" My excited screech makes her both wince and burst out laughing, and she looks so much younger despite the extra wrinkles and grey hairs. Almost like she's been reinvigorated by having me around.

"Good! Because the bakery almost didn't deliver on time. Want to help me set up the rest of the decorations? Your friends will be here any minute."

Friends? I never had friends growing up, unless you count Bebo.

This new me, though, is apparently pretty lucky. It's like I'm both me and her. I live through all her emotions, her joy, her complete innocence—this child has not suffered. She didn't go through all the crap I had by the time I reached this age. She's been sheltered.

Fury fills me, choking me, blurring my vision. Why the hell is the zmeu showing me this? None of it can be real!

Let me out! I shout in my head. *Pick another challenge.*

As the little girl—me—and the woman go about setting up pretty decorations, his voice resonates loudly and disembodied. "It doesn't work like that. This challenge is yours to face."

There must be a way out!

"Of course. Are you sure you wish to know?"
Yes!

"Very well. The only way out, if you refuse to finish this, is death." He pauses for a second, letting that sink in.

No… Has to… be… another way.

"You have been given the options. Will you run away from this challenge and die, or face it head on?"

It's the running away part that gets me, more than the threat of dying. I've been threatened with that one too many times in my life, to the point it stopped mattering at all. But running away? *A coward, I am not.*

At the back of my mind, I wonder if maybe I'm not already dead, and this is just…whatever it is. But no, something tells me while the zmeu is relentless and ruthless, he won't lie. So instead of backing off, I say, *Fine. I'll stick with it.*

He says nothing, and I'm forced back to the scene. Without knowing what it is I'm looking for, I keep my eyes peeled for everything. Each object the little girl touches, I try to make sure it's not a weapon, or something else.

Peine perdue, as the French would say. A complete waste of time.

Nothing out of the ordinary happens, other than a bunch of kids popping out of nowhere. And yes, that qualifies as out of the ordinary, given that when I was that age, I didn't even know the meaning of friendship. No one to count on but myself. Even my teachers hated me, though they couldn't deny I had brains. It was, maybe, the only thing that kept me out of trouble.

Unsure of what's going on, I watch the little girl enjoy her birthday, and receive presents. A sense of peace and happiness surrounds her, and the complete innocence in her eyes strikes me again.

This could have been me. In another life, if I'd been picked up by another priest… Instead, I got the foster homes, and by the time I turned ten, any prospects of having a real family or being adopted were gone. No one wants a teenager. So I got the shitty end of the stick, through and through. From there, the rest is history.

This little girl though…

The picture changes once more and, after a couple of flurries, I've grown again. This time, it's winter and I'm in a skating rink, surrounded by a group of teenagers. We must be around fourteen, maybe fifteen.

I'm wearing new clothes, new skates—I don't even know *how* to skate, but apparently this version of me does—and my hair is pulled up in a ponytail. Girls and boys surround me, two of each. I brace for the rush of insults, of beatings—what I was used to, at that age—and it takes me a second to notice everyone's smiling, their expressions open, soft.

One guy, next to me, is holding my hand in his. When I move, my skates slip, and he wraps his arm around my waist to steady me.

"Careful, babe. If you hurt yourself, I'll have to answer to your mom."

"We wouldn't want that," another girl says from afar. "Though Elena's totally the best, isn't she,

Katya?"

The mention of my name startles me, but the girl—teenager—whose body I'm inhabiting grins widely and nods. "Totes!"

The guy by my side laughs at my response and kisses the side of my cheek. "You're a weirdo, but I love that about you."

Butterflies spread in my stomach, and I grin back. Again, the teenager is filled only with happiness, and joy. I wait for the telltale sign of impending doom, for one of them to make a snarky comment, but nothing happens.

We skate, we laugh, we eat, and I'm filled with such odd nostalgia, that I get lost in the dream. Illusion. Whatever.

At some point, I split from the group to go to the washrooms, but they're set up a bit farther back in an isolated corner. Inside, I take care of business then wash my hands and rearrange my hair. My cheeks are rosy, my eyes bright—alight with something I didn't know at that time. Love. Innocence. *Joie de vivre.* Pure, freaking bliss.

When I come back out, a beefy-looking guy is waiting for me. "Just the gal I was looking for." He smirks.

The hair at the back of my neck stands up. This is it. This is the moment I'd been waiting for. He's about to try to hurt me—her—and I'm going to have to defend myself.

Can the challenge really be that easy?

Once again, I'm wrong. Because when he does move in, cornering me against the wall, the teenager I am starts shivering. She doesn't knee him in the balls, doesn't move away. It strikes me then that she's sheltered, doesn't know how to defend herself—she won't be able to stop him.

He lifts his hand, touches her cheek. She tries to move away but he grips a fistful of her ponytail. "What, you too good for me?"

Move! Hit him! DO something! She's deaf to my shouts, instead turning away and whimpering, avoiding his mean look. Then another voice cuts through the isolation.

"Let her the fuck go." The growl comes from behind.

The guy—my boyfriend—is there, along with two others. As I stare in awe, he wrestles the attacker from me, then pulls me into his arms while his two friends intimidate the attacker until he takes off.

"You're okay, babe. I'm so sorry, I should've come with you."

I shake my head in his arms, trembling like a leaf, but I'm safe once more. Safe, protected, cocooned...

The scene shifts again. This time, I'm graduating from university. The navy caps are a tell-tale sign, and Elena, with her wrinkled face, is in the stands. So is the priest, looking much greyer than before. And when I get off the podium, the guy from the previous frame is waiting for me.

He's older, also with his graduation cap, and grins at me. "Well done, babe!" His kiss makes my toes tingle, and then we're joined by Elena and the priest.

"Who's up for a celebration?" she asks, tears of pride in her eyes. "Tyler, joining us?"

"Wouldn't miss it!"

The picture changes again. This time, I'm volunteering somewhere—some other country. A tent is set up, sand blows everywhere, and I'm helping out packaging supplies. I get the feel the work is lengthy but fulfilling.

My phone rings. Tyler's picture is across the screen. Older, wiser, but still as gorgeous. I grin but when I answer, it's another person on the line.

"Katya, something happened. Tyler was on a plane, delivering supplies to a war zone, and it was shot down. We managed to get him back, but he's badly wounded." The voice breaks up, then comes back online, but huskier, as if he's choking on his own words. "You should try to get here as soon as you can."

My heart drops in my chest, and I feel his pain as if real. I'm so lost now in this illusion, in this life, that I don't care about the challenge anymore. What's going to happen? That's all that matters.

In Adult Katya's body, I run everywhere across camp, trying to get transportation. Everyone is overwhelmed, but we simply don't have the resources. And then, out of nowhere, a knight in shining armor.

A guy that looks suspiciously like Dante steps out from a tent. "I'm only in the area to deliver something and am heading back out. I can take you to the nearest airport."

I jump on the opportunity, and follow him out to his truck, driving for miles upon miles with nothing but sand around us. Rather than take advantage of a vulnerable woman, he's a perfect gentleman the entire drive, and drops me at the airport with a wish for wellbeing for my fiancé. The ring on my finger…

I twirl it nervously while waiting for the plane to take off. My heart plummets up and down, but in two hours the plane lands, and I'm back in a car, trying to get to Tyler, praying he's still alive…

I get to his camp and am greeted by another doctor. His shirt full of blood makes me seize with panic, and I drop to the ground. He rushes to me, saying something. It takes a moment for the words to sink in.

"He's okay, Katya. He'll live."

I rush inside, by Tyler's side. He opens his eyes, grins weakly. Glances at my hand. "So, you finally decided to say yes?"

Adult Katya's answer is lost on me. The picture changes again, this time much further into the future. We have children… And then, abruptly, it stops. I'm back in the pond, water in my nose, lungs constricting, ready to collapse...

And just as suddenly, I am released. Coughing and sputtering, throwing up water, I struggle to my feet and glare at the zmeu. He's back on his haunches, watching me carefully.

"What the hell was the point of that?"

His head turns, one blue eye settling on me. "Reflect on it, Flama. What do *you* think it was?"

Eyes narrowed, I throw, "Some twisted mind game! What, is this some new tactic to make me lose my shit before I do the challenge? Was that the point?"

He shakes his head. "Why would I want you to lose the challenge?"

"I..." No plausible answer comes to me, because nothing makes sense.

"Exactly," he says, and moves around the cave. His massive body is sluggish, as though whatever he did also took a lot out of him. I also realize the exit to the cavern is now freed.

"What... Am I done?"

"It depends," he says. "Have you figured out the point of this challenge?"

I think back to everything I'd seen. It was a life I could've had, if only fate had been kinder to me. But why show me this? Why torture me with images of something that would never come true?

Like a child, I end up whispering, "Was it to give me hope?"

The zmeu laughs, and the entire cavern shakes. Enough so that pieces from the ceiling fall around me, forcing me to hop from foot to foot to avoid being trampled.

"Hope? There is no hope in this quest, Flama. Only pain, agony, and a choice that will rip you apart."

I gulp at the ominous words. "Then why? Why show me her innocence, the life she could've had, the nice people helping her—"

The words die in my throat. A *good* life. *Nice* people. *Happy* endings, even to situations that could have turned disastrous. Strangers that help, rather than harm.

Clearing my throat, I say, "You're showing me the good in people."

"Yes." He nods. "In a way that you could see, feel, and understand."

"But I don't! Why would this be a challenge? I thought my guardians were supposed to influence me towards Light or Dark."

The zmeu snorts. "This is not about influencing you. It is about showing you what is out there, what could be saved. There will be others after me who will show you more… Less happy things, believe me. *Regina Zânelor* will want to take her time toying with you, and she will not be pleasant about it."

Regina Zânelor—*regina* means queen in

Romanian, and the other bit... "The fae queen? Is that my next task?"

He doesn't address that question, instead saying, "This challenge was meant to show you the good that could exist in the world, and what could be saved, if you make the right choice. You were not fated to have an easy life, but you could have been. And if you had, you would not be the person you are today. One who chose to face off against these demons, against everything you could have had but never would... It takes a lot of courage to get up after losing everything. But it takes more courage sometimes to see everything you could have had and realize it will never be yours. To live with that knowledge, and not let it corrupt you, make you envious, or jealous. To be the best version of yourself that you can be."

I'm silent, unable to think of anything to answer this. The zmeu sets his massive head on his paws, and says, "The wounds on your back will heal. If you go back the way you came from, you will re-enter the Ether, and return back to your world."

I can feel myself go pale at his words. "Are you saying this entire time..."

"You have been in my realm, yes. The veil between the worlds is lifted, and your presence at the Fortress has been felt and reverberated across many others than me. This place—much like the next ones you will visit—exists in the *Lumea Dintre*, the Between world. Neither dead nor alive. Forever apart." He blows out a puff of smoke. "You could not have left here even if you tried, without proof you have accomplished your task."

Stinging on my back reminds me of his talons having dug in. "My blood being spilled, that's the proof?"

"Yes. And now, you may go."

On shaky legs, ignoring the pain in my back, I turn and walk towards the exit. Before I leave, I face him one more time. "What would have happened if I had died, while underwater?"

His eyes are closed, but still he says. "There are no second chances in the Lumea Dintre, Flama. If you die here, you are dead in your world as well."

All the strength I still had seems to pour out of me, and it's with tiny, exhausted steps I walk out of there. By the time I reach the initial cavern entrance, his snoring follows me. Up the steep climb I go, all the while getting clammier, and more feverish with each passing moment.

The wound on my back is bleeding, and I'm cold. In shock. This was a brutal introduction to the trials… And I still have two more to go.

That is, if I survive the journey home.

Chapter 13

I've lost track of time and space. My feet shuffle around as I desperately try to remember my way back. And all around me, the mist gets thicker, like it's unwilling to let me go.

Now that I semi-know about the Enlightened Ones, and the Lumea Dintre, it just feels all the more eerie to be stumbling about in here. I half-fear voices will arise again, telling me how I best do my duty unless I want the world to pay the price, but nothing happens, and my thoughts turn in another direction.

What the zmeu showed me runs through my head. The life I could have had. The life someone else could have, if I make the right choice. The good that exists in the world, the people that I never had the chance to meet.

Have I been wrong all this time? Is there really something worth saving?

I trip over something and my ankle gives way, twisting in an odd way. A yelp of pain escapes me as I crumble to the ground. Emotions well up inside me, exploding in tears and sobs. On my knees, I finally come to the one realization that has evaded me all this time—I *am* lucky.

Lucky to have survived everything I did. To have turned out as I have. To have become better, stronger, because of what happened. How could I have missed all that, and the chance at what I have now?

Someone meant for me… and me alone.

A need unlike any other burns in my veins, to be with Vasile, to get back to my world, where he exists. I pull myself up and push forward despite the pain in my ankle and back. With each step, it's as if I'm struggling against the mist, demanding that it release me.

And yet in its thickness, I also hear the dreaded voices. Whispers. Calling out to me. I can't make out the words, but I know the longer I stay, the harder it will be for me to leave. I need to get out. Have to. *Now.*

Hobbling, I increase my pace, hoping the extra kick in my step will help distance me from what else is around me. And yet no matter how fast I run, dragging my ankle, the mist still surrounds me.

Burning under my skin has me glancing at my hands. The redness of my veins is apparent, more so than ever before. Before I can do anything, the voices grow louder.

"The more you see, the more you crave…"

I glare at the mist. "If you've got something

to say, say it to my face!"

Only laughter echoes, and I close my eyes. The burning in me intensifies, and my body aches to shift. I give into the pain with a groan, letting it overwhelm me, my every sense, until I can't take anymore. Then flames consume me, leaving only my phoenix form alive.

My wings flutter, up and down, and I take off in a whirl of fire, refusing to be tied down any further. I don't know for how long I fly, but eventually I emerge from the mist close to the barrier, near the barrier between realms.

It's a shock to my system when I realize I never physically left. My body is sprawled on the grass near the ruins. Daymun and Dante are keeping watching over it, with Vasile pacing back and forth. His agitated form warms my heart. I cry out, but he doesn't hear me, his gait increasing with frustration.

I fly closer, enough to hear them, though they obviously can't hear nor see me.

"Should it be taking this long?" Vasile asks Dante.

The angel shrugs, his eyes never once moving off my unconscious form.

"It'll take as long as it takes," Daymun says. "These things can't be rushed."

"But how do we know if she's alright?"

"We do not," Dante says.

I try to fly through the barrier again, but can't. Something is still blocking me. Why? My first challenge is complete, I should be able to go back to my body. The worst thing is, I don't know how to fix it.

As I uselessly flutter my wings to keep afloat, I notice my cheeks are getting paler. Vasile stops his pacing, sniffs the air, then drops to his knees next to me. "Katya!"

My two guardians snap out of their passive forms and join him, helping to roll me halfway to my side. My back is soaked with blood, seeping through the shirt and into the grass. But it's recent, hadn't been there before, else Vasile would have sniffed it.

Why? Why now?

As I watch them, my unconscious form winces. Daymun's hand touches my knee, then drops to my calf. When Vasile growls a warning, the demon ignores it. He touches my ankle, then moves the jeans leg up, exposing the skin underneath. It's red, the veins swelling before their very eyes.

What the hell?

Recalling Daymun's warning about using that particular word, I watch more carefully, hoping they'll give me a clue as to how to get back.

"Ce naiba? What is all this?" Vasile asks.

Desperation fills his tone, unlike the strength he portrayed when I left for my quest. I realize in that moment he's been trying not to overwhelm me with his emotions, but there's no denying whatever fate put us together, did so because we really do fit.

The realization unleashes something inside me, and I cry out again. Daymun stands from his spot, his icy gaze glancing around, searching me out. *Did he hear me?* And if yes, why him, and not Vasile, or Dante?

While he keeps searching, Dante and Vasile peer over my body.

"Her wounds from the Ether are seeping into her physical body," the angel says. "She's been in there for too many days, this shouldn't be happening now. Something is wrong."

"*Da, crezi?*" Vasile's hardened *yeah, you think?* seeps to my ears. I try to focus on that voice, to see if maybe that's what I need in order to cross back. Nothing happens.

"She's stuck," Daymun says, still perusing the skies and their surroundings. "I heard her cry just a few moments ago, meaning she must be in the area."

"Her cry?" Dante frowns at him. "Why you?"

Daymun shrugs. "A connection, maybe." He cups his hands around his face, yelling, "Katya!"

I cry again, and he smirks this time. "Yeah, she's out there. Rather tired from the challenge, I'd wager, and unable to cross back."

"How do we help her, then?" Vasile says.

"She's not a princess you have to rescue," the demon throws back. "Katya, love, listen to me. You have to focus on your body, the one here, and reconnect with it. The longer you stay away, the worse your wounds will get."

I try to do as he says. Eyes glued to the unconscious form, I focus on my red hair, the muscles under the clothes, imagining my hands clenching. Vasile rushes back to me, gripping one hand in his. I think I can feel his heat, but that may be my imagination, too.

In the end, at one point I get the sensation of running under water—and then I'm slammed back into my body.

≈ ♠ ≈

"She's back!" Vasile's relieved sigh echoes above me, then he's pulling me in his arms. "How do we stop the bleeding?"

Daymun kneels behind me then, pulling the shirt up. Vasile goes to shove his hand away, "Do you mind?"

The demon rolls his eyes. "Get your wolf hormones under control and look. She's fine now."

And it's true. I don't feel the stinging in my back anymore. But a wave of tiredness washes over me, and I can't keep my eyes open much longer.

"Katya," Dante whispers, touching my shoulder.

My eyelids are so heavy, but I manage a, "Hmm?"

"This is important. Did you transform to your phoenix form, while in the Ether?"

"Had no…choice…" I mumble, then go slack in Vasile's arms.

≈ ♠ ≈

The next time I wake up, my guardians are gone, and Vasile's heat is around me. I slip out of his grip and grab a change of clothes. On tiptoes, I walk in the woods to relieve myself. Then I head to the river, shed my bloody, nasty clothes, and throw myself in the icy water.

By the time I come out, my skin is red from the cold and I'm shivering, but feeling way cleaner. I pull on new clothes, brush my teeth, and sit on a rock to breathe for a moment while I munch on a granola bar.

I survived the first challenge. The realization sends a heady thrum of something in my veins, and I grin at the moon above. The fullness winks down at me, its craters fully visible, yet I think I notice its farthest edge disappearing, like it's heading into its next phase. Which means my time really is running out.

Only two more trials to go.

The thought sobers me up, on account of having to decide the fate of the world right after. But in the meantime, nothing stops me from enjoying the life I have left.

"You should have woken me up," Vasile says, stepping out of the woods behind me.

I glance over my shoulder. "Was planning to

come back."

He nods and rubs his face, trying to erase the sleep from his features. Taking a deep breath, he jerks his head towards the water. "Cold?"

"Icy," I grin. "But refreshing."

It seems to be the right answer, as he takes off his shirt right after, and walks past me. My mouth waters at the sight of his corded muscles. He has abs of steel, biceps I'm itching to run my fingers over, and a pattern of tribal tattoos across his back and shoulders.

With a shock, I realize the largest piece, decorating his back, is different— a flaming phoenix. It's a beautiful work of art, done in a myriad of orange and red shades, and my breath catches in my throat.

Before I can comment on it, Vasile reaches for his jeans and strips. My jaw drops at the sight of naked ass, right before he hops in the river. A few strokes later, he turns on his back. A different kind of glint shines in his eyes as he watches me, but he says nothing.

I have to clear my throat before I speak. "How is it?"

"*Perfectă*," he says, and his use of the female adjective in Romanian makes me think it's not the water he's referring to.

When he ducks his head under, I let out a relieved breath. Under his scrutinizing gaze, I was starting to lose myself—and control of my hormones.

Then Vasile re-emerges, completely naked, from the water. I avert my eyes so I'm not staring like an idiot, but I can't miss the scrumptiousness of his physique. *Holy shit, this guy is...*

Made for you, my inner voice says.

Yeah. Can't deny that anymore.

A touch on my shoulder nearly makes me jump out of my skin. Vasile managed to pull on jeans and tiptoe near me without making a sound. A corner of his mouth is upturned in a teasing smile.

"Are you avoiding me?"

"Nope," I whisper, while my mind is screaming, *Yes!*

"Good," he says. "Then you won't mind if I do this."

He lifts my chin with his index finger, then bends over and claims my lips. We've shared soft kisses, tender kisses, and comforting pecks. A few days ago, before my trial, we even shared passionate embraces, our bodies tightly wound in his hammock.

Nothing has prepared me for this. When Vasile sets his mind to seducing me, I'm left a puddle at his feet. With more skill than I gave him credit, he coaxes open my lips and plunders my mouth, taking his sweet time until a needy moan escapes me. My arms lift around his neck, playing with his hair, and I try to pull him closer.

He doesn't give in. Rather, he deepens the kiss further than I thought possible, before finally pulling back. My grip on him tightens, refusing to let go, and he lets out a shaky laugh.

"Let's take this somewhere a little more private, da?"

"Da." I nod, and he turns away to grab his shirt and my other clothes.

His movements seem rushed, with none of the relaxation I've come to expect from him. The thought makes me smile that at least he's not unaffected.

Grabbing his extended hand, I follow him through the woods. It takes us longer to get to our destination, as every few minutes Vasile tugs me to him for a kiss, or lets his hand linger on my lower back in a teasing caress, which nearly makes me attack him.

By the time we get to his little heaven of peace and the hammock there, we're both so strung high on lust, it's all we can do not to rip each other's clothes. Vasile throws my dirty rags under the hammock, then tosses his shirt off.

Eyes intense on me, he backs me into the nearest tree. I'm ready this time when his mouth descends on mine, and I give as good as I get. His hands roam my back, my waist, down to my ass… I arch towards him, silently begging for more.

His grip on me tightens, then I'm up in his arms, my legs wrapped around his waist. Pulse racing, all I feel is his hardness against me, his touch on me, his earthy scent in my nostrils. I'm surrounded by Vasile, and I want more. So much more.

Yet not even my growls of frustration are enough to get him to speed the pace. After a few failed attempts to unbutton his jeans, he lets my feet touch the ground again and shakes his head, laughing.

"Not so fast, *frumoasă*." He reaches up to my knotted hair and pulls the elastic off it, then arranges it around my shoulders. His eyes are a dark violet as he takes me in, and smiles. "I've pictured this moment for so long, I'm not about to rush through it."

He holds out his hand for me again and leads me to the hammock. The heat of the moment has sizzled down to a gentler flame, and I flush as I realize anyone could have walked in on us. When I mention it to Vasile, he shakes his head.

"No one crosses this territory. I've marked it as mine, and it's about as impenetrable as Fort Knox. If anyone even gets near, they'll have the forest's creatures to answer to, and we'll be alerted."

More things to wrap my head around. Then Vasile moves behind me and touches my hip, nuzzles my hair aside to kiss my nape, and I forget all about the rest of the world.

"I want…" The whisper dies on my lips. His hold on me tightens.

"I know," he says.

Ever so slowly, he reaches for the bottom of my sweater and pulls it off me. I lift my arms to make it easier, then shiver in the coolness of the air. My tank top follows soon after, before Vasile moves on to my jeans.

Wrapping his arms around me, he trails down my stomach, undoes the buttons, and slowly peels them off me. I kick off my socks and sneakers to make it easier, and a gasp escapes me when my bare feet touch the earth.

An odd vibration runs through me, like I'm being centered and protected all at once. "What is this?"

Vasile chuckles, now flush against my back, but still in his jeans. "The earth, Katya. A Flama's connection. It's welcoming you, trusting you. If you trust it back, the world is yours for the taking."

I don't have time to mull over his words. In one swift movement, he whirls me around to him, then picks me up again in his arms, only to deposit me in the hammock. His lips graze mine, but when I try to deepen the kiss, he pulls back again.

"One second," he says, then turns away to shed his jeans before joining me.

Butterflies run through me. It's not like I'm a virgin, but with Vasile, none of the previous experiences matter. The coolness of the air seeps through to my bones, and my teeth start chattering. I notice a blanket at the bottom of the hammock, and nearly reach for it when my mate returns to me.

With slow, sinuous movements, he

straightens his body by my side in the hammock, resting on one elbow. He reaches for me, and then I'm in his arms again, his heat warming me, his touches driving me insane. The last barriers of clothing are removed, and then Vasile's kissing me all over, driving me to an edge as perilous as it is alluring.

"Please…" I whisper at some point, drunk on the feelings he's evoking in me.

He rolls to his back and pulls me on top, his hands going to my breasts, palming them and playing with my nipples. My hips wriggle in place, trying to soothe the ache between my thighs, and he chuckles—though to my satisfaction, his brief moment of hilarity ends of a hiss.

"You're really trying to move this along, *iubirea mea*?"

I look down at him, seeing the adoration in his eyes, and I'm done waiting. "Yeah," I whisper, then feel him sliding inside me, inch by inch.

Head thrown back, I ride him, enjoying the complete connection between us. I've had great sex before, but this… Is more than that. All at once, I feel both grounded and like I could fall apart at any moment. The moon filters through the trees, and stars glint above me. It's a surreal experience, like I'm outside of my body again, yet fully there—even more so than ever before.

When it becomes too much, when the pleasure reaches a peak I cannot control anymore,

Vasile grabs my hips, dragging my gaze back to him. His thrusts become deeper, less careful, more primal, until I explode in a million pieces—and then some.

Each time I think we're done, Vasile just switches positions, showing me just how little I know my body and the true meaning of pleasure. In the end, I fall asleep with his whispers in my ears, his body covering mine, and the woods watching over us.

≈ ♠ ≈

Hours later, the sun is almost peeking over the horizon. My body feels sated, reinvigorated, and I don't even feel the chill in the air anymore between the blanket and Vasile's heat.

"Did Dante and Daymun leave us alone because of this?"

Vasile stops playing with my hair and snorts. "Maybe. They must have sensed this coming on."

I hide my blush in his chest. The thought of them feeling what happened, well, I'm not sure how to feel about that.

Then Vasile says, "How was the challenge? You're… changed. Of sorts."

"Am I really?" I look up at him then. He nods slowly, which makes me think. "I guess, in a way. I've always felt like this world had it in for me. But, in the end, I've been given the best gift ever—you."

He grins, and it's brilliant in the new dawn.

"I wish I could come with you on these

things," he whispers. "The thought of you in danger…"

I shake my head. "It wasn't so bad." I don't tell him about nearly dying, about the water in my nostrils, and what the zmeu forced upon me. Those memories are all my own, and I'll cherish them, as much as dread them.

"I think this one was meant to show me the good in the world—good things that are worth saving. Great futures awaiting." I drop my head back on his chest, biting my lip. "It's given me a lot of stuff to think about."

"And the wounds? How did you get those?"

"Let's just say I disagreed on a couple things with the zmeu who was harassing me."

Vasile grows still. "Zmeu?"

"Yeah… Turns out you were right. Why? Is that so crazy that he'd be my first challenge?"

He shakes his head, then stands up and goes to his jeans. From the back pocket he pulls out the small black book, its leather spine glinting with the sun's rays.

The last time I'd seen it, was when I'd found out about Flamas dying in this quest, and Vasile being my mate. Daymun had it before, which makes me wonder if Vasile wrestled it from my demonic guardian. The thought makes me smile, wishing I hadn't missed such an event.

I'm too busy staring at his naked body, wondering how the hell I got so lucky, when Vasile rushes back to my side. He pulls me into his chest and thrusts the book in my hands.

"Read this."

It takes me a moment to decipher the handwriting and the Romanian script, but then I translate it as I read out loud. "First, there came the cavern, and the zmeu deep in its depths. Then the Fae queen, fickle as they come, with her treachery. And finally, the undead arose, and that alone made me wish I had never embarked on this in the first place. The Flama may well rise from the ashes, but what is left to rise from, when the soul has been torn apart?"

My voice has gone all quiet towards the end. Vasile's grip on me tightens. "There has to be something I can do... Some way I can provide protection."

"There isn't." I know the truth of it deep in my bones. This is my quest, and mine alone, and none can help me finish it. "But you can give me knowledge. That may prove the biggest weapon of all."

Vasile pulls the blanket over us again. "Tell me, what is it you wish to know?"

"This fae queen... The zmeu mentioned someone called *Regina Zânelor*. He also said that each of my trials will take place in the Lumea Dintre, and the various realms that exist there. Now, I'm not all up to date with Romanian folklore. But I remember some tales of faes, who did white magic.

This… doesn't sound like it."

"It's not," Vasile says, confirming my worst fears. "The queen he speaks of is one that was cast out. She's the Fallen One—living in the bowels of Hell itself, or rather, at one of its entrances. None who go to her ever return."

Dread fills my stomach at his words, eclipsing the happiness of the last hours.

Chapter 14

"So… just to make sure I understand, by Fallen One, you mean this fae queen is, um, bad?" Must be the understatement of the year given what I've read, but I'm too tired to figure out a better way to say it.

Vasile nods, his mouth set in a grim line. "That's one way of putting it. A few thousand years ago—and I only know this because the story was passed down in my family—she got desperate, trying to gain control of this entire region. This was way before the legends of vampires and wolves took over. The thing is, the immortals in the area had always kept to themselves, hidden from humans. Her greed exposed them all."

Something tells me this story won't have a happy ending, but I keep my mouth shut.

"Anyway the queen, Daria, received a missive to explain her actions in front of the elders of each immortal race. At the time, there was a council for such crimes. Daria pretended she would listen.

Instead, she used her beauty on the fae men to enthrall them to her will. She unleashed the entire horde onto the unsuspecting council, while she herself went to take care of their offspring."

I go rigid in his embrace. "No…"

"Da," Vasile's voice lowers. "The carnage was found only later. It was a threat to never try to best her… But it also brought the immortals together. The fiercest of them joined in a hunt unlike any others, and once they found her, they banished her and those who had helped her to the gates of Hell."

"But why not in Hell, period?"

"They didn't want her to gain more power. Daria strives in the world of Darkness, and her being in Hell would have given her access to all kinds of new temptations. At its gate, she can never return to the Living, nor enter the world she would have in her passing."

"Stuck forever in the Lumea Dintre…" I snuggle closer to him, wrecked by shivers now. The journal is limp in my hand. "And that's who I'm meant to face next? What about the undead, in the third challenge?"

Vasile shrugs. "Could be anything. Undead is what all immortals were called at some point or another. But either way, the same way you bested a zmeu, you can survive them. I know it."

Warmed by his heat, I soon fall into a fitful sleep.

≈ ♠ ≈

When I next wake, Vasile's getting dressed. He hands me my clothes with a soft smile. "Your guardians are heading here. I smelled them from miles away, they'll be here any minute."

I practically jump to my feet and tug the clothes on, as though trying to hide what we did. Which is practically impossible, given my tangled mess of a hair, and the blush heating my cheeks. "I thought you said this place is like Fort Knox, that no one wanders in?"

"And it's true…unless it's your guardians. Special privileges they demanded, and all." Despite the bite of sarcasm, Vasile simply stands there in jeans, bare feet and bare chested, laughing under his breath.

"Stop laughing!" I yell, but fail to deliver an angry tone.

"It's impossible not to," he says. "You're cute when you're embarrassed."

"Of course I am! I'm supposed to be on a quest, not—not—"

Vasile stops my rushed efforts to pull on my sweater, and instead traps my arms above my head. "Breathe, draga mea."

Then he drops his mouth to mine, and I forget what I was doing. Rising on my tiptoes, I return the intensity of the embrace, off balance until the only thing holding me up is his strength.

Someone clears their throat, and I jump apart

guiltily. Rather, I try. But Vasile shifts us so his bulk hides my half-naked torso. He also takes his sweet time bringing our kiss to an end before releasing me. Flushing even harder, I pull on my sweater and try to fix my hair. When I'm semi-decent, I glance around his frame.

My guardians are at the edge of the forest, watching us with amused expressions. Dante is, anyway. Daymun seems more annoyed than anything. Which makes little sense, given he admitted having orchestrated this whole thing.

"You've had your break. Now you need to tell us what happened in the challenge, from the beginning."

I bite my lip. "Do I have to?"

"Something blocked you in the Ether," Dante says. "We have to stop that from happening again, otherwise it could put your life in jeopardy. And if it is something out of your control, we may have to link ourselves to you further."

"How would you do that?" I ask.

At the same time, Vasile growls and tugs me back against his chest, the gesture more protective than possessive. "Absolutely not."

His tone is cold, without doubt. But I shrug him off and position myself to have an unobstructed view of all of them. "What does that *mean*, exactly?"

Daymun interrupts. "Before the wolf gets all up in arms, tell us first what happened."

His demand is all the more serious as I don't

want Vasile to hear what kind of a psycho the zmeu is. Instead of following my guardian's directions, I start in the middle. "After the challenge was done, I was walking back through the mist, trying to get back here—"

"No." Daymun takes a step closer, his eyes flashing. "From the beginning, love. We need to know everything, from the moment you went unconscious."

"But—" I look to Dante for help, and he shakes his head in response. My eyes betray my hesitation as they slide to Vasile.

"You don't want me here?" he asks. Hurt coats his voice, and I automatically start denying it, but he barrels through. "If it's because of what I said earlier, I promise I can take it." When I still hesitate, he crosses the distance between us and kneels in front of me. Head bowed and tilted to the side, he grabs my hand in his and kisses it. "I am yours, iubirea mea. And despite my primal instincts, I know this quest is yours and yours alone. I promise to support you in it, not hinder your efforts."

To say I'm speechless, would be an understatement. And not just because he called me his love. I'm used to jackasses like Bryan who think they own you after sex, but Vasile is the exact opposite of anything I've ever lived through. I tug on his hand to pull him up and interlace our fingers together. "Okay."

This time, I tell them the full story, without omitting anything. Vasile grows tense by my side when I get to the part about the zmeu appearing to drown me, but he says nothing, true to his promise.

By the time I'm done explaining how I was stuck, and shifted to my Flama form, mirrored expressions of surprise face me. "What? What's wrong?"

"You should not have been able to turn, in the Ether," Dante says. "But that is the least of our problems. The more you stay there, the more you interact with it, the link grows stronger. The fact you bled there makes you vulnerable, and those voices you heard…"

"They must be the Enlightened Ones," Daymun adds. "As well as the Flamas who were here way before, and whose mistakes led to your current curse."

"Who are the Enlightened Ones, though?"

Daymun is silent, in complete contradiction to his usual chatting and annoying self.

Dante throws him a look I cannot interpret, and instead says, "No one really knows. They are powerful beings who were here before all else, some think not even the Creator had a hand in their existence. And since they've been gone for ages, no one can communicate with them, either."

The explanation leaves much to be desired, but I move on from that to a more pressing matter. "So what do I do about the Ether, then? What should

I watch out for?"

"Next time you are in there, do not bleed."

"That's easy for you to say," Vasile throws at my angel guardian. "How about you give her something useful?"

Daymun rolls his eyes. "Ignore the celestial, love. You *can* turn. Your phoenix is much stronger than your human body, harder to bleed, too. After your next challenge is done, when you've exited whatever realm you entered, shift forms. It should make your return to your body rather easier, too."

"Okay, I can do that. But you still haven't explained about the extra linking." They share a look, and Vasile grows tense again by my side. "What am I missing?"

"They want you to drink their blood willingly," he tells me. "If you open yourself to it, it won't kill you as it would if it's being wielded by someone with the intent to hurt you. It's the only way to strengthen the link, by putting a little of their essence in you." His jaw is so tight, I'm afraid he'll hurt himself. It's at odds with the tenderness in his hand.

"Granted, that's nasty," I say, "but why is it such a big deal?"

Vasile grips my chin and forces me to look him in the eye, as though to underline the importance of what he's about to tell me. "By doing so, their blood will mark you. A Flama's scent can be hidden, but the mix of celestial and demonic on top of it… It will be impossible to cloak. Immortals will flock to you, Katya, and they will not be doing with good intentions."

I gulp, the warning clear now. And it's not like I haven't felt the shadows of the forest watching me, at times… A shudder runs through me. "Is there any other way?" I ask my guardians.

"No," they say in tandem.

Then Dante adds, "But if we do not, and you are stuck in the Ether again, we have no way to bring you back."

"What about Vasile?" I ask. "Is there a way he could, since we're mates and all?"

They shake their head again. "No."

In the end, there's not much of a choice. I dread becoming fodder for immortals, but I dread even more being stuck in the Ether with those voices. "Let me try this one challenge without you… And if I get blocked again, we can do it."

Vasile sighs, relieved, and the two guardians nod.

Daymun then looks at the sky. "Ideally, you should have had days to recover in between trials, but the delay in the Ether has worked against us. It's getting close to mid-morning. The place you need to go to will not open until midnight, so you have the rest of the day to yourselves."

"Why only midnight?"

"Because it is the entrance to Hell."

I frown, trying to reconcile his words with what I already know of Daria. "I thought only my words could open the gate?"

"Yes," Daymun explains patiently, "but this is an entrance, not a gate, love. One of many that exist on Earth, in the Lumea Dintre. The gate allows for Hell's minions to exit. An entrance only allows entry, but no exit. Given you'll probably be going through in astral projection mode once more, I wager you'll be alright."

They leave us with that explanation, and I sigh. Between our arrival here and my first challenge taking longer because I was in a different realm, too much time has passed. We're heading into the second week of November, and I try not to think of the speedy days, and what they're ultimately leading me to.

"Well. A few hours are better than nothing."

Even as I say it, I'm aware of the time slipping through our fingers. And judging by the look in Vasile's eyes, so is he.

≈ ♠ ≈

That night, it's harder for us to separate. I had gone wide-eyed and innocent in the first challenge, but now I'm fully aware of how dangerous they can be. My feet are heavy as I follow Vasile and my guardians downhill, walking in silence until we reach a small valley.

Two mountains intercross, forming a V shape in the middle. A river runs through, creating a valley that looks nothing like it's close to Hell. Vasile stumbles, and I look at him, noticing beads of sweat on his forehead.

"What's going on?"

He clenches his teeth, and his grip on my hand tightens. "The energy here."

A few steps later, something crawls over my skin, sucking all warmth and freshness out of the air. It grows thick with humidity, almost like we're in a rainforest. Clouds gather above, obscuring the moon and stars, and each step becomes heavier, and heavier.

Ahead of us, Dante's movements seem robotic, as though he senses it, too. Given we're getting close to one of the entrances to Hell, I'm not surprised. Daymun, on the other hand, is in his domain, strutting about like he hasn't a care in the world. It makes me want to hate him, but I can't. Not really.

Finally, we all come to a stop in front of a cave. Its depths are completely obscured, and Daymun is closest to it. Dante takes a few steps back, as close to the river as he can, in an attempt to distance himself from it. I don't want to force my mate any further, so I turn to him.

Vasile pulls me in his arms like last time and hugs me tight. "Be wary of Daria," he says. "And come back to me."

I nod, not trusting my voice to speak. Then Dante grabs my hand in passing. A zing goes through my forearm, and I sense an odd burning on my flesh. When I look, a little indent has appeared right under my wrist, in the shape of a wing.

My gaze meets his chocolate one, and he smiles sadly. "A small protection, nothing else."

"How come?" I whisper. "You didn't seem to think I needed it last time."

His eyes are unreadable, and he leans over to kiss my forehead. "Be careful, sweetheart."

Then I pass Daymun. He remains stoic, not saying anything. We're far enough from the others that they can't hear us, but I lower my voice anyway.

"What, nothing to say? No protection to give me?" I'm only trying to get a rise out of him, given I still have his tiger's eye necklace under my sweater. Not that it works.

He shoots me a glare out of the corner of his eye, then stares straight ahead. Without moving his lips, he says, "Nothing can protect you down there, love. You should have taken our blood."

"I can't."

"Won't, is more like it. Does he mean so much to you, that you'll willingly risk your life to put him at ease?"

"Vasile?" When he doesn't answer, I say, "This has nothing to do with him. It has to do with everything *but* him. And the fact I don't want a bunch of creatures scenting me like bitches in heat."

A surprised laugh escapes his throat. "Well, then." He reaches for my cheek, the blue eyes digging into mine. A flash of lightning passes them, even as he brushes a lock of hair over my ear. "Good luck, love."

Then he struts away, leaving me shaking my head after him. Vasile meets my gaze one more time and, with a half-hearted wave, I cross the threshold into the cavern, desperately hoping I'll survive this, too.

≈ ♠ ≈

The switch to astral projection happens seamlessly, like before, and darkness immediately surrounds me. I inch closer to the cavern wall, and make sure to follow it with my fingertips. Like with the zmeu, the area soon fills with mist, and I emerge into a clearing. For a moment, I'm confused as to where I'm supposed to go.

Then, in the distance, I hear beautiful music. I follow it and emerge out of the darkness into a forest. Everything is massively sized, including the trees, flowers, and fruits around here. Vivid colors abound, making me squint my eyes at their brilliance.

After a few moments of walking, I stop in front of some sort of palace, perched atop a massive, pink flower. I don't recognize the plant. None of this makes any sense—unless you're in some fantasy world. And then, I realize, that's exactly where I am.

Without knowing it, I must have crossed into the fae realm. Or, at least, Daria's realm.

Something flies down to greet me, zigzagging so fast I can't keep my eyes trained on them. It's about half my size, with long, wavy blonde hair and blue eyes. Translucent wings protrude from its back, and it wears some kind of clothing wrapped around its body. The skin is wrong though, too pale for such a colorful place.

It must be a fae, I think, and lo and behold I'm proven right by its introductory remark.

"Queen Daria awaits you," the messenger says, and flies off.

I look up at the towering flower, and the palace there, and realize they expect me to go up on my own. Unwilling to show weakness, I close my eyes and reach for that burning inside me. Flames engulf me, and I'm in phoenix shape once more, reaching for the sky—more or less.

I fly to the top, then turn back human the minute I reach the pearly surface. Rather than picture myself with my regular clothes, I keep the starry dress this time, hoping it'll earn me some intimidation points.

The ground here reflects the sun in a soft, ivory color. I walk past it, surrounded by so much beauty, yet feeling as cold as if I stepped into a freezer.

"Over here," the same fae says, and opens

doors that appear made of petals—dead petals, that is.

Once I pass through, they close behind me with a soft *woosh*, and I gulp. A throne is set in the middle of the room. Its back is made of thorns, but the queen seems to be sitting on something cushy. When I get closer, I realize they're crushed flower petals.

She shifts, and some fall to the floor. A cold smile accentuates her beauty, and she has the same blonde hair as the other fae. I get that feeling of something not quite fitting in the décor, and I realize what it is. Her wings are not the shape of butterflies, but rather like bats. Edgy, ugly, and completely unbecoming.

"Yes, they're quite ghastly," Daria says. Her voice is like honey, but it drips bitterness and acidity. "A curse from those who imprisoned me here."

I take in my surroundings. "I don't understand. How is this near Hell? It's as far from it as it could be."

"Ah, they've sent me a true innocent this time." Her smile widens, as though she knows something I don't. "Let us simply say I make it what it is."

"Right…" My eyes narrow on her. "I wouldn't be so quick to judge me, if I were you."

"Hmm," is all Daria says, and continues observing me. I can't help but feel like an insect she's examining. "So. You are the new savior."

I don't like the way she says it, nor how her gaze remains fixated on me. But I came here with a purpose, so I simply nod. *Keep your head in the game.*

The queen grins widely. "Do you even know who it is you are supposed to save?"

"I know enough."

"I doubt that. Come closer."

Hell to the no.

"*Vino, draga mea.*"

Her voice drops lower, raspier, and the Romanian words tumble past her lips. *Come, my darling.* Her eyes glint and before I know it, my feet move. Of course she has magic, and of course it's activated by Romanian words. I should've expected nothing less of her.

With that realization, I recall Vasile's warning. *Be wary of the queen.* Thoughts of him remind me who I am, and of my free will, and something snaps in me. Fire burns in my veins, and I don't have to glance down to know they're reddish, once more. The ground under my feet becomes solid, and my muscles listen this time. Daria's eyes narrow on me with frustration.

"What is my challenge?" I defy her, knowing the worst decision I could make is to piss her off this early in the game.

The queen watches me for a few mere moments, then smiles sweetly. Her voice is all bitter honey when she speaks again, no hint of Romanian in it. "Use the Clarity Stone and, should you survive, your challenge will be complete."

"Okay."

I probably should have asked what the stone actually is, but I'm too eager to get away from her insistent gaze.

Daria lifts a gold pendant with an amber gem from her neck, and it floats to me. I hesitantly touch it, surprised to find its surface cool. I pass it around my own neck, and she settles back in her throne expectantly.

I don't know what for, since nothing happens. I'm about to question her, when the thing hits me with such force I drop to the ground and scream in pain.

But it's not mine. I can see, feel and experience the pain of millions. Burnings, rapes, beatings, anything... and everything... from centuries and millennia past.

The queen cackles. "Let's see just how much you'll want to save them after this, *draga mea*."

The throne room fades from around me, the ground disappears, and I'm left alone with the pain.

Chapter 15

This agony in my veins, it's the only reality I know. Vaguely, in some long-forgotten corner of my mind, I realize my muscles are trembling from being too long connected to the floor, but I can't move them. My entire body is curled up in a fetal position, unable to let go of the stone, and even less to stop the rush of images being thrown at me.

Unlike with the zmeu, I don't have to wait to determine what the point of this challenge is. It's quite clear from what I'm being fed—crime after crime, betrayal after betrayal, atrocity after atrociy.

Husbands beating their wives. Women killing their children. CEOs making reckless choices for the sake of money versus human lives. Nature being harmed. Rainforests destroyed. Human scavengers invading houses, destroying lives, hurting women and children.

It goes back and forth, forth and back. Images of conquistadors destroying Aztec and Mayan empires. Gory scenes of Romans killing everyone in their wake. The use of religion to subjugate, to control, to do more evil than good…

And then it goes to the present, showing me attacks like mine—only millions of times worse. I live through these women's pain, their inability to defend themselves, and watch as no knight in shining armor comes to their rescue and they suffer unseen atrocities at the hands of the cruellest of men.

I'm there as foster children, much like myself, are abused and thrown away, shuffled from home to home, put on medications that do them more harm than good… and eventually become part of the problem.

Everything shown rips at my soul, kills at the last hours of happiness, and leaves me devoid of anything, barely able to hang on to my sanity.

I'm panting, breathless, gripping the floor by the time I return to myself. My skin is clammy, sweat making the clothes stick to it. My hair has fallen out of its ponytail and swings, lifeless, in front of my eyes.

How long have I been here? Why does it feel like I've been doing this for hours?

"Feeling under the weather?" Daria cackles. "I am impressed. Not many can withstand the Clarity Stone's influence for eight hours. Let alone someone who was not born to magic. To be perfectly honest, I expected you to fail."

I lick my parched lips. Try to flex my fingers. They're numb, as if I've been clenching them for too long. My knuckles are bruised, like I've been punching the ground.

"Eight… hours?" I manage to croak.

"Yes… Of course, in the world of the Living, I imagine it was much, much longer." She tilts her head to the side, taking in my exhaustion.

It seems to give her more satisfaction, which alone pisses me off. The return of that rage inside me makes me almost drop to the ground in relief.

After all the pain, all the emotion from these last hours, my spirit is numb. I don't know if this is what being tortured is like, but my body, my mind, my very soul feel like they've been ripped apart.

Can I even pull myself together long enough to get out of here?

I push the thought away. I don't want Daria to get ideas, not until I've got more strength left to leave. Once I'm out of here, I'll be able to analyze and overanalyze what I've seen. For now, Vasile waits for me. Dante and Daymun do, too. I need to get out of here, and back to them.

And given this queen is a sadistic bitch, no way she'll let me go if I ask nicely. I recall what the zmeu told me—that after each trial, there has to be proof I've completed it, usually in my blood. Though I'm exhausted, sitting in a pool of sweat, I notice no blood anywhere. Clearly, Daria's got more in store for me.

So as I mentally prepare my muscles, I glare

at her. "You've had your fun. Now answer some questions."

A smile tugs at her lips. "If only it were so easy."

"What is the Clarity Stone?"

Daria looks at her nails, inspecting them for dirt. Even from here I can see their black tinge and want to recoil in horror. But I don't, standing my ground instead.

"Long ago," she says, "my father gifted me a crystal. He said it would help keep me grounded, make the right decisions as a princess in his kingdom." She purses her lips. "He was wrong."

"I don't underst—"

"Do you think I care for your understanding?" She flies in my face, her wings obscuring what little light is left in here.

My reaction surprises me. Instead of standing and facing off against her, I flinch and scramble backwards in reflex, much like all those victims have done. It's as if their suffering has suffused my being to the point I can no longer fight, and it's clouding my reactions. I don't have time to think more on it, instead desperately trying to catch the last of Daria's words.

"You are here for my satisfaction. And I fully intend to make you see what *I* see."

"You're crazy." I shake my head, willing my fists to clench so as to stop their trembling. "Probably why your daddy gave you the stone in the first place."

The words only anger her more. "You think yourself better? Foolish one. You want to know what the stone does? Very well. It was meant to provide guidance but got twisted along with my energy. And so, it has been lost."

"Like you." And then it dawns on me. "You hate that I was able to survive its influence."

She turns away and paces back to the throne. "You think you know everything, but you haven't even scratched the surface. Nothing matters in this world—nothing except *them*."

Oookay, crazy bitch, I think, but manage by some feat to keep my expression calm. "Them?"

Once more, she's gliding back towards me, those eerie wings shivering in the air. Her eyes are filled with a feverish gleam, something I've seen before—in movies, in psychos, and generally crazy people.

"They, the *Enlightened Ones*!" Her tone is impatient, as though she doesn't have time for my silly questions. "They are a force greater than ours. The greatest that has ever inhabited the Earth."

Recalling my guardians' words, I shake my head. "I thought no one knows who they are."

A hysterical laugh explodes past her lips, making me jerk and drop the stone. It clatters to the ground, rolling over as if attracted by a magnet until it's by Daria's feet. She bends over and picks it up, and her maniacal guffaw stops abruptly.

When next her eyes settle on me, they are filled with more disdain. "Who told you such lies, your guardians?"

I refuse to answer, not that it matters. She walks back to her throne, perching herself back onto it. "We *all* know who the Enlightened Ones are. The stories were passed down through generations of immortals. Would you like to know?"

No, I want to say, but the word won't come out. Taking my silence as agreement, Daria's gaze becomes faraway, and her voice grows deeper.

"Long ago, when the immortals walked the Earth, they were created equal. Different, with unique abilities, yet equal. Neither was meant to rise above the other."

I can't resist the dig. "Like you did, you mean?"

Daria chuckles. "So, you do have a bite, then. Good. But no, I was not the first. In that time, a group of different creatures mixed with us. We only knew them as the Enlightened Ones, and thought they were the same as us. Very soon, we discovered that was not the case. They were… so much more. Their knowledge was immense, spanning millennia and galaxies. They could shape shift, and see the future, and they warned us of things to come."

She goes silent for a bit, lost in memories as she plays with the stone. "Those of us who listened were awoken, allowed to see past simple things. We were given tools to think beyond, to demand more, and to realize the mortals were a threat. But some decided to remain ignorant and shunned the Enlightened Ones. Eventually, they left."

Her voice is filled with sadness now, as though the loss was personal to her. "And when they did, the Flamas took over. Having been favorites to the Enlightened Ones, they developed new ways to use their powers. They were able to cross the Creator, to open the gates to Heaven and Hell, and *he* did not appreciate that."

Daria laughs then, and I realize the story has come to an end.

The reverence filling her tone makes me question my own sanity. And then I remember the whispered voices in the Ether, and gulp past my fear. "Where did the Enlightened Ones go, exactly?"

Her sneer conveys how little she thinks of my question, but I pay it no mind. The information she's sharing is way more important than her disdain.

"No one really knows. They were able to overpower all immortals, to cross any barriers or gates, and that is why they were feared. Some say they lie in wait, just beyond the Ether of Flamas, waiting for the day they can return here and wipe the planet clean. But no one really knows… Not like I do. They were strong, they were great, our mentors and friends. And now…we are set against them." She pauses, and her face hardens. "But we are not strong enough, and never will be."

"I don't understand," I whisper. "Strong enough to *what*? The Enlightened Ones are gone, and now one of my kind shows up only every five hundred years to clean up mortals' mess. Probably as penance for rising above in the past. So tell me, what is it you want from me, exactly?"

Daria leans forward, elbows on her knees, and smiles maniacally. Madness glints in her eyes, and not for the first time I catch myself wondering if she realizes it.

"Let them come back," she says. "Refuse your task. They will see our superiority, yours and mine, and allow us to join their ranks. We will have power the likes you have never seen, enough to free your kin."

I ignore her jab about freeing Flamas—how can you free someone if they're dead? Instead, I say, "You are deluded." Shaking my head, I step back. "That's impossible. It'd be like raising the dead."

She throws her head back and laughs then. "And what makes you think that is impossible?"

My entire body rebels against the idea, and I try to quell the disgust rolling in my stomach. "The Enlightened Ones are gone, Daria. You've lost your marbles completely if you think anything's left to bring back."

"How little you know," she smirks. "But it's all in the little book, just read it."

"How do you know about that?"

She says nothing, instead resting her back

against the throne. Her eyes go glassy. "Read everything in there, not just what the wolf wants to show you."

"I…" The words get stuck in my throat. I try to say something else, but between one blink and the next, I'm no longer in her palace, but somewhere else. In a dark tunnel, in the middle of nowhere, not sure whether I'm in the Ether or somewhere else completely.

To top it off, my starry dress is gone, and I'm back in my old clothes. *Fucking hell.*

The air is chilly, but I don't let it get to me. Instead, I pull my jacket tighter and push my feet onwards. Ignoring the tightness announcing a cramping of my muscles, I move one foot in front of the other, keeping my eyes on the ground. The last thing I need is to step into a hole and land into some other land.

Wait, wasn't that a movie?

In the cold bowels of the earth, movies, fantasy worlds and fictive characters seem so damn removed from my life. Or at least, the life I now know. The one from before is like a long-forgotten dream, one I'm pretty sure was ages and ages ago.

Wasn't it?

Muttering under my breath, I shake my head. "I have to do this, come hell or high water. Have to.

No other way about it."

Hah. *Hell*. What a fucking joke.

A nervous laugh bubbles out of me and echoes eerily in the cavernous walls. Like multiple versions of me are chortling, though what they're finding so funny, I can't tell.

And then among them, one voice sounds different. I freeze in my steps, a chill running up my spine. Suddenly, it feels a hell of a lot cooler in here.

Hell—there's that word again.

I perk my ears for the sound, that other voice, trying to get my bearings. Am I still going up, or down? Can I even tell at this rate? These quests don't come with a damn instruction manual, and I have no way to reach my friends.

If I can even call them that.

"Come on, Katya." I hope the sound of my voice is enough to give me a semblance of courage. And it does, for about a millisecond. Until I hear that *other* voice.

"Come onnn, Katya," it mocks.

I gulp and unclench my fists, forcing them by my side instead. Katya. That *is* my name, and this is my story. Whether or not it'll have a happy ending… That remains to be seen.

Nothing around me says I will survive this. With the challenge completed, I should have survived, should have been able to exit. Except for the little fact I have no proof of said completion… Obviously Daria has something else in mind, maybe in an effort to force me to see things her way.

It's a wasted cause, I think. Only, what she showed me is very much present in my head, going on a loop. So much pain. My chest still hurts from it, my eyes unable to unsee what I witnessed.

And the stupid voice echoing in the bowels of Earth, that I'm trying to escape—or run towards. Who even knows, now?

"Come onnn, Katya," it mocks me again, and another shiver rakes up my spine.

I gulp, and unclench my arms, forcing them by my side instead. Katya. That *is* my name, and this is my story. And my happy ending? Well, I won't find out unless I fight for it, right?

It takes me another moment of breathing, getting myself under control, then I manage to move my feet. Inch by inch, I trek down—or up?—the runaway. Then I emerge into another corridor, this one darker.

Only an instinct of preservation saves my life. Before setting another step, as I automatically want to, I glance down. Half of the ground is gone, leaving only a ridge—a super thin, tiny ridge. To its left side lies a massive abyss, hinting at incoming death.

"Shit I'm supposed to get across this?"

On impulse, I try to shift to my Flama form, and find I'm unable to. Rather than panic, I reason that it's probably exhaustion from that stupid stone, or even some spell of Daria's. I should've known the queen lied. She wouldn't let me get out of here alive, not unless I see things her way. Well, I'm not about to let her win.

I pull the sleeves back from my hands. Yeah, I'm risking loads of scraping, but I need to hold onto the wall and not slip to my death. That drop looks deadly—not that I can see the bottom.

Shit.

As I inch my way across, not for the first time, I wonder why in hell I agreed to all this. It was bad enough facing the zmeu and seeing all that I could've had. Too damn real.

And now this fae queen, apparently determined to kill me. Maybe I should've played along… It wouldn't have been possible. What she showed me was brutal. But—

A flutter of wings draws my attention, and I grip the wall tighter. I'm moving at snail speed across the ridge, which seems about twenty, thirty meters long. Not incredibly so, but long enough for me.

Especially when I could drop to my death at any moment.

I need to shut my thoughts, so I focus on drawing in small breaths. If I inhale too much and my chest expands, it'll get me off balance. A few more tentative steps to the side, and the flutter draws my attention again. But I can't see anything when I glance to the side.

"It better not be bats," I mutter to the darkness. My dislike for them stems from being a city gal, and also not wanting some creature to nest in my hair.

Silence descends at my whisper—and somehow, I know it's bad. Real bad. I just don't realize how bad until I sense a presence at my back.

"Boo."

My little startled yelp is enough to cause a knee-jerk reaction, and my foot slips. I dig my nails into the cavern wall, managing by some miracle to hang on. Muscles trembling, I glue myself to it and search for footing.

After a panicked moment, the tip of my sneaker finds a rock. I'm frozen to the wall though, unable to move for fear of falling. And still I sense a cold gaze on me, watching me, waiting for me to fail.

I can't fail. I need to get out of here... See the sun. Breathe the air. Be with Vasile.

"Foolish one," the voice cackles. When I refuse to look back, it moves to the side, and I see it out of the corner of my eye.

It's a fae—or something. The wings are tipped at the top, and the skin is glowing, but of a sickly green hue. Pale grey eyes stare at me, and the mouth turns into a sneer.

"If I repulse you, then this will be much too easy."

It flows closer to me, and its sweet breath blows in my face. Something crawls in my thoughts, an unwelcome invasion testing and sniffing for weaknesses… The fae vanishes from my vision, and I freeze again. My mind is yelling at me that I need to move, to get the hell out of here as fast as I can, but my body won't listen.

Then something whips across my back. It feels almost like a feather hitting me, light and airy—and then the agony starts. I scream, unable to hold it in, and my echoes of pain are returned to me tenfold.

But still I hang onto the wall and move to the side. *One more step. One more step. One foot next to the other.*

My back throbs, and something trickles down the skin—blood. The smell of metal is in the air, or is that my imagination? *I can't…*

Vision goes blurry. Fingers go numb.

Need… air…

Nails digging into the wall, I clench and unclench my muscles, forcing them to be limber, to be what I need. A second creature floats next to me, this one even uglier. The ones with the queen had been pale, but these ones are…

"Foolish one," the second thing says. "Did you really think Daria would let you escape?"

Its claw-like hand goes to reach for my wrist, and my heart beats wildly. If they manage to injure one of my hands, I'm lost. I'll topple down to the darkness below and never get out of here.

Only, when the claw tries to touch me, a blinding light escapes my wrist, and they all fly back. Their invasion in my mind leaves, too, and I'm able to breathe more freely. I remember Dante's *protection*, and wish I could hug my guardian angel, because he obviously foresaw I would need some type of help.

Steeling myself against the sudden brightness, I force my feet to move. This is my one chance to get out, and I might as well take it. Step after step, I manage to inch forward, though I keep my senses alert in case those creatures return. Then I'm reaching the end of the stupid tiny walk, and I hit the ground running.

My lungs feel like they'll seize any moment, but I keep going, refusing to look back. I'm not even sure if I'm heading the right way, but at this point, I have no other option. Like a drumbeat, my soles hit the ground, and I'm running, running, running…

A root I don't see coming has me splatter to the ground, causing more bruises across various parts of my body. After the initial shock, I push myself off and get back up. I make the mistake of glancing behind—three creatures are following me.

Shit!

I pick up my pace and, in the distance, a light shines at the end of the tunnel. I've never been so happy to see something in my life. Just as I push my tired muscles, something yanks on my shirt and I topple backwards.

One of the creatures flies over me and straddles me. Her hands are on either side of my face,

and she grins evilly. "Nu aşa de repede, dulceaţă."
Not so fast, sweetie.

Her eyes glaze over and I feel something
trying to enter my mind. I jerk against the invasion,
bucking to try to throw her off, but my hands are
caught and held above my head by another creature.

"Stop it!"

She keeps digging in my mind, dredging back
to the surface all the things the queen showed me,
filling me again with the pain of so many. My body
breaks out in goosebumps and gets clammy. I barely
survived this the first time around, I can't do it again!

The creature shifts and somehow touches the
side of my cheek. A blood-curling cry escapes her,
and I hiss in pain when her claws dig further into my
face. Then the pressure disappears. I blink and see her
mouth open, but her entire body is burning, turning
to ashes before my disbelieving gaze.

The hold on my wrists lessens, and I scramble
away, then stay frozen in fear for a moment. This
must have been Daymun's doing. *So despite his
words, he did add his protection.* His tiger eye
necklace lies heavy between my breasts, its heat
reminding me that I'm alive.

My flight instinct kicks in and I take off on a
run, straight towards the light. I don't want to be
around when these creatures realize this was all my
fault. I can only hope all my blood spilled since
leaving Daria's is enough to prove my completion of
the trial.

I cross the threshold to the outside and don't even bother breathing the fresh air. Instead, I let my Flama shape take hold, and fly into the skies, hoping I can find the exit before an entire army follows me.

Moments later, I get that feel of waterfall and I'm deep in the mists again. This time, the whispers are much louder, and clearer.

"The fae queen is a treacherous being," one says. "But she speaks the truth."

"Their protection saves you," says another. "A price will follow."

I don't know what it means, nor do I want to stick around and find out. So I keep flying through, ignoring their whispers agreeing with Daria. I don't want to think about what she showed me. About what she said.

Finally, I'm at the edge of the Ether. I burst through, and jerk upright in my human form. I'd been lying down on the ground, in the darkness. On wobbly feet I move into the light, and the first person I see is Daymun.

His scent of cinnamon surrounds me, and I pull him to me, desperate to feel a hug, anything. I breathe in, but already he's pushing me away, scrutinizing my face. "What did she do to you, Katya?"

I shake my head and inch towards Dante. Only then do I realize we're alone, no sign of Vasile. And my angel looks damn threatening, wings spread as if to cover us.

"Where's Vasile?"

"Getting reinforcements," Dante says. "A group of immortals is heading this way."

"Why?" My voice sounds weak even to my own ears.

"For you, love," Daymun adds.

My expression must remain confused, because he moves closer and wraps an arm around me again. It keeps me standing, albeit barely.

"They want to stop your quest, before you get to make a choice," he tells me. "Must have caught your scent in the woods, or perhaps they have spies. Either way, since we're not about to let that happen, your wolf went to get reinforcements."

"He should be back within the hour," Dante says.

"I thought you said this would only happen if we link."

Dante shakes his head. "Someone must have seen something and told them."

My thoughts go back to those wolves I'd met in the woods, and the black one taking particular interest in me. Then something way more important crosses my mind as I glance around at the setting sun.

"How long was I in there this time?"

"A little over eight days," comes the answer.

That's when my body crashes, as if the thirst, hunger and exhaustion wrap me all at once. I sink into Daymun's embrace. Maybe it's my imagination, because surely he doesn't panic, but in my dreams he tightens his grip on me and shouts Dante's name.

Then both their arms are holding me upright, and warmth envelops me.

"The queen caused this," Dante says.

"Then we need to undo it!"

The warmth continues to fill me, then I'm back in the darkness. Only, rather than a peaceful one, I end up in pain. The agony of millions, focused into one beam designed to drive me insane. As it turns out, Daria took precautions to make sure I don't forget what she showed me.

And I have no way to escape it, stuck in a never-ending nightmare.

Chapter 16

I'm in a half-awake, half-not-quite-there state for a while. My consciousness is enough that I realize I'm being moved inside Poenari Fortress, and I'm pretty sure at one point I open my eyes to see Daymun casting some kind of fire circle.

"Do you not think that is excessive?" Dante asks.

"About as excessive as your circle of protection," comes the retort.

My guardian angel stops talking then and returns to my side. Sleep overcomes me again.

When I next come to, it's in Vasile's arms. But something is wrong, because his arms are too tight—that's what woke me up in the first place. I stir awake, pushing against him for a breather, and he loosens his hold just enough for my head to poke through.

"What's going on?"

My sleepy rumble attracts Dante and Daymun, but I only see them as two shadows standing over me, with no faces.

"Do you recall anything after you came out of the cave?" Dante asks.

I think back, and by that action realize my head is throbbing. I haven't had a migraine for a while, and the sudden agony is debilitating. Nausea rolls in my gut, my eyes squint at the movements, and my brain's stuck in a permanent fog. It takes me a moment longer to answer, and when I do, it's in a whisper to avoid making the pain even worse.

"I remember coming out, Daymun holding me... And you saying Vasile was gone out for reinforcements. Because of... immortals?"

I'm frowning up at him, but still see only the shadow. It makes my pulse race quicker, and it takes me a second to identify the sensation—fear. The trial with Daria, everything I've seen, is making me wary, worse than before. I no longer feel safe with my guardians, rather I'm perceiving them as threats.

It's Daria's tricks, I tell myself. *Nothing but a trick.*

Yet even as Dante speaks, I can't help recoiling against Vasile's chest. I'm afraid to look at him, in case he's also a shadow, so I keep my gaze glued to the ground.

"Yes," Dante says. "We had to enter Poenari Fortress instead. Sent out word to the tourists and staff that the monument is at risk of collapsing, to avoid having mortals coming nearby. It will not gain us much time, but it will be enough until we push back."

"Push back?"

Vasile answers from behind me. "My pack is here, along with a few other reinforcements."

"More shifters?"

"Da," he says and kisses my shoulder. It's only then I realize I'm in a tank top, and my skin is clammy.

"What…"

Vasile brings up a sweater around my shoulders. "You had a fever."

I pull the material tighter, trying to avoid a shiver. "So, these immortals?"

"The forest warned me first," Vasile says. "As soon as you entered your second trial, I got wind of a large group of *strigoi, pricolici, vârcolaci* and others heading our way."

Vârcolaci is what they call the werewolves around here, and I've already had the pleasure of meeting a strigoi, but I'm unfamiliar with the other word. "What's a *pricolici*?"

"It's a type of werewolf that feeds on dead carcasses."

Another shiver runs through me, and I dig my hands in my sweater. "Wonderful. Is there a particular reason why your wolves are on my side, but those other creatures aren't?"

Vasile rubs my back, and the friction from his palm sends some heat into my frozen muscles. "Remember the whole bit about Light and Dark, and

Flamas having a choice from the beginning?" When I incline my head in assent, he continues, "Well, strigoi and pricolici from the start were on the side of Dark. In order to multiply, they take lives—souls. Vârcolaci that have sinned, usually also by killing innocents, tend to lean towards Dark too. They are the most affected by the expanding corruption in this world, because they feed off it."

Not even his movements can warm me now, and my teeth start chattering. "G-go o-on," I whisper, desperately trying to tune out the part of my brain warning me of incoming danger.

Vasile hesitates, then adds, "They are afraid of what you will choose. If you cleanse the world by opening Heaven's gate, their entire existence will be wiped. This is a cowardly attempt to get to you, one I will not let stand."

"And what makes you believe your own wolves won't turn against you?" I mutter. My voice is toneless, devoid of emotion.

If Vasile is surprised by it, he doesn't show it. Instead, he kisses the side of my head in a gesture so sweet, it brings tears to my eyes. "They stand with me, aligned with Light. And they will help me protect my mate, to the last wolf standing."

To my guardians, he adds, "I got help as soon as I could, but it's still going to be an ugly fight."

"Would it help if I go talk to them?" I ask.

"Absolutely not!" Dante thunders, and I back

into Vasile even further. Flashes of what Daria showed me run through my head again.

Daymun crouches in front of me, reaching for my chin. I scramble away from his touch, refusing to look him in the eye. Silence grows deafening around me as they notice my skittish behavior, then his voice comes, neutral.

"Are you afraid of us, love?"

I shake my head, but it's useless. Their energy pulses around me, and the shadows thicken. I curl into myself, trying to fight against the pull, but the energy of the souls is too much and I'm dragged once more into nightmares of others' despair.

Voices overlap in my head, visions of what happened to others. They have nothing to do with me, and yet they have *everything* to do with me. Faces intermingle with those I know—Dante, Daymun, even Vasile. Then it's no longer strangers being beaten, betrayed, murdered, but me. My body, in their stead. My pain, for theirs.

It's all in my head, and on some level buried deep down, I realize it. But not enough to fight it or snap out of it.

≈ ♠ ≈

Minutes, or hours later, I'm outside of my body again. Unable to keep up with constant barrage of pain, my mind extrapolated and removed me from myself, perhaps in an attempt to protect whatever's left of my sanity.

As I hover in mid-air, I catch sight of Vasile's concerned expression, mirrored by my guardians. He leaves my shivering body, and heads to Daymun. Dante is overseeing the mountain, a lonely figure cast in anger on the fortress wall.

Daymun, oddly, is at the entrance of the tower they've brought me to. He's throwing me side glances. "The queen did a number on her."

"There must be something we can do," Vasile says. "I know you're bound by some laws, but there has to be something."

Daymun looks away, frowning at the ground. His jaw is tight, as though he's warring with some internal decision. In the end, he says, "There are things we can try, but none will help unless Katya shakes it off." His gaze shifts to me, and I swear he can see my hovering form. "She is in the Ether now, she is safe. But we must be quick about these immortals."

"They are climbing," Dante warns.

Vasile heads out, his face a stormy mask. Once he's further down the stairs, Daymun sets fire to the door, I presume so no one else can enter. Him and Dante remain around me, protecting me. My body remains unmoving and, still in midair, I stop fighting the pull and let myself be dragged into the Ether. Maybe there, I'll get some much-needed answers, and consequences be damned.

In the mist, voices whisper all around me,

then coalesce into one. Or perhaps one is louder than the rest. Whichever the case, the presence surrounds me.

"You have been tainted by the queen of faes."

I look around, but I'm definitely alone. "Is that why I'm seeing things differently?"

"That, and more."

Silence grows, but I break it. "So how do I snap out of it? I can't afford it messing with my head. It's making me not trust my guardians, and I can't do this without them."

"It is only affecting you because it forces you to lean towards Darkness, towards destruction."

Which is what Daria wanted, in a way. If I'm leaning towards destruction, I'm more likely to eventually walk away from all this.

I try another tact. "Who are the Enlightened Ones? Is any of what she told me true?"

"Truth and reality are not always the same."

Useless answers, the bunch of them. Rather than scream my frustration at the invisible, I force myself back into my body. When I blink awake, the door is still keeping me protected. I reach to the corner for a bottle of water and some berries and bread that was left for me, gulping everything down.

The food feels good in my otherwise empty stomach, but still I'm glancing out the door every few seconds. I can sense my guardians' agitation outside, and despite Daria's tricks, I cannot stay still. *They were there for me when I needed them. Much as it'll cost me, I have to try and help out.* Before I can change my mind, I shift to Flama form and fly through the flames.

Unmarred, I emerge on the other side. Daymun and Dante are on the rampart, surveying the fight below. They turn to me with equally surprised looks. This time, maybe because I'd been in the Ether, or because of the sun—either way, the shadows are gone, and it's their regular faces I see.

"You cannot be out here," my guardian angel scolds. "The whole purpose of this is to keep you protected."

I glance below the fortress, where a line of wolves is spread out in a semi-circle. I fly to the other side, noticing they're spread out into a full circle. Amid them, I recognize Vasile's white fur. He glances up as if feeling my distress, and howls.

Dante is there next, picking me up and cradling me against his chest. I try to struggle against him, but my form is small, and his arms are like iron around me.

He drops me in a corner of the fortress where I'm surrounded by wall. "You cannot put yourself in danger. If anything happens to you, this entire world is doomed and—"

A loud bang startles me, and brick goes flying everywhere. Dante is thrown backwards, a massive boulder atop him. He struggles to get freed, and Daymun comes to his defense.

They're both piss angry, and without another look at me, Dante jumps off into the fray below. Avenging angel, definitely. Before joining him, Daymun throws a glare my way. "Stay. Here." Then he's gone, joining Dante and Vasile.

I do as he says—for about ten seconds. Then I peek around the rubble to the mess below. Creatures of all shapes and sizes are trying to climb the mountain. Some are massive enough to require four humans to dispose of them. I'm seeing trolls, goblins, something that looks like vampires, and other creatures I can't identify.

What is unmistakable, however, is the rage coming off them. I remember something either Dante or Daymun told me. *The humans' hate corrupted even the best of us.* Judging by these guys, they were right, because they're focused on one thing alone—my death.

As I go back to my corner, shivering against the chill permeating my feathers, I also realize something else. Yes, humans have spread corruption far and wide. But my guardians, my mate, they're out there trying to defend me. As is Vasile's pack.

I can't just stand here, doing nothing, but what the heck *can* I do? Vaguely, I recall Dante explaining my powers… But what would be useful here? Regeneration? Hardly. Healing tears? Maybe after, to help out the wolves. Carrying heavy loads? *Yes!*

With a beat of my wings, I perch on the

remaining ruins of the wall. I close my eyes, letting the anger, the fear even, fill me. When I launch myself off the wall with a sharp cry, more flames consume my body until the phoenix grows to the size of a wolf.

Elation fills me, fighting some of the fear off. I am strong, and I am powerful. *I can do this.*

As I circle above the fight below, I try to look beyond, to figure out the best way to help. And also, not panic when I see the only three people who've given a damn about me smack in the middle of very angry creatures. Rabid dogs have nothing on these guys.

Forcefully, I fly away from the battle, and find a couple of trees that have been cut down. Diving down, I dig my six-inch talons into the trunk of one, and lift it up. I expect to have to flex muscles, but it's as easy as lifting a feather.

Returning to the battle, I avoid some arrows being shot my way—*what is this, the sixteenth century?* I stop midair and take aim before dropping the trunk. My tail has sparked it with fire, and it gathers speed in the air, the blaze growing until it's all-consuming. When it smashes down onto the creatures, their startled cries fill the air.

As does the smell of charred flesh. *Yuck.*

"Katya, get away from here!" Daymun yells at me.

His face is filled with the dirt of the fight, his

shirt shredded to bits. An animal gleam shines in his eyes, as though he's no longer restrained. But I refuse to listen. Instead, I distance myself—but only to find another tree.

A couple of times, I manage the maneuver, until the last time I go back for a tree, a welcoming party awaits me. I cannot avoid the arrow in time, and it pierces my wing. My cry echoes in the air, and I start dropping from midair.

My imminent capture is near—it was stupid flying in a predictable pattern. And the two trolls, three vampires waiting for me look like they'll be relishing my demise.

But when I land on the ground, my phoenix shifts to human form. Already, the wound is closing on my arm, healed by my transformation. I stand, dressed in the stupid starry dress once more. The vampires have to avert their eyes, no longer covered by the clouds in the sky—at least *some* things are predictable.

"You wanted to capture me?" I ask sweetly. "Well, here I am."

One of the trolls grows bold and stomps towards me, making the ground shake. He's two heads taller than me, and looks like a dead, bloated human with grey, dirty skin. A ripped cloth covers his swollen underbelly, but it's his chunky feet and arms that cause the vibration in the earth.

I'm not sure of what I'm doing, but it's like instinct has taken over. When the creature attempts to touch me, the veins in my hands flash red and rather than cower away, I grip his ugly, rotten skin by the wrist.

To my surprise, not only does he stop moving, but his beady eyes widen in surprise, and it's like he's paralyzed. Then a gagging scent fills the air, and I realize smoke is sizzling from my touch. I'm burning him!

He staggers back, and the wrist I'd grabbed falls as if cut from his arm. When the lumpy mess hits the ground, he screams and scratches at his face with his remaining hand, tearing himself into pieces. In front of the others, he turns to ashes.

One of the vampires uses his speed to rush up behind me, wrapping an arm around my neck. I lift my hands to him, and the same thing happens, causing him to release me.

I make the mistake of turning to him, thus leaving my back wide open. The other two vampires are by my side in the next breath, each catching a hold of an arm, but making sure they don't touch skin.

Their grip is strong, and firm. If I try to move, I'll end up dislocating both my shoulders—or worse, dismembered. So I force myself to remain immobile, and instead turn my head slowly to the vampire on the right.

Black locks surround a young face with an aristocratic profile. He wears a suit much like Daymun, but the cut and style are older—a few decades, at least. He sneers, transforming his otherwise beautiful face into a mask of cruelty.

"So, the rumors are true," he says. "A Flama walks the Earth once more, ready to make her choice and ruin everything for us."

"And she has figured out how to externalize her fire, it seems," adds the other vampire from my left.

I glance at him out of the corner of my eye. He's dressed similarly to the first one, but with brown hair instead. Despite the inclination to face him as he speaks, I focus on the dark-haired strigoi. He's the leader, I'm sure of it.

"Ce vrei?" I ask simply. *What do you want?*

His eyes narrow at my use of Romanian, a hint of irritation in the irises. "Ceva ce nu—" *Something that you can't—*

He never finishes his sentence. A silver arrow whooshes through the air, implanting itself in his head. The strigoi lets go of me with a howl of agony, and staggers backwards. A wolf jumps out of nowhere, tackling him to the ground.

I don't miss a beat. Whirling to the last strigoi, I lift my now free hand and slam it on his face. As with the troll and the other vampire, he starts sizzling under my touch, and releases me. Underneath my watchful gaze, he becomes ash, as well.

Before the rest of the welcoming committee can try anything, a pack of wolves emerges from the forest, Vasile at their head.

Faster than I've ever seen wolves move, they lunge and attack the remaining creatures, ripping their flesh apart. Howls and shrieks permeate the air, as does the stench of death.

All becomes background noise as Vasile stalks towards me. Anger brims in his eyes, and despite him being in wolf form I can sense it radiating in the air around him. Aimed at me, for putting myself in danger, if I were to guess.

I decide to leave that particular fight for later and instead tell him, "Take me to your wounded. I can help."

After a slight hesitation, he bows his head. I morph once more into my Flama form and follow him from above.

≈ ♠ ≈

Between the wolves and other shifters Vasile summoned, as well as my guardians and my own meagre efforts, it seems the fight is won. Bodies litter the grounds near Poenari Fortress, but Daymun takes care of burning them one by one, until nothing but ashes are left. A wind picks up and before we know it, the air is fresh again, the scent of death gone, and Poenari Fortress and grounds are as they were before.

Well, except for that rather spectacular hole at the top of the Fortress, which Dante seems to think will be explained away to humans via their other warnings of the building collapsing. Not that he told me that—neither of the three men in my life are talking to me right now.

For hours, I go around to the shifters, tending to their wounds. For the most part, they're able to heal themselves by turning back and forth from human to animal form. But some have injuries that are beyond even those meagre healing abilities.

Then I remember Daymun whispering on our flight here about tears. The first time I approach anyone in Flama form, I'm met with wariness and a dose of fear. Instead of letting that push me away, I near the poor wolf and tilt my head to the side, blinking until one pearl-shaped tear falls on his torn leg. Within seconds, the skin shines brightly, then healing begins and the wound closes in front of my eyes.

Wow. The angel knows his shit, I guess.

After that one success, word spreads among the survivors and my help is easily accepted.

Between Dante, Daymun and the wolves, the assault was stopped in its tracks. I count it as a victory for us. It's only when I get to my guardian angel to heal his wings that I notice his angry expression.

Not you, too. It comes out as a croak since I'm still in phoenix form, but Dante must understand, surely.

He shakes his head and turns his back to me, offering me his wings. He must be too exhausted after the fight to fix them directly, and it's the least I can do. After healing them, I shift back to human and try to talk to him, but he walks away. Stubborn, I stomp the other way, back into the fortress. I'll gladly relish solitude right now.

And still, I hear their whispers, feel their confused stares behind me, but I cannot face them. Now that the adrenaline is wearing off, I'm back to square one. Were my visions also the fruit of imagination, or something else? Was it normal that I feared my guardians, when they've done nothing but protect me?

I'm losing sight of reality, feeling it escape my grip. My fingers dig into the wall, scraping the skin, in a desperate attempt to ground myself, but already the Ether pulls at me. I shouldn't have sought advice from there last time, it's only tightened my link to it.

Despair threatens at bay, and with it the migraine that is never far off. It presses on me, and the slight link I have with my surroundings breaks. I tumble into the abyss... Only instead of darkness, I'm standing next to my guardians in my ghostly form—back into the astral realm.

"I do not like this," Dante mutters, frowning towards the fortress I disappeared through.

"I warned you that dodgy queen was manipulating."

"She cannot have gotten through to Katya."

"Really? Keep being deluded, angel wings,

but I saw the desolation in her eyes."

Dante says nothing, lost in thought. "Where is that damn wolf?"

As if on cue, something tugs on my sleeve. I snap to my physical body, just as Vasile shifts and pulls me in his embrace. But I don't need a friendly hug. I need to get lost in him.

He holds my gaze, anger brimming in his, and he opens his mouth to lash at me. Before he can, I press my mouth to his. When our lips clash and meet, he reads the need in me, and tugs me farther into the darkness of the fortress.

We don't bother with a smooth surface. Eager hands remove clothes, then my legs are wrapped around his waist and he takes me against the wall, driving deep inside me. The stone scrapes my back, our pants fill the air, until neither of us knows where we are anymore. Until we're both a panting, sweating mess, tangled in each other.

Later, as we lay in each other's embrace, I nuzzle closer, trying to quiet my trembling. Vasile touches the scrapes on my back, swearing under his breath. "I should've been more careful."

"It's okay," I mutter, burying my head in his neck. Tears stream down my face, not because of some scrapes, but because of the kindness in his voice. Knowing how it must look, I clear my throat and add, "I didn't mind it. Crazy as it sounds, I needed it—needed *you*—to ground me again." My voice trembles on the next words. "I feel like I'm losing my mind, Vas."

His hold tightens on me, drawing me closer. "This isn't you, iubirea mea," he whispers. I refuse to look at him, but it doesn't stop him. "Being afraid of your guardians is the worst she could have done. You know who I speak of."

He allows a bit of silence, then drives on, "What happened with Daria?"

I try to find the right words, but settle on, "It was horrendous and illuminating all at once."

Something in my tone must have tipped him off, because in the next moment he's shifting, bringing himself up on an elbow to look at me. "What did she say?"

Nothing fools Vasile, not even my futile attempts at avoiding the topic. He is my mate, the one who should understand... So despite the voices in my head warning against the contrary, I take a deep breath and tell him everything. He listens for the most part, only letting loose a soft growl of a curse here and there. His eyes narrow as I reach the end of my tale.

"Have you told Dante and Daymun any of this?"

"No."

For the first time, I see him hesitate. Then he kisses me, and I lose my train of thought... at least until he stops.

"Katya, the queen is manipulative by nature.

She is a trickster, nothing else."

I look away, hesitating to voice what I want. Vasile grabs my chin, forcing me to meet his stare. "What is it?"

"What if she has a point?"

It's a testament to his self-control that the only sign of his surprise is how he drops my chin.

"What if we were the monsters, as the queen believes?"

His body tightens around mine, as if my tension has seeped into him. Still, his expression is filled with kindness, not judgement, as he asks, "What do you mean, draga mea?"

"We talk about creatures we never knew or took the time to discover. Humans have corrupted everything, even the supernatural beings whose existence they ignore. We've taken everything for granted in this beautiful world and destroyed it. Instead of taking the time to discover, we've only hunted and killed the unknown. The special. How much longer can we really go on doing this, without expecting consequences of some sort?" My voice fades away to a whisper, but I don't miss the shock and recognition in his eyes.

"You really believe this?"

"I don't know anymore. But…what if… we *are* the monsters?" I answer myself with my next shaky breath. "In which case, the real monsters are much closer to us than we believe."

"Even if that is true—and I'm not denying it,

having seen the worst of it in war—there is still good to save," Vasile argues.

"Is there? Humanity is ruled by one thing now—greed. It will be its doom. And I don't think anything I do will have the impact needed to bring about proper change."

The words sound ominous with the night's noises in the background. Yet Vasile doesn't try to change my mind. Instead, he makes me forget with his touch, as though that alone would clear my head, and bring me back to him.

Chapter 17

Something nudges me, and I blink awake. Daymun is scowling over me, and it takes me a moment to realize I'm naked under a blanket and wrapped around Vasile's body.

"A little privacy?" My mate growls, thereby informing me he's been awake longer than me.

Daymun turns his back to us and talks to me over his shoulder. "Care to explain what got into you, love? Putting yourself in danger like that?"

I glare at his back as I pull on some clothes. "You can turn now, I'm decent. And I thought it was self-explanatory—I was trying to help out."

"You could have been killed."

"I'm immortal. Practically invincible."

Lightning crosses his blue eyes and he takes a step forward. "Let's put it to the test, then."

Dante peeks inside the tower, his hand a restraint on Daymun's shoulder. But nothing can keep my mouth shut, not even Vasile who got up to his feet and dressed as well—much less shy than me.

"And if you two had gotten killed, wouldn't

that have been dangerous for me? Given your blood can kill me?"

"We took precautions," Dante says. His voice is calm, or trying to be, but I can sense the edge of control ready to slip.

"Really? Is that why your wings were bleeding only hours ago?"

His chocolate eyes lose some of their gentleness as he glowers as me, all hard jaw and crossed arms. "If you must know, we set up a perimeter of celestial and demonic barriers, ensure none who survive get to escape."

Oh.

"Well, it's not like you told me any of that!"

That does it. Dante drops his hand from Daymun, and side steps him to tower over me instead. "When would we have? When you were busy cowering away from us in fear?"

I open my mouth to say something, but his hurt expression stops me. Vasile touches my lower back in a small gesture of reassurance, but it only chokes me up more.

"You cannot even deny it," Dante says. "After everything we have done for you, you allowed some queen's tricks to get into your head?"

I look away, unable to face their honesty anymore. "I'm sorry."

"It's not an apology we seek," Daymun says, his tone cool. "But an explanation."

"What do you want me to say? That she showed me all the evil humans are capable of?" I search their gazes, trying to make them understand. "She made me use some stone, and I got hours and hours of agony drilled into me. Or what I thought were hours but were days instead. Details of crimes I would've been better off not knowing. Humanity at its worst, and its lowest."

I pace away to the lone window that oversees the grounds. Not even the river and mist surrounding us are enough to quiet me. "I lived through all of it, unable to stop the barrage. Their pain ripped at my soul. When I came to, she told me she didn't expect me to survive it." A bitter laugh escapes me. "Is that what you wanted to know? That all of it warped my mind, and made me see things where there are none? That it made me ask for advice from the last place I should've?"

I turn to them again, shrugging. "I went to the Ether again. The link is stronger now. I've screwed up, time and time again, just like you thought I would. Does that answer *all* your questions?"

Dante stares in shock and wariness at me, while Vasile simply waits. He's heard all of this earlier, and worse. Nothing surprises him, and I try to draw strength from his unyielding demeanor.

Daymun, typical of him, zones in on the one thing I didn't give details about. "What stone did Daria make you use?"

I glare at him, angry that's all he cares about

after they forced me to bare my soul. "She called it the Clarity Stone."

Curses escape him, swift and deadly, and his aura changes in front of my bemused gaze. Ripples of rage emanate off him as he turns to the closest wall and thrusts his fist into it—over and over, until his knuckles are bleeding. Dante snaps out of his stupor to stop him, but it's too late.

Daymun escapes his hold and comes at me. I think for a moment he's about to pick up where he left off before—show me how vulnerable I really am—but all he does is cup my cheeks. His gaze if filled with regret, with pain. The metal scent of his blood fills the air.

"I should have seen it coming."

"Seen what?"

He lets go of me, and sighs. Runs a hand through his dark locks, leaving them coated with blood. "The stone, it comes from Hell."

"No," I contradict him, "Daria said it was given to her by her father. And that it was supposed to help her choose wisely, but it got twisted and turned by her aura."

Daymun snorts. "And part of that is true. However, the stone already had an aura, something her father probably didn't know. Weapons from Hell, and from Heaven, are not handled unless by celestial or demonic entities for a reason."

Silence lengthens, and I snap it. "So what

does that have to do with me?"

"Your challenge, what it did… The stone tainted you. Shifted you towards Darkness."

"I've gathered as much already, from the Ether. But isn't that the point? That everything I go through on this journey eventually influences me towards one side or the other?"

"Not like this," Dante says. "This is against the natural order, warping your very sense of free will. It is why the Creator linked us, to protect you from such things."

I gulp, taking some of the water Vasile hands me and draining it in a few seconds. After I wipe my mouth, a sigh escapes me. "It's not like we can undo it, though."

"No, we can't," Daymun says. "Which means now you have to do something to shift you towards Light. To even the balance."

I look at Dante. "So, what? You need to bless me or something?"

"Not quite as easy. I must bring you to a holy place, for a fast."

"I've never been religious."

His small smile is encouragement. "And you do not have to be. Trust me."

When I still hesitate, Vasile tugs on my hand and turns me towards him. When his gaze catches mine, everything else stops existing, and a sense of calm descends on me.

He drops his forehead to mine and says, "It

won't be for long, and it will help you."

"You think so?" I bite my lip, unable to voice my real fears. That Daria's tricks are so far ingrained in me, nothing can cleanse them out.

Vasile's eyes flash, and he nods. Then he drops his mouth to mine in a soft kiss, a promising embrace. Something about it tells me he knows—all my fears, all my doubts—and he'll be with me through it all.

Without much of a choice, I step away from him, grab Dante's hand, and we fly out.

When Dante said something about a holy place, I didn't clue in that he meant a monastery. Nor that his idea of healing me was to drop me at the bottom of a mountain and let me make my way up there. And yet, that's exactly what he does.

With more will than I gave myself credit for, I force my beaten muscles up the broken stairs, trying not to trip and incur more wounds. By the time I get to the top, I'm greeted by an old man in a monk habit. It's a dusty brown, but despite the color and his overall wrinkled appearance, I can't help but think there's more to him.

I try to look past him, expecting to see a skeletal face staring back at me—like what happened in Chinatown—but… nothing.

"Bine ai venit," he welcomes me. A strong

scent of incense wafts towards me. "Follow me."

I hesitate. Dante wouldn't have dropped me somewhere dangerous, but the way he welcomes me seems... weird. "Did you know I was coming here?"

He throws me a smile over a shoulder. "Much before you did."

I follow him into the monastery and am surrounded by incense. Its sweet-like aroma does something to me, and I stumble. My vision becomes blurry, my limbs feel like lead. The monk doesn't stop in his footsteps, not even when I fall to my knees.

"Please..." My pleading ends on deaf ears, and a different kind of darkness swallows me.

≈ ♠ ≈

When I next come to, I'm in a courtyard. The ground is covered in cobblestones, looking worn and ancient. A fountain stands in the middle, and my throat is parched. I crawl to it, cup my hands and drink the cool liquid.

As it cascades down my throat, I sense a presence behind me. The same monk as before is there, watching me with unreadable eyes.

"What happened, before?" I don't want to accuse him of doing something to me, but the thought isn't far from my mind.

"The incense," he says in a smooth voice that doesn't match the wrinkled face. "You reacted to its holiness when it entered your tainted body."

"How…"

A smile. "There is much I know, Flama. Including your purpose here."

I give up trying to see his angle. "So, help me, then. That's why Dante brought me here. I'm supposed to realign myself, or whatever."

He takes a step closer, and his gaze becomes harder to withhold. Is that a golden hue in its depths? "Do you think it is that simple?"

"Huh?" Yeah, way intelligent reply, I know. But his nearness is causing my brain to go haywire, and not in a physical chemistry kind of way. More like my senses are overwhelmed by something outside of my comprehension.

"You have been shown a side of humanity that is the ugliest. No one contests it. But this broken balance in you will not right itself unless you can make yourself see the good, too. Not in order to complete your quest, but in order to not become a bitter, old harpy."

I open my mouth to deny it, but he places an index on my lips. "No. Do not speak. *Ascultă.*" I try to do as he says, to listen, but he doesn't give me a chance as he barrels on. "Do not argue, but hear me. Truly. It is self-reflection you need, not an easy way out."

He removes his index, and I find I can't move my lips. Like they're sewn together, except they're not. He did something to me, the old bastard, and now

I can't speak. And in front of my bulging eyes, he turns and walks away.

"It is no use asking for help," he tells me. "Once your period of self-reflection is complete, I will return and remove the curse."

I'm going to strangle Dante when I get out of here.

≈ ♠ ≈

Despite my vengeful desires towards Dante, a few hours later I'm screaming his name in my head, hoping he'll come to my aid. As it turns out, I can't even morph to my phoenix shape, let alone undo this curse.

In the end, I curl up by the fountain and do as I was asked to. Reflect.

At first, anything I hope to achieve is drowned away by my thoughts. Now that I'm unable to speak, it's like my mind is going crazy, refusing to shut up. The trials run through it on repeat, but any lessons learned from them are overshadowed by the utter panic gripping me.

Holding onto the edge of the fountain, I bring my knees up to my chest and drop my head onto them, taking deep breaths. As a child, when I saw those skeleton faces, I was prone to panic attacks. They went away with my teenager years as I toughened up, but now that same sensation of my chest clenching, unable to draw in a breath, makes me almost hyperventilate.

Eyes shut tightly, I focus on the sounds around me. Murmurs in the corners from monks and nuns, birds singing in the trees, the water in the fountain trickling. A flutter of something makes me blink, half-expecting an angel to drop from the sky, but it's only a hawk.

No, not just a hawk. With a start, I recognize it as the one Vasile called to him, way back in the woods. One golden eye is fixed on me, and he slowly inches closer. My trembling hand lifts in the air, and he allows my caress. The smoothness of his feathers, the calmness in his gaze, washes away the remnants of the panic in my chest.

Vasile promised he'd help me with whatever I need, and this is him doing that. With a sigh, my breathing regulates, and I close my eyes again, even as my hand lingers on the hawk.

Reflecting...

The zmeu showed me the good in the world, but it was in a fictive setting. What he demonstrated wasn't real kindness, but possibilities. Daria, on the other hand, made it a point to showcase true crimes and vivid pain.

And yet... The utter darkness of what she showed me, doesn't that in itself expose that it was a biased account? The zmeu might have intimated possibilities, but Daria picked and chose what I would see. The Clarity Stone was her means, based on what Daymun told me.

So, really, in the end I was fed what they both wanted me to have knowledge of. The problem is no matter how much good exists in the world, if one bad thing happens, it's human nature to focus on it. I've done it before in my personal life, and yet I managed to stop that destructive habit while with Vasile.

Maybe that's all I have to do this time again. Curb that habit and choose to see both sides.

The realization makes me blink, only to notice the hawk is gone. The monk decides that moment to come back, his steps soft on the cobblestone path. I glance up and, to my disbelief, the sun is high up in the air, almost setting. With one touch to my lips, he releases my voice.

"You didn't have to do that." I glare at him, still irked at being treated like a disobedient child.

"Oh, but I did."

Standing up, I stretch here and there to loosen out the kinks in my muscles. Then I look at him—*really* look at him. "Yet you're not human. No way in hell you could be."

Dark eyes shine with laughter. "Be careful with that world. And no, I am not. My name is Michael."

In front of my eyes, he unfurls gorgeous white wings—angel's wings. And then I clue in to his real identity. *An archangel!* Yet just as quickly as he appeared, he is back to the old man with wrinkles.

I shake my head, surprised no one else noticed the sparse moment of craziness. "So that's all

I needed, according to you? The magical cure to Daria's machinations was a few hours of self-reflection under an archangel's watchful gaze?"

He tilts his head to side, silent for a few moments. When he speaks, his voice is low. "You tell me, Flama. Did it help, or harm you more?"

I want to deny it, and tell him to shove it. But when I search deep down, the burden and fog in my head *has* abated somewhat. And when I next look up, Michael is walking away.

I'm free to leave, after all.

Dante's waiting for me at the bottom of the stairs, earning another glare. "You could've warned me you were bringing me to an archangel's monastery."

"I am bound, unable to speak truths that are not mine."

I glance back over my shoulder. "So, Michael, he'll forever be there?"

"In one form or the other." He inspects me up and down, arching an eyebrow. "You seem better."

"A bit, yeah."

"Good. Let us get back to your wolf, he is getting impatient."

We fly back to Poenari, and the minute I've landed and morphed to my human form, Vasile pulls me into his arms.

"Cum te simți?" He's asking me how I'm feeling.

"Better." I grin at the softness of the Romanian in my ear and clear my throat. "Much, much better. Ready enough to take on a new trial."

Daymun, of course, goes and spoils all my fun. "Not quite yet, love."

"Why?" I try not to get defensive, but it's hard when I'm so exhausted. "Time is running out, and the twenty-first of the month is less than two weeks away!"

"And you've only just escaped the clutches of a manipulative queen, who was able to make you see us as the enemy." Daymun's tone is cool, vibrating with anger. "A few days to rest won't kill you."

"They may!" I shout, effectively losing my cool. Rage builds up inside me, and the rest of what I've been keeping away floods out. "I've done what you asked, went to the damn holy place. But it's all a waste of time—all of this. Stop focusing on me. Yes, I'm important, but it's about something way bigger than me at this point. And any delay is just keeping us from the truth... And making us weaker for the danger to come."

"Katya."

"No, Dante. I won't be responsible for the Enlightened Ones descending and making the choice I'm too weak to. So, enough."

"Enlightened Ones?" Dante repeats. "What do they have to do with this?"

"You are correct," another voice interrupts us, and I turn in surprise.

Vasile is glaring at me, his face set in a stony mask of disapproval. "Enough *is* enough. Come with me."

I hesitate, and the silver in his eyes overpowers the violet, flashing like lightning in annoyance. "Katya…." He growls, and my ears pick it up. My feet move of their own accord towards him, leaving my guardians behind.

Dante tries to stop me, presumably wanting to hear more, but Daymun blocks his path. "The wolf's got this. We'll find out the rest later."

The amusement in his tone predicts nothing good. When I reach Vasile, he grabs my hand in his iron grip and practically drags me back to the woods.

As soon as we're out of sight, he shifts, and I know he expects me to do the same. I follow suit, choosing my smaller Flama form, and fly just a little above the trees so that I'm able to keep an eye on him in the darkness. The moon offers very little light tonight.

About an hour later, we emerge from the wilderness into a village. Brick houses are set in a wayward pattern, with a path that looks like a little road between them. Smoke comes out the chimneys, and I hear laughter and low murmurs of voices.

Sweeping down, I join Vasile by one of the houses. He's back in human form, so I return to mine, picturing my clothes from before. Luckily, it works, and we remain in the shadows concealed, without risking being found out due to an overly bright starry dress.

"Why are we here?" I whisper.

Vasile lifts his index to his lips, indicating for me to be silent. He bends his head by my ear and his voice is even lower than mine had been. "You seem to think this danger that's coming is something humanity can't handle, and you're using it as an excuse to rush through this trial, draga mea. In a way, you're still scared by Daria's words, and what she said of the Enlightened Ones. And I understand that. But you have to see this, to understand just how untrue her words are."

"I don't get the point, Vas!"

"You will." Then he grabs my hand, and we walk to the first house.

Inside, a woman is screaming. My thoughts immediately go to her being in danger, but Vasile's hold is restraining on me. He gestures for me to peek in the small window, and after a brief hesitation, I rise up on my tiptoes.

Unlike what I'd been thinking, the woman isn't being beaten, or otherwise abused. She's giving birth, standing over a basin with a midwife in front of her. A man is by her side, holding her hand in his— though judging by his grimace of pain, it seems she's crushing his fingers.

The woman screams again, an unholy howl,

and this time a baby drops from her womb straight into the midwife's hands. The husband helps his wife over to the bed, wiping at her sweaty forehead and brushing the loose hair off her face. His gaze is proud, his touches soft.

And then the midwife brings their baby, and their faces are filled with the purest happiness.

Vasile tugs on my hand again, and we head to another house towards the end of a street. This time, as I glance in the window, I see an elderly woman on a bed, with an equally grey-haired man by her side. He's holding her hand, though she seems fragile, and her breathing is almost nonexistent.

I glance around the house. In a corner are two women with their husbands, presumably the old couple's children and their partners, watching the scene unfold. Real tears run down their cheeks, and the entire scene is filled with sorrow. And yet, the old woman's face is filled by an odd serenity.

Gulping back my own tears, I turn to Vasile. "Why show me all this?"

He cups my cheek, resting his forehead against mine. "Happiness and sadness, two sides of every coin. Daria only showed you the bad, but you must realize in every bad, good also exists. Though the old woman is dying and causing heartache to her family, she has lived a happy life, and left behind a legacy. And the birth, though it brought so much joy, was probably the most painful thing that woman has had to go through."

"Yin and yang," I murmur.

"Da." Vasile exhales in relief at my finally getting it.

We walk away from the village and shift once more. In a daze, I follow him again, thinking we're going back to the campsite. My thoughts go back to what I witnessed, and Daria's words. Everything she showed me was tainted, true. Then, maybe, her talk of the Enlightened Ones wasn't all true, either.

When we land again, I'm still struggling to get a hold of myself. Vasile wraps his arm around my shoulders and tugs me closer to his side. "I have one more thing I'd like to show you before the night is complete."

In silence, I follow him until we emerge onto a cliff. Beyond us is the valley, and in the distance, Poenari Fortress. Two lonely figures atop it indicate my guardians have been watching over me all along, albeit from a distance.

A golden glow is cast on the whole place, making it look unreal in the sunset-bathed light. I lean my head against Vasile's shoulder and fall asleep, free of nightmares for once.

Chapter 18

A kiss at the back of my neck wakes me up. I stir, blink awake, to find Vasile staring down at me. He's holding himself up on his elbows, caging me in, and I've never felt safer. He drops his mouth to mine, and I gladly allow him access. My body strains towards his, craving his touch.

We're secluded here, in the middle of nowhere, and the sun hasn't yet risen. When his hand impatiently goes under my sweater, I arch to give him more access, panting and murmuring words I don't even understand.

Like we're driven by something much, much deeper than either of us understand, we shed clothes, and underwear, and then Vasile pins my hands above my head, and drops his mouth to my nipple. I'm outright begging now, wishing for nothing more than the pleasure of being filled by him.

And then he gives in, spreading my legs and settling between them, driving in me with one thrust. I'm panting against his shoulder, my teeth biting his skin and leaving a mark. We're moving together, losing all sense of self and time and everything but each other, and the pleasure between us.

Afterwards, nestled in his arms, I sigh against his chest. The night air is chilly, but Vasile's heat is akin to being close to a radiator. I don't know what prompts the question, but it passes my lips in a soft whisper.

"Do you think they'll let me embark on the last trial, now?"

His hands stop drawing circles on my back, and I sense his pensive state. "I'm not sure."

I pull back to look at him, trying to see his reasoning. "I know you talked to them, while I was out of it. Help me out. What is it they're worried about?"

"You, losing yourself."

A grimace tugs my lips at his too-honest response. "Why? I did Dante's cleansing thing... And this quest needs to be completed, one way or another."

"True, iubirea mea, but you still have two weeks. Why rush?"

I tear my gaze away from his. "It's hard to explain, but for the first time in my life I feel like I belong, like I'm meant to do something. And the sooner it gets done, the better it will be for everyone."

"What if you don't survive?"

I shrug. "Then the world will be better off."

Vasile stands up a bit, forcing me to follow.

"I disagree with that."

His tone is firm, but it doesn't detract from my thoughts. I reach for his cheek, trying to explain what I mean.

"We can't know how long this last trial will take me. The first time, it wasn't a few hours as we thought, but days. The second, over a week. Now, what if it's more? I can't leave it to the last minute."

"I'm not asking you to," he says, dropping his forehead to mine. "But you can't rush into this when you are still recovering."

"But I'm not," I say. "I'm fine, and ready to go now."

Vasile shakes his head and gets up, pulling on his clothes. The chill of the wind gets to me at his abrupt dismissal. It's only when he hands me my clothes, his expression shuttered but his eyes filled with pain, that I clue in.

"It's not because I want to leave you, Vasile. It's something I have to do."

"I know that," he says. "But it doesn't make it any easier."

We get dressed in silence and head back to my guardians. Once we reach them, Dante and Daymun are crowded around a bonfire, chatting animatedly.

"What's going on?"

"Come here," Dante says, waving the little black book at me.

I'd completely forgotten about it, despite Daria telling me to read it from beginning to end. They must've gotten it from my belongings, and I can't even find it in me to be annoyed at the invasion of privacy.

I share a look with Vasile, then head closer. By the firelight, I can make out a few words, but the ink is smudged. "I don't understand."

"We might have found clues to your next trial. At least, more than we were told."

When I still say nothing, Daymun pushes off the earth and comes to stand in front of me. With gentler hands than normal, he flips the page and points to a diagram. It depicts a mountain, and above it, an empty sky. Writing I don't understand explains what it means, but all I focus on is the sky, and the shiver that racks my body at the sight.

≈ ♠ ≈

I should've known this last trial would take place in the skies. Or, as high as you can get there. Moldoveanu Peak, or *Vârful Moldoveanu* as they call it here, is the highest mountain peak in Romania. Its eight thousand or so feet seem daunting now that I'm up here, but the sight below leaves me breathless.

I'd thought Vasile's sunset had been wonderful, but this… Green valleys extend as far as my eye can see. Behind me, clouds gather, and spread across. It's getting close to nighttime, but according to my guardians all I have to do is wait here until the moon's light hits the right spot.

Of course, nothing is ever easy with these challenges.

They'd warned me to be careful, to watch my back, because I wouldn't know when the portal would be revealed. Or the task, whatever the hell it is. Despite this, I catch myself closing my eyes, breathing in the scent of the pure Southern Carpathian Mountains, lost in the beauty surrounding me.

The moment my guard drops, so does he.

A golden eagle larger than my entire forearm dives for me. Only the wind announces his presence, and the brief second of warning is enough to help me snap out of it. I duck, and he grazes my back with his massive talons.

When I lift up from my crouch, intelligent eyes stare at me, with a beak that looks way too mean for a simple bird. Its tilted head and perusing gaze warn me right away this is no regular bird. First off, eagles are not usual in this particular area. And, second, that intelligence cannot be masked.

"Shifter?"

He croaks at my words and dives again, this time for my neck. *Must be another one of those crazies who wants me dead before I can make a choice. Just my freaking luck.* I tuck into a ball, having enough self-preservation instinct left to protect myself. Still, he clucks around me, and I sense

297

his claws dig into my back on more than one occasion.

Since I'm not ready to become its food, or whatever it is he wants, I try to inch out of his way, but only succeed in getting more hurt. Without realizing what's happening, I'm heading closer and closer to the edge of the mountain—and then I lose my footing.

Like a snowball, I go down, down, down... Wrapping my arms around my head, I make sure it's protected, but that leaves the rest of me at the mercy of the stones, branches and debris I roll over. Everything digs in me, and still I'm not coming to a stop—and then I fall *through* something.

It feels like water, but it's not. It's another portal. And when I emerge on the other side, it's not a cavern, or the Ether that I land in. Nor does it feel like an astral projection. Rather, my body feels my own and I'm in a deserted field, and a farm awaits in the distance. I frown at what I'm seeing. Bodies move around it—three, all redheads by the look of it.

Without much of a choice, I head closer. The air is humid, my clothes stick to my back, and beads of sweat run like rivulets over my face, down my back and between my breasts. By the time I get to the farm, my throat is parched, and I would give a kingdom for a glass of water.

The three people I'd seen before are nowhere around now. "Hello?" They couldn't have vanished, could they?

And yet, no one's around. When I walk around the farm, what I see is an ocean. It makes no damn sense, here in the middle of all this dryness, but it's there. Waves beat the shore gently, its beautiful blue waters scintillating at me under the sun. The dried grass gives way to a sandy beach, of the purest beige.

I want nothing more than to throw myself in the water and bathe, but something stops me. And the moment after, movement behind me snaps my attention.

Three guys are facing me, all redheads as I'd thought, all with blue eyes. But they're of different ages and builds.

The tallest one smirks and says, "I am Ștefan."

"And I am Cristian."

"My name is Ion."

I stare between them, mouthing the names. "Who are you? Here, I mean?"

"We are the guardians of this place," Ștefan says.

I glance pointedly at the shabby farm, land and the vast ocean. "And what is it that needs protecting here? Better question—what am I doing here, for my third trial?"

Cristian chuckles. "Did you not figure it out yet?"

A shiver runs up my spine. These guys are...

They're built. Even the youngest, Ion, could easily toss me away. I'm hoping this trial doesn't involve fighting them. "Figure what out?"

"You are here for Apa Sâmbetei," Ion says in Romanian.

I've heard the name before, but I still throw him a confused look, and Ștefan takes over. "What do you know of the Romanian version of the creation of the world?"

A shrug escapes me, and I take a step backwards. I don't want to tell him what my guardians told me days—weeks?—ago. Something warns me the less I reveal, the better. At least I could always swim, or fly over the ocean, right? If anything does happen.

Ștefan's eyes zero in on my movement, but he doesn't comment. Instead, he takes my shrug as an invitation to continue. "In our version, it was animals who helped the Creator in designing the world. And while everything was carefully crafted, one spot was there since the beginning of time and would be there forevermore."

"Apa Sâmbetei," Ion repeats again.

I glance behind me, finally linking his use of *water* to what's behind me. "You mean this ocean?"

"It is the World Ocean," Cristian says. "Surrounding the entire planet. The end of it closest to Hell boils as hot as the underground, and some areas are cold, nearing the Kingdom of the Creator."

"You mean Heaven," I clarify.

All three of them nod, and I shiver again. Something about that synchronized movement makes their whole appearance even creepier.

"Okay, so basically this water behind me is the World Ocean, and, what's the link with me, and my quest?"

Ştefan lifts a hand. "Shush, Flama. Listen to the story, and all will be revealed."

I cross my arms over my chest and lift my chin. He seems to get the meaning that I won't be bossed around and resumes his story.

"This Ocean you see behind you, is where *Nefartatul* and the Creator lived together in harmony."

"Nefartatul?" This, I'm not familiar with.

"The Devil," Cristian supplies.

That explains why Dante didn't mention it.

Ştefan goes on as if he hadn't been interrupted. "Nefartatul did not like being used. See, back before the split of the world, when they lived together in semi-harmony, the Creator tried to get him to bring forth clay from the World Ocean, to create his precious mortals. It was not an easy task, and while Nerfartatul tried, the earth would not listen to him. Until he invoked the Creator's name, trying to be something he wasn't. Because of how fast the earth listened, and because he realized how truly inferior he was, he decided to push the Creator to the side, to get rid of him. But the earth was protecting him… And so Nefartatul tried to get rid of him in the North, and the South, and East, and West… Not realizing that with each time he tried, he was creating a symbolical cross in the ground. It was, ultimately, his demise."

Cristian points to the Ocean. "And he was cast into Hell, with the Creator taking the other Kingdom. The water separates them to this day."

This is definitely not a version of the creation of the world I've ever heard before. I look back at the ocean, and something else dawns on me. "That's why they talk about opening the gate. And cleansing with fire or water."

"Da," Ion says by my side. "Humanity needs your choice, and time is running out."

"I don't understand what that means, though. All this link to Apa Sâmbetei. Why here? Why now?"

Ștefan jerks his chin towards the ocean. "No woman has been able to pass over."

I stare back at him. "That's my task?"

Ștefan smirks then. "No. Your trial is to fly over the ocean, without being pulled towards either Heaven or Hell."

"Why?"

"Because you were recently tainted, and such an influence cannot be erased so easily. Not even with a self-reflection period under the archangel Michael."

At his words, the shivers and sense of wrongness intensifies in me—how do they know all this? Yet I swallow past my dry throat. The faces staring back at me are open, not skeletons or anything implying they're rotten. What I feel must be because of Daria's machinations, similar to how I doubted Dante and Daymun.

With a struggle, I focus back on Cristian's words. "If neither side pulls you over, it will signify your purity, and prepare you for the last choice."

I glance back at the wide expanse of water. "And if I fail?" I think back to the fae queen and what she'd shown me. "If I do get pulled in a certain way?"

"Then you may not get out of here alive."

I hug my arms to my chest, fearing the outcome. Vasile had been angry when I left, and Dante. They were worried I was pushing myself. I didn't get to say goodbye to either of them. Or Daymun. I need…

Looking back at the three brothers, I ask something to which I already know the answer. "Can I say goodbye, at least?"

"No." The answer is unanimous, unequivocal.

Well, shit.

Without another choice, I let flames engulf me, and return to my Flama form. I lift high up in the skies, trying to empty my mind as I do so. I need to be strong, unwavering… To escape this and get back to the real world.

Beat by beat of my wings, I move across the

wide expanse. Behind me, the three brothers watch me go. When I next look back, they're gone as if they had never existed. And, worse, so is the land, and the farm.

I am alone in the middle of the ocean.

A line from a poem comes to me, by John Donne. *No man is an island entire of itself.*

Well, I think, *you were damn wrong, Donne. 'Cause I'm sure feeling like one right about now.*

As I fly, there is nothing to do but think. And that, I do. Of the first trial, and the zmeu. Of the second trial, and Daria. Of Vasile, Dante, Daymun, and everything I've learned. Everything that has been shown to me. About me, about the world… Things I never thought existed, that do live among us. Things I wish had never existed but have always been there. Nightmares disguised as dreams, and dreams disguised as nightmares…

A burning sensation in my wings pulls at me. I glance back down, noticing the color of the water has changed. A reddish tinge taints it now, vapors rising from it like in a sauna. My wings flap, keeping me in midair, yet the energy is unmistakable.

Is that Hell?

Sure enough, the more I look below, the more I sense its pull. I remember Daymun's warning about the word and try to keep my mind from thinking it. But it's hard. A perverse beauty emanates from what I see below, probably completely at odds to what hides underneath.

Shadows move in a circle, almost like in a dance, awaiting to be freed. I see a kaleidoscope of colors, as if hinting at treasures hidden beneath. I know it's not true, but the illusion is pretty damn good.

To think, all I would have to do is focus on it, say the name of the second kingdom out loud, and it would open for me... Unleashing everything else within it.

Another piece of Donne's poem comes back to me. *Any man's death diminishes me, for I am involved in mankind.* No salvation can be found here and wasting time around the gate isn't a good idea.

I tell myself that, yet even as I try to fly away, the pull intensifies, dragging me closer. It pulls and pulls at me, and the panicked beating of my wings doesn't help. All I do is fall further down, until I'm right above the gate.

Trembling, I dare to glance below—a startled croak escapes me.

The kaleidoscope of colors is gone, instead replaced by beady, red eyes. Faces smudge against the barrier, staring up at me. Skeletal arms, rotten cores, mouths open in agony. And beneath them, the powerful blaze of Hell's fire, churning and burning.

The creatures state at me in excitement and pleading, as though begging me to release them. To let them loose upon the world. And it would be so easy...

The link intensifies even more, dragging me within a few inches of the barrier. They push at it, as if getting ready to drag me into the depths of Hell itself. And as I close my eyes, all the memories Daria infiltrated my mind with are there again, at the surface. Tearing at me, pushing me to make a choice I am not ready for.

I cry again, this time in anger, and beat my wings faster. Forcefully. With determination. Fire burns through me and my form lengthens, growing again, gaining more strength. I refuse to glance below, instead focusing on *my* will, on *my* choice.

Which, right now, is to get the fuck away from here.

With a lot of willpower, I wrench myself from the pull, and fly away. My tiny heart is thudding in my chest. Unsure which direction to go to, I allow the panic to veer me East, then North.... And finally, the heat dies off.

For a while, I'm free. For those precious moments, I can breathe.

And then it feels like I've entered the Arctic. The ocean beneath me becomes icy blue in color, hard in some spots, less so in others. Same as with Hell, a connection tugs at me again. A gust of air comes from below, pushing me upwards, closer to where I don't want to go.

When I glance up, the clouds look way too painted-like, parting to reveal a flicker of gates—I think. A fairytale design, glinting with inner light...

Beyond them, I don't see anything. But I *feel* them. Heaven's warriors, ready to descend upon the Earth and cleanse it. The Creator's angels, prepared to believe the best of humanity.

They don't send me images of dread, or happiness. But their voices linger in the air, whispering of babies deserving life, of teenagers with so much potential, of soldiers who save the world, of charities who make a difference. They murmur of hope, and faith, and above all, man's ability to change.

Without even realizing it, I've allowed the pull to bring me closer to the gate. If I reach a talon, I could touch it, feel the bars in my grip. The moment I catch on, I turn my gaze away, forcing myself to beat my wings faster, to carry me further away.

For a moment, I think I notice a shape in the clouds. Maybe more. Tips of spears, shields, like warriors ready for war. But then I blink, and the only thing surrounding me is the puffiness of the clouds.

It takes more force to fly away from Heaven's pull, and retake my spot below, but I manage it, though I'm left panting and weakened by the time I get back on track. On, and on, I fly away, forcing myself away from either impulse.

I cannot make that choice now… It's not yet time.

Chapter 19

The wide expanse surrounds me, drowning me. I almost feel the beginnings of a migraine, or is that wishful thinking? And then the horizon is no longer, and I'm back at the beach. Ștefan, Cristian and Ion are there. Only, they're no longer the great-looking men I left behind. Rather, their faces are skulls, their arms skeletal, but with thin membranes like wings attached to their bodies.

I hover in mid-air, hesitating to join them by the shoreline. Surely I must've missed something… Aren't they the good guys?

Ștefan's face flashes as though he's grinning, and he hops in the air with a powerful push of his thighs. His wing-like arms blow air, and he cocks his head at me. "So. You survived without being pulled in either way."

I nod, wishing I could speak—then thinking it's just as well I don't.

"You must see us differently, now. The Ocean wipes away all illusions, restoring the power of true Sight." I try to mimic a shrug, but don't quite manage it.

"We are the keepers of the Ocean, here since the beginning of time. We have seen all types come and go, but you, Flama, you can release us of our curse."

What curse? I tilt my head to the side, hoping to accurately convey my confusion. Cristian and Ion join us in mid-air, but rather than be by Ştefan's side, they spread around me, effectively closing the circle. A sixth sense warns me of danger even before Ştefan speaks.

"We need your blood, Katya. We were thrown in here by the Enlightened Ones and have never been able to leave. The time has come, and your blood will lead the way."

"And tears," adds Cristian.

"*Scuze*," Ion apologizes, his voice softer than the others'.

I don't stick around to wait for their attack. Instead, I dive down, wings flapping urgently, willing the wind to work with me. I can't be caught for their purposes. If nothing else, what I learned from my guardians is the natural balance is affected by everything I do.

That certainty pushes me faster, though they're hot on my tail. It won't be easy escaping, but maybe if I go back by the farmhouse? As I fly, my eyes scan the area—*where is the stupid house?*

Thoughts of Vasile run through my mind,

nearly crippling me with dread. I cannot die here, not without saying goodbye to him. And doing my duty to the world. None of this is right. I finished my trial, why is there nothing protecting me? Is this what the black book meant, about the undead being the last to overcome?

If so, what the fuck was the point of sending me across the ocean?

Thinking and flying don't work well together, so I focus on the former. Ștefan is hot on my trail, but I let my fiery tail swing and hit him in the face. *Where is the damn— there!*

I dive down, heading straight for the house in shambles, in a single-minded focus that proves to be my downfall. Ion and Cristian emerge from a corner in front of me, catching me by surprise. They hold a net, like for catching fish, only it's made of silver. Dante's words come back to me. *Only our blood can kill you, but silver will hurt you.*

NO! I scream in my head and turn around, flapping my wings wildly. But I'm too panicked— too slow—and the movement doesn't gain momentum.

Ștefan blocks my way out. I'm trapped, and my hesitation gives them the upper hand they need. The net falls on me, silver scorching my feathers and making me cry out in pain. My shriek echoes across, but to no avail. Not like anyone's going to hear it.

I drop on the sandy beach in a tangle of net and feathers. My body is weak, unable to shrug it off.

I've spent so much energy fighting the pull of Heaven and Hell, probably as they wanted me to. *I'll die here.*

Ștefan, Ion and Cristian land next to me, still in their triangle formation, and start closing in on me. I was so stupid to have hesitated, to not see this coming. And now, I'll pay for it.

One hand holds me to the ground, the other brings out a knife. At the flash of the blade, something snaps in me. I refuse to be a victim again. The memory of my beating in Chinatown comes to mind, and the promise I made to myself—I wouldn't be a weakling again.

With desperation and uncaring of the consequences, my beak rips at the net. I taste the burn of silver on my tongue, but it doesn't stop me. My flurry of activity has them drop on me. My wing is spread. The knife comes closer.

My vision narrows and everything in me rebels. Then, just like when I shift, flames coat me entirely, burning through the silver, melting it and the trio away from me.

It causes them to let go of me as pain—the pain they'd wanted to inflict on me—hits them. My song of fire is no longer soft but sending out an unholy note. They drop to the ground, blood coursing out of their ears. I shrug off the net and fight my way upwards, to the skies.

Without a portal to get out, I head back to the gates, and this time it's like I'm retracing my steps.

The coolness of the Arctic hits me first, and the tug towards Heaven. This time, I let it drag me until I'm closer to the skies, closer than I think is possible, through the clouds—and right back in front of the silvery gates. The metal—or whatever it is they're made of—glints in the sun, making it hard to look at. Behind it, I see more clouds, and something tells me I'm being watched.

Help me! I cry out mentally.

A moment, two, and by my third cry, an angel emerges. Blonde hair falls to her waist, a beautiful white robe covers her body, and creamy wings protrude from her back. Regret flashes in her expression, and then a second angel arrives by her side. With a shock, I recognize him as the one who'd chided Dante—Gabriel.

His expression, unlike hers, is cold. "We can only help if you have made your choice."

Made my choice? It dawns on me, then. My life for that of humanity? No. I have not gone through all of this just to get forced into a choice by celestials.

Spitting fire, I turn around and fly further, waiting for the tug of Hell. I've been spoiled by my guardians, it seems, because neither has tried to use me for their own gains. And yet, that is exactly what is happening now.

I give in to the tug of Hell, letting it pull me forward until I'm floating above the pit. Water boils underneath me, shadows dancing within. I hesitate. Dread grips me. All I need is one word, repeated three times, but I'm at the same conundrum as before.

"Flama!" Ştefan's roar echoes across the water and I know I'm running out time.

The shadows underneath me agitate, as though feeling it, too. But just like with the gates of Heaven, I refuse to give in. If nothing else, the realization pours over me that this quest—it's not about me.

I've been so busy internalizing everything, when in reality my fate is the one least important. But like all humans, I've made it about me. My beliefs. My wrongs. Wrongs done *to* me. But that's not it— at all. What matters is what's out there, and the best way to preserve what is left of the world.

And I will not make that decision on a whim. Humanity deserves more than that, even if half of it is rotten to the core. I never considered myself a hero, and I've been fighting against these responsibilities since they were thrust upon me. Yet now, it's with a sense of calm I acknowledge that once I'm out of here, I will make my choice, but as a Flama and nothing else, without outside influences.

With one last glance, I shift away from Hell, roaming mindlessly.

Where can I go for help? Or, worse, am I really on my own? Shadows in the distance warn me that my time is up. I had my chance, turned my back to it, and now I have no other choice but to meet them head on.

So rather than turn tail and run, I head straight for the trio. If they're surprised by my stupidity, they don't show it. It seems we're about to collide in midair when thunder rumbles. I stop, my gaze rising above me.

A moment later, lightning crackles despite the clear skies, and it seems like the force of it makes the clouds crack open. Through the small tear, multiple Flamas burst out. Of all shapes and sizes, they surround me, as does a mist leaking from above.

I'm not sure what's going on, but I try to fly in their midst. One such bird—a larger one than most—stops me. Its wings are spread in what I've come to know from Dante as a defensive gesture.

Its beak opens and out comes a pearly cry, as beautiful as it is mournful. But what truly stops me in my tracks are the words I hear within the musical notes. "Go. We will handle this monstrosity."

I look back in confusion, uncomprehending. Two more phoenixes come to me, flying closer and pushing me backwards. I stare at the large one again.

"We heard your plea for help, but this is not something you should witness."

And just like that, they turn their backs to me and go to meet the trio. Ştefan, Cristian and Ion are taken aback by the swarm of Flamas descending on them. Just as I had been, they're forced backwards, all the way onto the shoreline.

Despite the warning, I don't disappear. What can I say? I never did respond well to authority. So it's with wide eyes I watch fire and mist surround the trio, then hear more musical notes that end up into words.

"You dare defy the balance of natural order, and hurt one of our own?"

Ștefan I think, tries to stand in the circle, but he's forced down by some other power. "You cannot kill us," he says. "The Enlightened Ones put us here to avoid killing us, and to protect that same balance."

Another pearly note echoes in the air, short, like a laugh. "And who do you think cracked the Ether open for us?"

A stunned silence answers, but soon the fire and mist envelop Ștefan. Agonized screams echo across the distance. Something in me says to move, to help them, but their agony is also music to my ears.

The larger phoenix looks behind again, dropping one short cry. "*GO!*"

A gust of wind hits me, knocking me out of the sky. And then I'm tumbling through the water, drowning, swirling…. Until I'm not.

I emerge into a cavern, in full human form. Everything hurts, but I know from experience it will get better once I return to the world of the living. I push myself up, annoyed at the starry dress that once again covers my skin. At least it also illuminates the way.

No sooner do I move, that something comes out of the shadows. I'm dizzy, my head a pounding cry, my limbs heavy and numb, except for a burning in my shoulder. Blood… a wound? It takes me a minute to sort through the blurriness and see… a wolf.

"Vasile?" The wolf looks at me. Its fur color is white, familiar, too much so. On wobbly legs, I pick myself up and head closer, holding out my hand. "Need…you."

It takes me holding out my hand, and his answering growl, to realize this isn't my mate facing me. Gulping, hand now trembling, I meet its gaze again.

The eyes I thought were dark violet are now revealed to be fully black, glinting with coolness. A pink tongue licks the muzzle, and the wolf inches closer to me.

Fuck. Fuck. Fuck.

My eyes scour the surroundings, but it's no use.

Then he morphs to human. Or, what I think is human. It's definitely not Vasile. Pale skin. Sunken eyes, rimmed with red. And when he opens his mouth to speak, I see sharp fangs.

"*Pot să fiu cine vrei, Flama.*"

I shake my head, deny his claim. No matter how he tries, he can't be the one I want. "I made a mistake. I'm looking for a way out."

The guy is dressed all in black, making the pallor of his skin even more obvious. Dark eyes continue to stare at me, his mouth twisted in a sneer.

He's not about to let me go, and he's blocking the only way I see forward.

His eyes catch mine as he moves closer, a hypnotizing glare to them. I try to shake it off, but I'm so dizzy, lost…

"What are you?"

He laughs, a dark chuckle. "Flama, your ignorance betrays you. Have they not taught you the dangers of crossing into *muroni* territory?"

"Mu…what?" I move my hand over my wounded shoulder, trying to staunch the blood. His eyes fixate on it in a way that makes me uneasy.

"Muroni," he repeats. "Night walkers."

"V-vampires, you mean?" My voice shakes, trembling, and I hate it.

But the shock of the last trial, the coolness of this area, and that fact I'm definitely in my physical body, hurt and without being able to heal… Dizziness spreads through me, and I force myself to stand upright, hoping he doesn't notice the weakness.

If this is another one of those immortals intent to have my skin, I'm not sure I can defend myself. Not right now, and not alone.

The muroni—whatever that is—shrugs, his gaze still on me.

"Mind tearing your eyes from my throat for a second?"

He does as I ask, licking his lips. "*O secundă*, of course. But only one."

I gulp, and he takes another forward. "What do you want from me?"

"Come, now." His voice is soft, hypnotizing. "Will you really tell me you're not tired of being pulled in different directions?"

I look away, his words touching a chord inside me.

"I can take it all away, you know."

"How?"

Silence answers me. When I look at him again, he's closer, staring pointedly at my throat. One finger reaches up, tracing my vein. "You know how."

Death.

It shouldn't be seductive, but it is. Not have to worry about billions of people, about making the wrong choice, about losing Vasile… Then I try to shake myself out of the mood, knowing the thoughts are not really mine.

I don't want to die. I want a happily ever after. Having never had something good that lasted so long, I…

"You think too much."

He shifts in front of me, his broad shoulders suddenly dwarfing me. My pulse thuds in my ears, and his smirk widens. "Yes. Fear."

"I need to… go… challenge…"

He bends over me, his mouth by my ears, and still I'm frozen. "I'll let you in on a little secret…I *am* your challenge."

Realization runs through my tired mind like

lightning, a brief flare of consciousness. The undead in the black book—could it have meant the muroni, or strigoi, or vampires, or whatever the heck? Is *this* what I've been meant to be doing all along, not…

Then what the hell was all that talk of the World Ocean for?

A shudder runs through me, but it's nothing sexual as he bends his head to my neck, fangs on my skin. "Let me give you what you crave, Flama…"

I don't move away. And my immobility is followed by a sharp pain, then darkness.

Before I can think on it, his teeth sink into my neck, and a rush of adrenaline runs through me. In the movies, they always make it seem seductive, but this is anything but. I can smell the metallic taste of blood in the air, and bile rises in my throat. I can hear his slurping sounds, like I'm the best of liquids. And above all, a heaviness weighs on me, dragging my limbs down.

What I crave? I wonder aimlessly.

Death.

Fight it!

It would be nice, not having to worry anymore.

Fight it!

My hands, curled into fists and ready to push him off, fall back to the ground, as does my body. He moves with me until he's hovering above me, his mouth still glued to my neck.

So, this is what dying feels like...

For a brief moment, everything is more vivid. Then it fades way, like a blurry photograph. My eyelids flutter closed, and just as I'm was about to fall into the unknown, I hear him.

"Katya!"

Chapter 20

I fall into darkness, but that's not the end of it. As my eyelids close, I hear a roar of pain, snarls…

And then Daymun is standing over me. Sounds of fighting echo in a corner. My bleary eyes see two wolves tearing each other apart, then Daymun's whispering in my ear.

"I've got you."

And then I truly give in to the darkness, gone… floating. Another astral projection.

Only this time, there's more out there... More than me. I look around, aware of being watched, but not understanding where it's coming from. Below me, Vasile and the muroni—now in wolf form—are going at it, and I can't tell who's winning. But beyond me—there's more. So much *more*.

An entire universe of knowledge, beyond these mists, beyond what my little brain can comprehend. My mind gets pulled away, and clarity overcomes me.

They're the ones who saved me not that long

ago. Or was it a long time ago? Their pearly notes fill the air, both praising and disappointed. I should be doing something, or not doing something? Clarity eludes me now, wiped away by my throbbing head. A light pulsates, promising answers within it. I head towards it…

Then wings block it, and I'm being pulled back—far from the temptation.

"Katya! Katya, wake up!"

"Why isn't she waking?"

"She headed towards the light, I tried to pull her back."

"Would you two stop your squabbling? She's waking."

I blink to find Dante over me, frowning. Then Daymun and Vasile pop up next to him. I try to stand, but dizziness overcomes me once more.

"I wouldn't if I were you," Dante says. "Muroni are known for drinking all the blood of their victims. It's quite possible you need some rest."

"I don't have time for rest. They're… coming." Before I can explain, I pass out again.

≈ ♠ ≈

The haze lifts once more. How long have I been under? Hours? Days? Weeks? Panic spreads through me—a deadline fast approaching… Then voices get louder—Daymun and Dante.

"Are we seriously not going to talk about what she said?"

"We knew it was bound to happen."

"But she's the first to have connected with them since..."

"Since eons ago. And we know how that turned out, yes."

A pause. Someone's holding my hand. I squeeze it, and everyone shushes.

"Katya?" Vasile' voice is hoarse. "How are you?"

I blink awake, finding the dark circles under his eyes. "Better than you, it seems."

He doesn't laugh, not even a chuckle. There's so much I want to heal for him, to take away... but will I have time?

"I survived the last one," I whisper, even as he reaches over somewhere and brings me something to drink.

"You did," he says, looking even more miserable.

I know what he's thinking—that our time together is nearing an end. The idea is unbearable. Why couldn't we have had more years? More decades? We've known each other forever, and yet...

"It's not fair," he adds. I squeeze his hand.

And it's not. But what we have, and what I have to do, it's so much bigger than us. I'll explain it all to him...but later. Right now, I need answers to so many questions, my head is swimming.

Without me asking, Vasile helps me to a half-sitting position and I glance at my guardians, not too far away. "I liked it better when you were only in my head," I mutter. "So much more silent."

They chuckle and inch closer, crouching next to us. Dante speaks first, asking the question that's been on everyone's minds.

"What did you mean when you said *they're coming*?"

I shake my head. "When I was above, it felt like I wasn't... alone. It's hard to explain. But like something more exists out there."

Vasile frowns, glances at the angel. "Like the Creator?"

I shake my head. "No.... More like me? Maybe. Maybe not, maybe… more enlightened. Superior to anything that exists here. The queen alluded to something, but I thought she meant the dead Flamas. Now, I'm not so sure. Is any of this making sense?"

Dante sighs. "Yes. Very much so. We should have been upfront with you earlier."

"When we first talked about them, you mean?"

"Yes," Dante says. "It was untrue, when I said no one has interacted with them in ages. The Flamas have, they must have. They were the favorite ones, the ones chosen by the Enlightened Ones to carry out purging of the world, cleansing of it."

I wait for him to continue, but it's Daymun who speaks. "When the Flamas started scaring the angels and demons by showing no limits, no rules applied to them... Well, let's say they were imprisoned in the Ether."

Dizziness threatens to overwhelm me, and I sense Vasile's hands rubbing my back soothingly, his touch grounding me. "I don't understand. I thought only dead Flamas ended up in the Ether?"

They both stare at me, and I remember that line in the black book about rising from the ashes... "You're saying all of them were killed?"

"And forced to live in the Ether, where they could not affect the balance of the world unless called upon," Daymun says.

I stare between them, trying to wrap my mind around this. Such a power *would* be threatening to Heaven and Hell, but eliminating them from the Living world seems...

"Harsh, I know," Dante says as he follows my thoughts. "And I do not excuse it, but you have to remember by this point, Flamas were uncontrollable. The best—and worst—of the immortals, with too much power."

"And that excuses it?" I counter.

He shakes his head but says nothing more. As they let me collect my thoughts, Vasile ends up breaking the silence.

"What happened with the last challenge, iubirea mea? You're shaking all over."

And I realize then that not only are my teeth

chattering, but I can feel sweat slide down my back, and my entire body is trembling.

"Everything went wrong," I shake my head. Then I remember that I'm here, alive, and having survived three rather daunting trials. *I can do this.* "I'm not even sure which was the challenge, in this case... But anyway. When I crossed into the trial realm this time, it wasn't via an astral projection, but my full, physical body. I was in some kind of field with a farmhouse. And behind it, though I didn't see it at first, was this massive ocean."

I pause, staring at my guardians as I say, "Apa Sâmbetei."

Vasile's hold tightens on me. Dante narrows his eyes on me. "Someone was guarding this place?"

"Yeah, three men. I thought at first they might have been angels, but..." A shake of the head. "They said all I had to do was cross the Ocean and resist the pull of the two gates. If I did, which apparently no woman has ever been able to do, then I could walk out, my last trial completed."

I fall silent again, thinking back to the events. Something strikes me. "How long was I away this time?"

In my ear, Vasile whispers, "Over a week and a half. Another three days to recover from the Muroni's bite."

Which means I have three days from now until I have to make my choice.

I shudder in his arms, and file that away for a

later question. To my guardians, I say, "So I flew over the Ocean. And I passed by both gates, feeling their pull, but I resisted." Noticing their stunned expressions, I stop again. "What?"

"How…?" Dante shakes his head. "Katya, the pull of the gates, in that environment, should have been like a magnet to you. You should not have been able to evade it."

A glance at Daymun shows him oddly thoughtful. "Neither held you?" he asks.

I nod my answer, not trusting my voice to speak. Eventually, as the silence lengthens, Vasile breaks it again, his tone low and angry. "Explain yourselves, *naibii*! Can't you see you're freaking her out?"

It's enough to snap them to attention.

"Did I do something wrong?" I ask. Maybe I broke another rule to do with the balance.

Dante shakes his head. "No, at least I do not believe so. I have never heard of such a feat, is all."

Daymun adds, "But then again, neither have we heard of a Flama being asked to cross the Ocean." He rubs his chin, then gestures for me to keep going. "What happened next, love?"

"Well, after I passed both gates, I thought there would be a way out, but I only ended up taken back to the beginning and the three guys. And then…" I trail off, recalling my panic. "They wanted my blood and tears, to break their curse and release them. Said they'd been stuck there by the Enlightened Ones."

Vasile swears heavily behind me, his arms coming around me as if to shield me, but it's too late. The flow of words won't stop, pouring out of me like lava, scorching my tongue with the truth.

"I tried to pass them, to outrun them, but they captured me with a silver net. I fought against it and something happened with my Flama form, it burned, and I escaped. I ran to the gates, but that angel that talked to you, Dante, he wouldn't help unless I made my choice then and there. Same with Hell. And I couldn't. Because it's bigger than me, this quest, and I…"

It's only as I trail off that I realize my face is bathed in tears, and Vasile is rocking me gently back and forth, trying to calm me down. I wipe my nose on the sleeve of my sweater, and sniffle some more.

"How did you escape, love?" Daymun's oddly soft question falls heavy with meaning.

I look up and he's kneeling in front of me, his blue eyes searching my face.

"The Ether opened," I whisper, "and out came a flock of Flamas. They attacked the three guys and pushed me in the water. Then I woke up in the cave."

"That explains your cryptic warning," he murmurs, almost to himself. Then he glances over my shoulder to Vasile and his face hardens. "Those creatures got what they deserved. But I need you to answer honestly. Did the Flamas say something?

Anything at all?" I nod. "What did they say, love?" he asks patiently, as if to a child.

"They said to the guys... When they were circled, they said their existence, interfering with it was against natural order, against what the Enlightened Ones would want. The biggest Flama said, *and who do you think cracked the veil to let us through*?" I stare at him, waiting for the miraculous words that will explain everything.

But Daymun only asks another question. "And did you feel anything, when you watched them burn?"

I don't want to answer, not at first. But unwillingly, the words leave my lips. "I felt I should help them... but I also relished their punishment."

A flash of satisfaction runs over his expression, gone as quickly as it appeared. Then he's standing, walking to Dante. "This screams of celestial interference."

"Or demonic," Dante retorts.

I slowly rise to my feet, Vasile a supporting shadow behind me. "What do you mean?"

"Your challenge should have ended with the Ocean," Dante says, his features betraying his warring emotions.

"There's something else," I whisper, staring at the ground. "The muroni in the cave, he said *he* was my last trial. And whether or not I would give into the temptation and pick the easy way out—

death."

Silence descends for long moments, followed by a sudden burst of noise. Daymun is yelling at Vasile, Dante is yelling at Daymun, and they all move away from me as their bodies get more filled with tension than ever.

The cacophony of noise makes my head throb and I touch my temples, massaging them gently. On weak legs, and holding onto the tree behind me, I try to keep my balance. "Stop!" None of them hear me, so I try again. "*Enough,* all of you!"

This time, silence descends again, and I bite my lip as I take in their expressions. "What's the point of fighting over something that is done?"

"You were forced to do an additional trial!" Vasile argues.

"And this is proof of celestial interference, alright," Daymun repeats. "It's no coincidence we were given a talking to only weeks ago, and then you were forced to make a rubbish choice when you weren't ready."

I shake my head. "But I didn't, did I? Even if it wasn't fair, it's done."

Dante adds his voice to the other two, refusing to let it go. "Those three should never have confronted you directly, not like this."

"Yeah, I figured as much." I shrug. "It's not like we can do anything about it though, is there?" They stare back expectantly. "Neither of you can start a petition. And besides, whatever it was meant to do, it failed. I'm here. Alive. Ready to make my choice."

Vasile intertwines his hand with mine, and I squeeze it back.

"It is clear the extra ordeal was meant to force you into a choice," Dante says. He looks almost perturbed by this possibility, as if only now realizing something is truly wrong. "Regardless of whether it was your true trial or not, the muroni attack still does not fit."

"What's a muroni, anyway?" I ask. "Why could he be a wolf, too?"

Vasile answers, his tone dripping with scorn. "They're a lower race of vampire. The strigoi are the strongest, able to walk among us, even live among humans. Muroni dwell in caves, and are able to shift into various animals."

"Like a wolf," I reply, thinking back to the resemblances. "Why did it look like you, Vasile?"

His gaze is angry, and with a jolt I realize it's at himself. "I've run into that particular creature before, ages ago. I was more focused on saving a fellow shifter than hunting him down." He clenches his free fist. "If I had, he never would have touched you —*he'd be dead*."

My hand rises to my neck, and the smooth skin there. No scar. I didn't expect one, but something about its swift erasing bugs me, leaving me almost bereft. Like it never happened.

To Vasile, I say, "But I'm okay."

Daymun intervenes. "Yes, and you did your duty now, wolf."

"But it still doesn't explain how you all were able to enter that realm," I say. "Because it was one, wasn't it? I wasn't truly back in the regular world."

Daymun nods, confirming my suspicions.

"All except me," Dante says.

Daymun jerks his head at Vasile, as if the answers lie with him. As it turns out, they do.

He shrugs at my questioning gaze. "I can't explain it. These two bozos know all about what we're allowed and not. All I can say is, I felt your distress. It was in the earth itself. I know it makes no sense, but it's what I felt."

"He came to us," says Dante. "Ranting about how something was wrong. We could not figure out why he would be pointing to the cave, when you were atop a mountain. Then we realized something was really wrong, because your tie to us was loosening."

"At first," Daymun adds, "I wagered it was the Ether. Then we arrived at the cave—the same one from your second trial—and realized something worse was going on."

"I jumped in," Vasile says, "and even though it's territory we're not supposed to cross, Daymun followed through. But Dante was blocked."

I look to my guardian angel, registering his regret. "Celestial blood is not welcome in the fae territory."

I nod and turn back to Daymun. "But yours

is?"

"In a way. When I got to you, you had been deprived of most your blood. I focused on getting you out, and Vasile took care of the muroni."

I bite my lip. "Will Daria come after either of you, for killing on her territory?"

"She can try," Daymun says, "but she will not dare. She can do nothing to me. As for your mate—" He stops and throws Vasile a look.

My gut churns. 'What?"

Vasile sighs and lifts the sleeve of his shirt, showing me a new tattoo. He must have gotten it done while I was unconscious, because the skin still looks irritated. The design is small paw prints around a full moon. "Mihai marked me as protected by them. If nothing else, Daria will fear the Dacian blood in him, as well as my own pack, and won't go against us both."

"These are all guesses, though," I say.

A part of me also points out I'm supposed to be distancing myself, to care less, so I can make my choice. But it's impossible. I can't control my emotions, especially where Vasile is concerned.

He misreads the tears on my face and gathers me in his arms again. Despite myself, I cling to his shirt, inhaling his scent, trying to imprint him on my very soul. We can't end up together, not once I make my choice, but in such a short time he made me feel things I never thought possible.

When I eventually pull back, Dante and Daymun are gone, leaving us alone. "They're getting pretty good at this disappearing act."

Vasile ignores my comment, instead grabbing my hand in his and tilting my chin up. "I thought I lost you."

"For a moment, so did I."

When our lips meet, it's burning fire, scalding ice, and all that matters is the present moment. Vasile tugs off my clothes until I'm naked in front of him, shivering in the night wind. His lips move down my neck, to my shoulder, then lower across my breasts, my stomach…

And then he's kneeling in front of me, parting my folds, and looking up at me with all his emotions in his eyes. "There are no words for what I feel, so I will do the second best thing, and show you."

Before I can answer, he's touching me, and kissing me, and my knees shake as wave after wave of pleasure descends on me. The stars seem brighter, the moon within reach, and my body is floating…

Then Vasile tugs at my hips, and we're on the ground. He rolls over so I'm straddling him, and then he's inside me, cupping my cheek, kissing my lips, moving within me until all I'm aware of is him.

As if he, too, is trying to imprint me on his soul.

As if he, too, cannot bear for the moment approaching when we'll be wrenched from each other, torn apart.

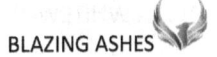

So I give in to his touch, and forget everything but the heat of his kisses.

Chapter 21

Dawn finds us awake in each other's arms. Every time either one of us would sleep, the other would shift, and we would start kissing anew. Neither of us wanted to waste a single, precious second, which really means we're even more tired by the time the sun comes up.

"We could run away," Vasile says, seemingly out of nowhere. But I know where the thought is coming from—it's been brewing the entire night. I place my chin on his chest to look at him, even as he adds, "You don't owe anything to them, to humans."

A slow chuckle rises out of me. "If I run, I'll be no better than the rest of them shying away from responsibility. Blaming others for the state of the world." I pause, spreading my fingers on his chest. "I can't avoid this, Vasile." *Please don't ask me to.*

He grips my hand in his with an intense expression. "I'm not ready to lose you."

No reply is good enough, because we both know we can't guess how things will carry out. We can hope that by some miracle I'll survive my choice, that I won't get dragged to the Ether... But that's all it is—hope.

I set my head back on his chest, listening to the heartbeat so close to my ear. Much too soon, it'll be the last I hear of it, and I try to commit it to memory, so I never forget it. Tears come to my eyes, but I blink them away, refusing to waste our last time together being sad. There will be plenty of time for that.

Another hour later, Vasile stirs, as though coming to a decision. "We have one more night, right?"

I glance at the waning moon, feeling that countdown in my bones. The full moon is fast approaching again, and it will demand a choice. The problem is, I'm nowhere closer to knowing what my decision will be.

"Yes," I say softly.

He nods and stands, taking me with him. "Let's have a swim, then I want to take you somewhere."

Meekly, I follow him. His sudden mood makes me wary. It's not excitement, not really. More like an awareness of some secret weapon that will make things right. But such a thing is impossible. Surely Dante or Daymun would have mentioned it.

We dip in the river, and once more the coolness catches me by surprise. "Vas—"

He turns abruptly at my words and cuts me

off with a kiss. His hands roam my backside, pulling me closer, heating me and stoking my desire higher. Before I can say more, Vasile latches onto a nipple and hooks my leg around his waist, driving inside me at the same time.

Anyone could come across us, but that doesn't stop his stride. On the contrary, his thrusts go deeper, and I can't hold back anymore. The angle of his thrusts, the primal way he's taking me…. I let go on a scream.

Vasile drops his mouth to mine again and comes with a groan. Something in his eyes as he pulls away and washes me tells me to stop asking questions. So, I do. I let loose to his ministrations as he cleanses me gently, then follow him back to our love nest.

We get dressed in silence, then he turns to me and holds out his hand. "Ready?"

With the way he looks, sun behind him, a perfect picture of an avenging warrior, I can't help but nod. I'd follow him anywhere, so long as I can return to my quest after.

≈ ♠ ≈

"Won't the two Ds wonder where we took off?" I ask Vasile after a bit of walking.

He snorts. "They can find us if they need to, so I'm not too worried."

A few moments later, the path we're on converges with a familiar one. Sure enough, about another half an hour later we emerge back in the Dacian village. Vasile tugs me along, but after a few strides he lets go of me and hails out Mihai in the distance.

I watch their intense talk, and Mihai shoots me a look I can't decipher. He shakes his head, but Vasile grabs his arm in an abrupt way that's unlike him. I take it as my cue to intervene and walk towards them...

Just in time to hear Mihai say, "*E alegerea ei.*"

"What's my choice?" I ask.

Vasile freezes, obviously so intent on their conversation that he didn't even hear or feel me approach. That alone should warn me something else is going on here, something deeper than just friends meeting up.

"What's my choice?" I repeat.

Mihai appraises the situation and shakes his head again. "You haven't even explained why you brought her here? Great, Vasile. Just fucking great."

My mate has the grace to appear contrite, rubbing the back of his head. He seems about to say something but ends up silent. His friend, meanwhile, is half-angry, half-afraid, unless I'm misjudging his expression.

"*Bine,*" Mihai says. "I will untangle this mess you created. Come with me."

We follow Mihai deeper into the village than

before. Near one of the houses, an old woman is sitting on a log, preparing a fire. She's at least in her seventies, wearing a worn-out navy skirt with a polka dotted shirt tucked in, and a red wool shawl wrapped over her shoulders.

My gaze is drawn to the flames at her feet. At first, I think she's using a lighter, but when we get closer I realize it's…her hands. Fire jumps out of her fingertips, stopping me in my tracks.

Mihai continues onwards, then bends down and kisses her cheek, making sure to stay away from the flames taking hold. "Meet *Baba Oarbă*." *The blind hag.*

When she looks up at me, her eyes are glazed a light blue. Her wrinkled face pinches and stares straight for a moment, then she points an index finger towards me. "*Nu eşti de aici.*"

I glance at Mihai, hoping he'll explain the cryptic statement that I'm not from here, but he shrugs and points to the tree stump opposite her. "Take a seat."

Vasile goes first, and I follow reluctantly. Of course, I'd realized during our last visit that this place is special, but to see magic so close, it's…weird. Beyond weird. Out of all the things I've seen so far, this old woman wielding it as easily as she takes a breath is quite easily the weirdest.

Again, Baba looks at me and says, "Nu eşti de aici."

Gulping, I whisper back a reply in Romanian.

"Where am I from, then?"

She points to the sky, but whether she means Heaven, Ether or just the plain old sky, I don't know. All that does is make me remember the countdown, and then I'm filled with an odd wave of annoyance towards Vasile. Why bring me here, out of all places, during our last moments? I only want to spend time with him, surely he must have realized that?

Mihai clears his throat and Baba stops her staring, instead returning it to the fire. The flames crackle as if being fed anew, and they rise higher and higher, until all I can see of Mihai and Baba are their faces and hands.

"How is she doing that?" I ask.

He grins. "Remember how you thought we were gypsies?" I wince at the memory, ready to offer another apology, but he waves it off. "My branch of the Dacians, well, we're…"

"A different breed," Vasile finishes for him.

Mihai nods. "We have hidden in the mountain because we prefer solitude and the old ways of the Dacians to what is out there."

"The old ways?"

He nods to the fire. "Magic's in our blood, but we choose how to use it." A glare to Vasile. "And what you demand is too early, given we used it not long ago on you, *prietene*."

"You know I would not ask," Vasile says.

Mihai inclines his head and turns to Baba,

whispering low. After a beat, she gets up and brings an old kettle filled with water. She sets it on the fire, and I watch as it boils. Next to her, she prepares a cup and throws herbs inside.

"What is she doing?"

Without glancing away, Mihai says, "Preparing a brew for you, my Flama friend."

I realize then it was stupid expecting them not to know what I am. "A brew? Why?"

"For protection," Vasile says. "Same as I got."

He points to his tattoo, and my expression softens. He'd gotten it to protect him from Daria, and somehow he thinks it might help me out, too.

"You know this won't—"

"I know," he cuts me off patiently. "But…please."

I turn back to Mihai. Baba reaches in the boiling pot and flicks water at me. I gasp, expecting a burn on my skin, but it's cool as the droplets slide on my face. With sure, precise movements, she pours water over the herbs and hands me the cup.

"*Bea tot.*"

I inhale deeply, and the scents of mint, cloves and other unidentifiable herbs hit my nostrils. I take a sip, surprised at the taste. As she instructed, I drink it all. It almost tastes like beer with peppermint—I hate beer. Still, I gulp it down. Then watch the leaves and ingredients mesh together at the bottom.

"*Dă-mi.*"

I hand back the cup to Baba as she demanded, and she sprinkles something else, then pulls out a mortar from the folds of her skirt and crumbles it all together. She waves her palm over it, mutters something, then gives it to Mihai. Her movements are slow now, exceedingly careful.

"*Cu grijă,*" she warns.

What's there to be careful about? It's just a paste.

I frown when Mihai passes the cup to me, his eyes on Vasile. "Are you sure about this?"

"Da," he nods by my side, as stoic as ever.

Mihai sighs and releases the cup in my hands. A glance inside only reveals a dark liquid, almost like ink. "What am I supposed to do with it?"

Vasile points again at his sleeve, but it's Mihai who explains. "The tea you drank opens your mind. We provide the protection, but we cannot choose the form it takes. Only the bearer can. Dip your index into the cup, and let your senses choose a spot on your body. Allow your mind to draw."

I stare at the cup, then at Vasile, and sigh. "Alright."

The minute my index dips in the ink, I realize I should've taken this more seriously. Warmth runs up my arm, followed by something akin to electricity. My finger throbs, but it's with sure movements that I bring it to my opposite wrist. The first swipe burns, the second more, but by the third, I get into a mindless rhythm.

A gasp, followed by a curse, almost makes me open my eyes, but I don't. Instead, I keep at it until a cooling sensation coats my wrist.

"It is done," Mihai says.

When my eyes open, I notice Baba is gone. Vasile seems transfixed by my wrist, an almost gleeful expression on his face.

I've never been the best artist, so I expect a horrid tattoo. Instead, what I find is a phoenix, drawn in long, sweeping strokes. I've seen this design before, on Celtic symbols. What's different though is its feathers have an infinity symbol etched across them.

"No way I did that with my finger," I mutter, staring in awe at the delicate lines.

Mihai moves closer, kneeling. "Oh, but you did. The ink only listened to what you told it. Show me."

The last bit is for Vasile, who obediently reveals his own tattoo. Mihai grabs my wrist and lifts it next to it. This close, I see now what I missed the first time around. The paw prints around the moon, they're also in a loop pattern. An *infinity* loop.

"Looks like you got your wish," Mihai says. He stands and runs a hand over his face, then salutes me. "Best of luck—or like we say around here, *noroc.* Here's hoping your choice saves us all." With one last wink, he's gone, leaving us alone on the tree stump.

Vasile looks at me as if expecting me to blow up. "Are you angry?"

I shake my head slowly. 'Should I be?" When he doesn't answer, I say, 'What exactly is this supposed to accomplish, Vasile? We have so little time, and I don't want riddles."

"It's no riddle," he whispers, and shifts so he's kneeling in front of me. "The Dacian protection has worked before. It was in the black book, towards the end."

The book I still haven't freaking read. Ugh. Maybe in another life.

"Protection against what?"

"Whatever comes."

It takes me a moment, then I understand. "You think this will help me not ascend to the Ether? To stay behind, to live a happy life with you?" He frowns at the edge in my voice. "Vasile, I don't want dreams. I'd much rather spend these last hours with you in reality than chasing some forgotten lore."

I stand, move away, and whirl back to him. Tears are streaming down my cheeks now. "Don't give me hope. My choice is already hard enough."

He jumps to his feet, grabbing my shoulders firmly. "But hope *does* exist, Katya. No matter what you choose. My clan has survived the end of one world before. We can do it again. And this time, I can be with you. That is why we've been thrown together, can't you see? You're supposed to save the world, and I'm supposed to save you."

His voice is so full of conviction, his eyes so filled with emotion, that I only cry harder. He kisses my tears away, and when I calm down, he lifts my wrist.

"These infinity circles are hope, iubirea mea."

I allow myself to believe it, if only for a moment. After all, who knows what will happen? Hand in hand, we leave the village, but barely a few minutes out we run into a fuming Daymun.

"What the *fuck* did you do?" he roars as he shoves Vasile into the nearest tree.

"Hey!" I yell and go to position myself between them—too late realizing my mistake.

Daymun isn't just fuming, he's downright furious. Pushing me aside as easily as a fly, he goes back to Vasile and punches him in the gut, then grabs him by the throat and lifts him up.

"We did you a *favor*," he hisses. "You could have lived your entire *fucking* life not knowing what's it's like to hold her, kiss her, *be* with her. All you would've had are dreams. We gave you reality!"

His words are so close to what I said only moments before that I'm rooted to my spot, only able to watch.

"Instead, you got greedy. Having her wasn't enough. Now you want to *keep* her, you fucking wanker. Don't you understand she's a wild creature, untamable?"

Vasile can't say anything, pinned by the force

of Daymun's rage.

"Daymun, stop it!" I cry, but to no avail.

Then Dante swoops down, grabs Daymun by the neck and tosses him a couple feet away. "Enough," he says, his features equally thunderous. "You always make a big case of things, Daymun. Let him explain."

Vasile coughs, then rights himself. "There is no explanation," he says. "At least none that will satisfy either of you. I've loved Katya since we were young. Distance may have separated us, but I knew she was the one for me way before either of you told her what she's been put on Earth for. So yeah, I want to protect her. To you, she's a tool—for Light or Dark. To me, she's everything."

He turns to face me. "And when you have a taste of everything, it's damn near impossible to let it go. So, I won't. I refuse to."

He stands defiantly, and my feet finally listen and move. Straight into his arms. I relish the way he hugs me, despite the disapproving gazes on our backs.

When we're done, I slowly face my guardians. They cannot deny our strength together, nor the fact Vasile has helped. Yet with everyone's tempers so high strung, I know only one solution remains.

"Will you take me to where I'm supposed to make my choice? I think I'm ready now."

Dante frowns. "You still have time."

"I know," I say. "But I'd like to get there early… and enjoy one last sunset with my mate."

They share a glance, then Daymun shrugs. "Why the fuck not? Everything else has blown up brilliantly so far."

I roll my eyes at his sarcasm and follow Dante out of the clearing. We go by our old campsite and I grab my hiking bag, then we head out.

"Where, exactly, do we go now?"

Daymun answers in a flat voice. "Where else but His Excellency's estate?"

Before I can retort, the world around us trembles, blurs, then we're in a different forest. The trees are taller, the sky is bluer, more vibrant. The air itself is charged with energy, like someone very powerful used to live here.

"Was that necessary?" Dante mutters, distracting me from my observations.

Daymun only shrugs and leans against a tree. "*That* is where you'll make your choice, love."

I glance up through the unfamiliar mountains, then glare at him when I recognize the historical monument in the distance—Bran's Castle. Brown brick aged by time, white walls dirtied by nature, standing insolent against an otherwise calm sky.

A shocked whisper escapes me as I call it by its more known name. "Dracula's castle? Seriously?"

Vasile mutters, "Well, I'll be damned."

Chapter 22

"What do you mean?" I turn to Vasile, picking up something in his tone and expression.

"When I was growing up, I was told an old legend about the Impaler." He slants a look at Dante. "That he was a fallen angel, and the reason for his fall was that he wanted to teach humans a lesson in behaving. The Creator didn't much like that."

I gape at him. "You're saying the guy Dracula's legend is based on, was a Celestial?" Vasile doesn't answer, instead staring at Dante for confirmation.

"It is true, but not many know it."

I shake my head at the revelation. "This is crazy. So, what am I supposed to do here?"

Daymun answers this time. "We head to the woods, climb to the top. Those were the instructions from my handler."

With dread creeping down my spine, I trail behind him. He and Dante are first, Vasile is by my side, but really, it's Daymun leading the way.

As we walk, I glance down at my tattoo and the slightly reddened skin around it. The phoenix stares back, and for a moment I could swear those infinity circles ripple.

Vasile grabs my hand, intertwining our fingers. "You okay?"

I nod, not really sure if I am. Fear grips my heart, at being unable to make the choice *and* at being able to make it. It's enough to make me claustrophobic.

Then Vasile squeezes my hand and grounds me. I take a deep breath, and my nerves settle. The forest around us thickens, becoming more and more, as if alive. Daymun and Dante are up ahead, and it strikes me that they could've flown or teleported to the area. Them walking side by side with me must be another part of the ritual.

'You can do this," Vasile says. His gaze is full of trust, of encouragement, and it warms me up.

"I'm not sure that I can, to be honest. They talk like it's a choice that'll supposedly come to me when I'm ready, but how will I know that?"

I wave my hands at the surroundings. "Shouldn't now be the time to feel ready? When I'm walking up to Dracula's castle? Because I'll tell you, I feel anything but ready." Without paying attention to where I'm going, I trip and scrape my hand on a tree. Shaking my head, I mutter about my clumsiness. "Case in point. I've always said I'm no one's hero, least of all the world's. Maybe I'll finally be proven right."

Vasile's there, in my space, cupping my cheeks. "And I always said that you are. As did your guardians."

No reply comes to mind, because his belief in me is lifting. So, I don't. Instead, I step closer and kiss him, letting it linger and deepen. With a groan, he pulls me closer, as if this moment could be ours and ours alone.

"Are you two coming?" Dante asks from afar, and we break apart like guilty children.

Vasile mutters something under his breath about angels and misplaced timing, but I'm laughing too hard to hear it.

"Come on," I say and move onwards. "It can't be that much further."

I glance behind when I don't hear anything, but Vasile has vanished. My eyes take in the surroundings, turning in a circle, but he's nowhere to be seen—like he vanished into thin air.

"Vasile?" I call out, but my gut tells me he's gone. And then it dawns on me that I've lost him, and it's no longer a whisper, but a full-fledged shout. "VASILE!"

Dante and Daymun descend upon me, but I'm blubbering through my tears, trying to explain. "He's just disappeared!"

I throw my hands up in the air, Dante moves downwards, to where Vasile had been—and then vanishes before my eyes. Daymun freezes, all senses on alert, and we wait with bated breath. After what feels like the longest moments of my life, Dante reappears, feathers ruffled and shaking his head.

I think I see the hint of a bruise on his right cheek, and the way he rubs his jaw confirms my suspicion.

"He is in one piece," he says. "Damn wolf temper."

"I don't understand, where *is* he?"

Dante vaguely points behind him. "On the hill towards Bran Castle."

"Aren't we on the same hill?" Daymun shoots back.

"No, apparently not." Dante's back to being by our side now, and ushers us onwards. "And we cannot stay here. That barrier is there to keep out all but the Flama. I suppose we got through because we are your guardians, but who knows how long it will last for?"

"But, Vasile—" I dig my feet in, but try doing that victoriously with two immortals dragging you away. It doesn't work, and I end up being whisked away despite my—very vocal—protests.

After a few more minutes of hauling me across, Dante drop my hand. "Enough, Katya! Stop acting like a petulant child and just *move*."

The panic in his voice is what stops my yapping. "I will," I say, "but tell me what you saw!"

He shares a look with Daymun, then rubs his

jaw again. "It is some type of barrier. I could not even feel it when I crossed, which alone speaks of its power."

"How did it get... I don't know, alive?"

"When you fell," Daymun says with a glance to my palm, "it must have activated it. With your Flama blood."

I glance at the scrapes on my palm, then back to where Vasile disappeared. "But he's okay?"

"Yes," Dante says. "Pissed at the barrier. Thought Daymun created it to keep you apart." He slants a look my demon guardian. "You did not, correct?"

Daymun nearly growls. "Fuck off, Dante."

Then he stalks away, leaving only us two. I gulp, and ask for the third time, "But Vasile's alright?"

Dante sighs this time. "Yes, Katya." He places a hand on my shoulder. "Let us get you to the top, shall we?"

"But if it's no longer Bran Castle we're going to, then..."

My whisper causes another flash of panic over his features. "No, it is not. Which means the instructions we were given purposefully led us in this mess."

I bite my lip, surrendering to his push and walking on. "If the barrier is there," I say, "then I won't get my last night with him, will I?"

Silence answers behind me, then Dante sighs again. "I am afraid not. I have no way to undo it, and we have no time to figure it out."

I try to fight the crushing disappointment filling me and fail. With each step onwards, more and more tears fall down my cheeks, wetting the ground.

"I just thought I'd get a chance to say goodbye, to tell him how happy he's made me... Even if there's no future for us."

More grudging steps. My entire being wants to turn tail and go back to Vasile, but I know it's too late. I can only hope he's realized, through the time we spent together, how much he means to me, and how much he helped me in these last weeks.

"Do you think he knows?" I ask Dante.

A prickle of unease slithers down my spine when he doesn't answer. Sure enough, when I look back, he's gone. Just like Vasile. I stand staring like an idiot for the longest time and scream at the top of my voice. "DANTE!"

Without thinking, I turn tail and run like the demons of Hell are chasing me, and without any direction. I run because whatever barrier that is, it's getting closer and eating the people who have been with me on this journey and robbing me of any chance I have to say goodbye.

As I run, not paying any attention, a shadow emerges in front of me and I smack right into it. Strong arms wrap around me, and I scream—but it's only Daymun.

He's shushing me, trying to quiet my trembles, all the while also trying to figure out what happened. I point behind me with one hand, hanging onto him with the other. "Dante, he's gone! Just like Vasile! This thing, it's taking each of you away from me!"

Daymun grabs me by the shoulders then, forcing me to face him. "*Listen to me.* You have to get to the top, love. To wherever this new forest leads, without fail. Even if it takes me next, you have to move on. Promise me."

I nod, albeit shakily, and it seems to satisfy him. He lets go of my shoulders, but I snatch his hand in mine, holding it tight enough to bruise. "No. Don't let go of me, please."

He glances down at our intertwined fingers with a look I can't quite decipher. Just when I think he'll refuse, he nods and relaxes in my grip. "Alright," he says. "But let's keep moving."

After a few minutes where he doesn't disappear into nothingness, I relax. At least enough to keep yapping away, trying to fill in the silence so I can quiet my own head.

"Why were you so mad at Vasile, earlier? With the tattoo?"

Daymun throws me an annoyed glance out of the corner of his eye. "Because he made you do something neither of you grasp the consequences for."

355

I wait a beat to see if more will follow. "You're wrong, you know. He didn't *make me* do anything."

"He took you to that blasted village, that was enough."

"But it was my choice! I could've walked away."

Daymun shakes his head then, and I sense ripples of frustration coming off him in waves. "What is it?"

When he refuses to speak, I tug on our joined hands. "Don't keep it in."

He growls, more than sighs. "You're so much more than a lover, Katya, or a mate. It was my idea to bring you two closer, it's true. I thought…" He shrugs. "I thought his worthlessness would make you understand how above all that you are. I thought—" His eyes glitter, lips pursing as he stops himself from finishing.

I do it for him. "You thought it would make me choose Dark. That it would change the parts of me that you like—ambition, selfishness—and make me play right into your hands." I shake my head at how stupid I've been. "And all along, I thought you and Dante were really looking out for me."

Maybe Daria was more on point than I gave her credit for.

"Love, we were—"

I let go of his hand. A flash of panic crosses his expression, but I turn and walk away. When I next look back, he's gone, just like Dante and Vasile.

For a moment, a sheer second, I wish he'd been gone for good, and not temporarily. But then I shrug it off and force my legs to move onwards. I've arrived where I least wanted to—all alone. And with a massive revelation on my hands, and yet another betrayal. Though, I guess it can't really count as one since Daymun was only doing what he was supposed to—albeit, in his own cunning way.

As I move through the forest, I can't help but think back to everything. In retrospect, that's probably what this barrier is meant to do. Let me have a moment of peace, away from all influences, so I can take stock and move onwards.

So, why then am I feeling so lost, so completely out of it? I thought I was alone back in my dingy Chinatown apartment, but I realize I didn't know what true loneliness meant.

Even with Bryan, I'd never truly felt that deep connection. And now I have—three times over. Two impossible immortals with hidden agendas, one guy who wants nothing but my happiness. And above all…. That leaves me.

Without those connections, untethered, roaming mindlessly in a forest far away from home— and that still feels exactly like home should. Maybe Vasile had a point, with what he'd been trying to tell me. Maybe I *am* meant to be here, as well as make my choice.

Choice…

And just like that, all thoughts of betrayal and loneliness disappear. I started off this quest—this journey—an unwilling hero. Some might even say an antihero. After all, what did I have to gain from saving a world that has never given two shits about me? Or about itself?

I'd seen the truth with my own eyes, both through fighting the immortals, flying over the Ocean, and seeing plastic, and so many others. I felt the pain humanity causes itself day in and day out, for a week—and it felt like forever.

And yet despite all that, I've also seen the good. Vasile showed me. And though I'm meant to choose Light or Dark, water or fire, Heaven or Hell, I find that I can't. I've been put in the seat of judge, jury and executioner, and my entire being rebels against it. I *can't* choose.

As if the forest hears my thoughts, a mist creeps around me. Whispers surround me, and here I am wishing for that loneliness once more.

"A choice must be made," they say. "You cannot go on without, or the world will know our wrath."

And just like that, I'm released back, the mist evaporates, and I emerge back to the trees. The weight of that brief encounter bears down on me, and it suffocates me.

I fall to my knees, digging my fingers into the earth to stabilize myself. Most people as children have at least one wise figure in their life whom they can go to for advice. I never truly had that. Bebo—Vasile—grew up at the same time I did. And as for adults, they were more interested in hurting me. So why does this burden lie on me, and not with someone else?

Because, in the end, it's not about my worthiness. It's about the world's. And regardless of what it will do to my future—my life—I need to figure out whether it is worth saving with Heaven's cleansing or needs punishment through Hell's purging.

That, in a nutshell, is my choice.

Not that I'm anywhere closer to making it.

Sighing, I stand from the earth and wipe my hands off. As I do, something else dawns on me. It's a deeper realization, one I sense in my bones. Humanity may have failed me, but Mother Earth has always been there for me—as were her bountiful gifts.

And, maybe, I'm luckier than I thought.

With that in mind, I emerge out of the last trees, shading my eyes against the setting sun. With a start I realize I'm back atop the highest peak in Romania, Moldoveanu Peak, and I'm not alone. Mere feet away are three figures, silhouetted against the setting sun—Dante, Daymun and Vasile.

Chapter 23

I stand there, stunned, and this time it's Vasile who runs to me, crushing me against his chest. His heart is thudding a mile a minute, and I grip onto his shirt just as tightly. Dimly, I realize the other two's silence.

Pushing away from Vasile, I march up to them. "Is this another game?"

"No game," Daymun says, looking contrite.

"Just us trying to do as we always should have done," Dante adds.

"Really?" I cross my arms over my chest. "And how did you get past this impenetrable barrier, then?"

They share a look and shrug. "We don't know."

"After it blocked me," Dante says, "I retraced my steps, hoping to cross the first barrier and head join Vasile. I managed, and he was trying to find a break."

"With no luck," my mate adds by my side.

"We were busy debating the finer points of

teamwork," Dante continues wryly, "when Daymun came stumbling down, looking all kinds of panicked."

"Nearly wanted to beat him into a pulp." Somehow, I'm not surprised Vasile felt that way.

"Anyway," Dante starts off again, "we were still lost as to how to get to you when a ripple went through the air, and the barrier was no more."

"But you were still in the forest near Bran," I point out.

"We followed our link to you," says Daymun, speaking for the first time. His hair is ruffled, like he's been running his hands through it in frustration.

All of them, I realize with a shock, look worse for wear. It's so at odds with how I feel—this put togetherness—that I can't help a wave of love for these guys. My guardians may have wronged me, but it only shows their own humanity, in a way.

A smile splits my face. "You all look like shit."

They glance at each other in surprise, and a low rumble starts in Vasile, then gets picked up by Daymun, and finally Dante. Before long, we're all cracking up, the frustration from earlier running out of us in fresh waves of hilarity.

Long moments pass, and then we all fall silent. The sun is setting, meaning I've got one more day before making a choice. Oddly, the thought doesn't make me as afraid as before. A sense of calm has descended through me, and I realize perhaps that's what broke the barrier, earlier.

Whichever it was, this is how I'll choose to remember my guardians. Smiling, solemn, godlike and human alike. Sexy as sin, and so completely unattainable.

"Thank you," I whisper, then clear my throat. "For everything you've done for me."

"We should have done more," Daymun admits.

"And at times, less." Dante throws a warning look at him.

"You've done plenty," I say, stepping towards them. "Plenty of good in my life, and for that, I'll always be grateful." I pause, struggling for words. "I hope you'll get back home alright, once... after, well, everything."

I trail off, and this time a tear slips, followed by another. They move closer in tandem, and with that odd synchronization proceed to wipe them away.

"You are amazing, Katya," Dante says. "And it has been my pleasure to guide you."

Daymun grabs my hand, looking into my eyes. "And mine." Two words, but like always with him, so much more brims beneath the surface.

He lets go before I can dig deeper, and then they both step back.

Dante spreads his wings. "Until next time, sweetheart." With one beat of his wings, he pushes off the ground and he's gone to the skies.

Daymun meets my gaze, a faint smile on his lips. "Don't overthink it, love," he says, and then he opens a portal and he's gone in the next breath.

Just like that, I'm alone with Vasile. He comes up behind me and wraps his arms around my waist.

"It'll feel so weird, not having them in my head again."

He chuckles. "They'll be around."

I tilt my head back. "What do you mean?"

"That was just for your show, to make it easier on you. They'll be around until you make your choice, iubirea mea. Here until the end. As will I."

"But—" I try to say I don't want them around, that I'm afraid for their own safety, silly as it sounds.

Vasile gently turns me, tucking a strand of hair behind my ear. "You won't see me. But I'll be here. Now, shut up and kiss me."

He takes the words out of my mouth. What starts off soft soon spirals, as it always does with us.

"We could live a hundred years," Vasile whispers against my mouth, "and I would never get tired of doing this."

I moan in agreement against his lips, and my hands travel upwards, tugging at his hair and nape to bend him lower. Vasile reads my cue and swoops me up in his arms. Before long, we're tangling in the grass, I've got one leg hiked up around his hips, and his hands are travelling under my shirt, touching my skin and slowly driving me insane.

"Vasile…" I break the kiss and groan in frustration.

He chuckles against my neck and makes quick work of my clothes until I'm naked under him. "Oh, nu, iubirea mea," he laughs. "I plan to take my time."

And he does. With each inch he bares, he kisses and licks my skin until I'm on fire, ready to combust. When he finally, finally closes his mouth around a nipple, I arch off the ground, screaming a little. He repeats the action to my other breast, then moves lower, and lower still. Pushing apart my thighs, he kisses every inch until he finally gives in to what I'm wordlessly begging for.

It doesn't take longer than a few careful licks, and I shoot off like a firework. Vasile sheds his clothes then and lies atop me. I hold onto his shoulders, trace his back muscles, my fingers trailing his tattoo. He gazes down on me, his features full of love, and then he slides inside me. So slow, it's almost painful. No matter what I do, he doesn't increase the pace. Instead, he grabs my wrists and holds them above my head, and with his free hand cups my cheek.

"Never enough," he whispers, then drops his mouth to mine once more. Then, and only then, does he increase the pace.

We come apart under the stars, and the only thought in my head is, *He's right.*

≈ ♠ ≈

The few hours we have are blissful, but what's harder is once the sun rises. Vasile stands and puts on his clothes slowly, as though each movement is painful, ripping at his very core.

I know, because that same sentiment is tearing at my insides. And when he finally turns to me, his eyes misty, I can't help my tears again.

I throw myself in his arms, clutching onto his shirt. "I love you." I finally whisper back. "I should have said it sooner. Don't know why I waited, and now—"

He places an index on my lips. "I will be here to hear it a thousand more times. I love you, my beautiful phoenix mate. And I firmly believe that whatever happens, I *will* see you again."

Then he kisses me again until we're both left panting. "I'll be here, Katya. No matter what you choose, which way it goes. Always here. You focus on the world, and I'll have your back." One last soft peck, and he takes a few steps back.

It's impossible letting him go, but I do, because I have no choice in the matter. The next hours are mine alone, and I have too much riding on them.

With my heart in my throat, I whisper goodbye. I watch as he makes his way downhill, staring until my vision is blurry and I can't see any more. He doesn't turn, true to his promise, trying to make it easier on me.

Not that it works. Agony in my veins has me crumble to my knees as the full weight of everything I need to come to terms with descends on me.

This is it. This is my choice.

After Vasile is gone, I cry. A lot. Then I think. And cry some more. Before I know it, the sun is past halfway up in the sky. I glance at my tattoo, tracing the infinity symbol, and sigh. Like before, an odd calm descends upon me—and that's how evening finds me.

Waiting. Ready as I'll ever be.

As the last of the sun's rays disappears, a mist picks up from the ground, surrounding me. I guess it makes sense I'll be having one last visitor from the Ether. Only, not in my wildest dreams did I guess who.

The two Flamas I'd seen before at the ruins face me. One who chose Heaven, the other who chose Hell. A Savior, and a Destroyer, two sides of the same coin.

"What are you doing here?" I whisper.

The Savior smiles. "We came to offer our support."

"What she means is, we came to give you the dagger."

I remember then that both the memories they showed me involved their blood to make the choice, and gulp. The Destroyer reaches into the pouch around her waist and pulls out a dagger no bigger than her palm. Its hilt is all black leather, and the metal blade shines with the full moon's glow.

Hesitantly, I head closer and take it in my hands. It feels… light. More than it should be.

"Thanks, I guess."

When I look back up, the Savior's expression is shocked. The Destroyer, on the other hand, is smirking. Her eyes no longer hold disdain, but curiosity.

My own gaze follows theirs, noticing it was the tattoo that drew their attention. Before I can ask anything, the mist evaporates, and they do, too.

An owl hoots in the distance. A wolf howls, further in the woods. I think I catch sight of fire in the forest, and hear wings flapping above. Scents of cinnamon, vanilla and pine travel to me on the wind, and I inhale deeply.

It is time.

I've started this life alone. And this challenge has been my own. Each lesson learned, each trial faced, has shown me more of what I knew, some of what I didn't, and some that I will never know.

Vasile is gone.

Dante, too.

As is Daymun.

Yet I sense their presence around me, their support. I shift to Flama form and fly in the sky, enjoying the feel of the wind under my wings, the breath of air, the moon high up in the sky. Its knowing shine, as though aware of what is happening.

The hour draws nigh... With a sigh, I drop back down onto the peak, and shift back to human form. My starry dress flows over each inch of my body, and I bend to the small heap of clothes, pulling out the dagger from within their folds.

I glance at it, then at the moon.

My two choices—Heaven or Hell. Which will I unleash to purge this world... to save everyone?

The challenges rise like a flood of memories, unbidden. And my heart knows my choice. It knew it all along, really.

I bring up the dagger and cut the soft flesh above my thumb. A sharp pain fills me, then numbness as the blood falls. The wind picks up in a song as old as time.

Whispery at first, my voice gains momentum.

I am Flame
Flame is light
I am fire
Fire is sight.

The blood burns, then turns into a ball of fire. My gaze shifts again—up, down... Then I close my eyes and focus on Vasile. And home.

The fire escapes, and from behind closed lids

I hear thunder. Then the earth shakes.

It is done...

And another voice answers. *But only the beginning.*

Epilogue

Beneath the ground, the creatures await. Swirling and growling, their souls lost to the Darkness beneath, the fire awaiting. They know she is near. They feel her choosing time has come.

Every five hundred years they wait, hoping it will be their turn. Sometimes it is… and sometimes it isn't.

This time, the rumbling of the blazes increases, and their cries grow stronger. A crack echoes above… and then through the earth. Excitement spreads through the horde.

Pieces of the ground fall apart, and light shines through in their prison. They stop their movements, staring in surprise, in amazement. The brief illumination is a promise, a dangling like a bone to a dog, yet it is real.

She has chosen.

She has released them.

And now… The time for purging has arrived.

With gleeful cackles and inhuman noises, they break through the earth, ready… hungry…

starving for souls…

What happens when Katya's choice comes to light? Will Dante and Daymun pay for the rules they ignored while helping her out? Find out in the companion series to *Blazing Ashes…. Demoni Sancti*! Pre-order Book 1 today and keep up to date via my newsletter!

Author's Thanks

I hope you enjoyed Katya's story ☺ If you could find it in your heart to leave a quick review at your favorite retailer, it would mean the world to me. Even a few simple words make a difference as an indie author!

And if you liked Dante and Daymun...

Their story continues in Demoni Sancti, as they face off with the consequences of their actions and try to clean the world following Katya's choice. The Enlightened Ones, the fae queen, and many more evils await them... In this paranormal suspense saga coming in November 2020!

And if you'd like more of Katya and Vasile later on, let me know! "Curse of the Dacians" is a novella sitting on the backburner, but I'm more than happy to bring it to light ☺

Love my books?

Want to get your hands on them and review them first,
before anyone else?
<ins>Sign up for my ARC team now</ins>
at www.alexawhitewolf.com/contact

And you'll get to read and review everything first....

Including the series set in the same universe as *Blazing
Ashes, Demoni Sancti*!

More angels. More demons. More drama. More love.
And mythology?
Always :)

About the Author

Alexa Whitewolf is a fiction writer, newspaper columnist of daily issues and author of the critically acclaimed *__Moonlight Rogues__* shifter series.

Alexa has been a lifelong writer and first began creating other worlds and characters at the ripe age of 12. Growing up in the Transylvania region surrounded by epic mountains and a never-ending stream of legends and stories was bound to create an overactive imagination. This shines through Ms. Whitewolf's writing by creating worlds filled with unique folklore, life wisdom and plenty of furry creatures.

An avid traveler, Alexa writes under a penname and spends her days between an office job and writing in Canada's capital, when she's not flying somewhere with lush landscapes and plenty of hiking trails.

Her series focus on strong heroines, kind yet sexy men, fights of good and evil and the never-ending learning curve of humanity's strong—and weak—points.

Romanian folklore is intertwined with her writing, more notably in her shifter romance series, the **_Moonlight Rogues_**. Her other series draw on world mythology, such as the Avalon myth and Arthurian legend (**_The Avalon Chronicles_**) and Ancient Egypt (**_The Sage's Legacy_**).

You can follow her blog at www.alexawhitewolf.com/blog or on social media. Her column in Observatorul also tackles various issues, including health, technology, and a writer's life.

If you want up to date releases, make sure you sign up for her newsletter. **For new releases notifications, you can also follow her on:**

Also by the Author

The Avalon Chronicles series
Avalon Dreams
Avalon Wishes
Avalon Nightmares
Atrox
Exclusive inside look in the series
www.alexawhitewolf.com/the-avalon-chronicles

The Sage's Legacy – YA series
The Dragon Medallion
The Dragon Manuscript
Relics of the Underworld
Exclusive inside look in the series
www.alexawhitewolf.com/the-sages-legacy

Moonlight Rogues series
Moonlight Rogues: Origins
First to Fall
Second to Surrender
Third to Tumble
Last to Love
Exclusive inside look in the series
www.alexawhitewolf.com/moonlight-rogues

Flaming Rogues series
Fanning the Flames
Igniting the Ice
Exclusive inside look in the series
www.alexawhitewolf.com/flaming-rogues

Demoni Sancti series
Fallen

Broken
Unshackled
Risen
Ascended
Exclusive inside look in the series
www.alexawhitewolf.com/demoni-sancti

Standalone novels
Blazing Ashes
Blood Ties, Love Binds
Unconditional Love
Exclusive inside look in the novels
www.alexawhitewolf.com/standalone-novels

More novels coming soon

Sign up for my readers' group **at www.alexawhitewolf.com/contact** and receive a copy of ***Moonlight Rogues: Origins*** for **FREE**, as well as first dibs on cover reveals, discounts, giveaways, prizes **and more**!